✳

MY ONLY LOVE

KATHERINE SUTCLIFFE

JOVE BOOKS, NEW YORK

MY ONLY LOVE

A Jove Book / published by arrangement with
the author

PRINTING HISTORY
Jove edition / April 1993

ISBN: 0-515-11074-4

Jove Books are published by The Berkley Publishing Group,
200 Madison Avenue, New York, New York 10016.
The name "JOVE" and the "J" logo
are trademarks belonging to Jove Publications, Inc.

PRINTED IN THE UNITED STATES OF AMERICA

10 9 8 7 6 5 4 3 2 1

This book is dedicated to the many readers
who wrote me asking for Miles Warwick's story,
and to my Arabian friend Perlagal, my horse,
for making my wildest fantasies come true.

A very special thanks to my editor, Carrie Feron,
and my publisher, Berkley Publishing Group—
What a delight it has been working
with you on this book!

And, as always, to the bookstores and distributors
who continue to support me—my heartfelt appreciation.

A Time for Roses

A rose just might be taken for dead
when covered with leaves and winter's snow,
but when it's again a time for roses
that rose will spring forth and grow.

Hurt can be hidden so no one can see
when covered with fear or with hate,
but love can erase all that is hidden
if you let it before it's too late.

Don't let the anger of your tortured soul
blind you to what could be;
a love that's as fresh as a rain-drenched rose
this love can happen between you and me.

I may not be the one you had chosen
and you're not the one I would claim,
but sometimes life deals us a hand
and we play it to stay in the game.

So what may now seem hidden or dead
like the roses waiting for spring,
if given the chance love can bloom too
when it's time for roses again.

—JOYCE JACKSON

Then be not coy, but use your time,
And while ye may, go marry;
For having lost but once your prime,
You may forever tarry.
—ROBERT HERRICK

CHAPTER ONE

THE SITUATION WAS PREPOSTEROUS. MILES WARWICK was having trouble believing that even his half-brother Damien, Earl Warwick, Baron of Middleham, could be so devious as to arrange such a meeting.

The courier had arrived at Braithwaite Hall at half past noon with an invitation that read:

"Sir: Would be pleased to receive you at Devonswick at three o'clock in the afternoon of November 6, (Today) or at your earliest convenience. Respectfully, E. Devonshire."

At the time Miles had believed the "E." stood for Emily, Lord Devonshire's petite, blond, beautiful but ill-tempered daughter, the woman Miles had dallied with a few years ago, just before she and her older sister, some spinster (he could only vaguely recall) had up and moved to the Continent. Rumors had occasionally drifted back to England of the golden-haired Emily's

1

being courted by this or that count, duke, or baron. Well, she was certainly pretty enough, but Miles had pitied the man who actually fell in love with the lovely little viper. Later there had been the *noise abroad* of the older girl's breach of respectability. Tongues had wagged for quite some time over—what was her name?—birthing a babe out of wedlock.

Shocking, to say the least.

Even more shocking was the fact that she had *kept* the child, rather than farming it out. Then again, Society had hardly been surprised, not after the wild and sordid chronicles that had drifted across the Channel of the elder Devonshire daughter dancing with Gypsies in Romania, and wandering the squalid night markets of Singapore without a chaperon. There had even been whispers of her submitting herself to the tortures of an Asian tattooist.

Imagine a woman with a tattoo!

Scandalous.

But Miles had always listened to the rumors with half an ear. First he barely knew the older daughter, and secondly he, himself, was usually the subject of such calumnies. As a young man he'd come to loathe the smug and self-satisfied expression the gossipmongers pasted on their self-serving faces as they spread their often erroneous rumors—always spoken with their voices lowered an octave because it added a sense of drama to the story. By the age of eight he'd heard his and his mother's names bandied about enough that he'd often feel physically ill before entering a room full of strangers.

In fact he felt a bit sick at the moment. At three o'clock Miles had stepped into Devonswick's warm, well-lit gallery and made the unpleasant discovery that

"E. Devonshire" hadn't meant Emily Devonshire at all. Her father *Everett* had offered the invitation, the wily son of a dog. Lord Devonshire had promptly invited him into a study gleaming with soaring mahogany walls and twelfth-century tapestries of knights in armor and fair damsels in distress. Undoubtedly, they were worth a fortune, as were the other antiques scattered throughout the room. Briefly, Miles had calculated what the treasures would be worth to his "friends" who dealt in disposing of misbegotten merchandise—then reminded himself that those misspent days were behind him. This trip to visit "Emily" would have been his first backward slip in months. He'd tried his best the last two years to straighten out his life—to put his rather sordid past behind him. Admittedly, he would never be considered a paragon. Respectability was an extreme load to manage; exceptionally weighty when he so obviously wasn't accustomed to it. But he was doing his best. Trouble was, time was running out. And he needed money desperately. Perhaps that was why he'd responded to the idiotic invitation to come to Devonswick in the first place. In the back of his mind he'd considered, for an infinitesimal moment, that Emily Devonshire had changed her waspish ways and wished to win him again. He'd even considered that this time he wouldn't play so hard to get. The girl's dowry was no doubt worth a small fortune and would go a hell of a long way to satisfy his creditors . . .

If only that *were* the case.

Miles regarded Lord Devonshire, who sat in a chair by the hearth. The old codger had made him an offer he would be stupid to reject, considering his dire financial straits.

But take a whore for a wife just so he could get his hands on her dowry? Good God. To what level had he sunk?

"As I was saying . . ." Devonshire cleared his throat and relaxed against the back of his chair. His liver-spotted fingers drummed the chair arm with impatience. "It's no secret that Olivia's reputation has suffered."

That, Miles thought, *was putting it mildly.*

"But the gal is not without her strong points. Since my wife died and my own health has deteriorated to such a deplorable state, Olivia has more than adequately taken over the running of Devonswick Hall. Aside from her rather lengthy sojourn to the Continent, she's skill-fully managed the books—she truly has a sharp mind for business. Yes, indeed. Mind you, such an attribute would not normally be nodded at in my circle, but considering her other shortcomings . . ." He pursed his lips in contemplation. "How shall I say this?"

Miles narrowed his eyes and did his best to recall Olivia Devonshire without success. Their paths had crossed so briefly those years before.

"My daughter is rather plain, I think. Not ugly," Devonshire hurried to add. "Just . . . unremarkable. In short, a man such as yourself would find my oldest daughter a more than suitable wife."

"Suitable except for—"

"Her mistake."

Olivia Devonshire's "mistake" let loose with a tantrum somewhere in the distance. Lord Devonshire's wrinkled face became masklike.

Miles uncrossed his long legs and stood. The heat of the dark room was stifling; his head pounded. Hothouse flowers adorned several tables in the room, and their too heady scent, mingling with the image of Lord Devonshire's transparent skin, caused an unwelcome churning in Miles's stomach. He considered shoving open the window to breathe some rain-fresh air. But that would be bad form. And besides, when a gambler was dealt an iffy hand, and there was his life and livelihood at stake, he didn't fold too quickly.

Sliding his hands into his pockets, Miles focused on his reflection in the windowpanes, watched his mouth take on that sardonic twist for which the Warwicks were so famous. He may not have inherited money or land from his father, the distinguished Earl Warwick, the pretentious son of a bitch, but he *had* become heir to Joseph's looks and temperament.

Without turning to face his host, Miles asked, "And tell me, Your Lordship, what exactly did you mean by 'a man such as yourself'?"

The chair creaked. Miles watched Lord Devonshire's image in the glass as the old man moved up behind him.

"Miles . . ." Devonshire smiled, aware that calling him that showed a certain disrespect. "You're a man without a title. Indeed, you're a man without a heritage. If you wish me to be blunt, I could point out that you are the illegitimate castoff of Earl Warwick and his Parisian mistress. You had nothing of your own until your half-brother Damien handed over the Warwick ancestral home to you, due strictly, I might add, to the fact that he and his family will soon be relocating to America. You have nothing to offer any young woman of breeding, yet you saunter over here assuming you could once again court my dear, sweet, innocent Emily."

Miles returned Devonshire's reflected gaze with a

cold, unreadable smile and lifted eyebrow. He thought of telling the old toad that "courting" wasn't exactly what he had in mind, and that dear, sweet Emily was anything but innocent.

"Everyone knows that Braithwaite Hall is a crumbling mess. They also know that you're struggling to revive those old played-out mines your brother had given up as a lost cause. Not to mention your gambling debts in London and Paris. Talk is you have a rather indelicate addiction to hazard, and that you've been known to frequent Hells in the Quadrant whenever the opportunity arises. Your markers at Crockford's have mounted, and word is that your credit has been cut off completely. You can no longer pay wages and three of your servants quit you only last week."

Miles slowly turned to face Devonshire. The old man's mouth curved in a smile. "If you marry my daughter the dowry will be large enough to see you out of debt and to tide you over for some years to come. If you spend it wisely, of course."

"May I ask why you're in such a hurry to get rid of the young woman?"

Devonshire shrugged. "Convenience. You see, my youngest daughter, Emily, has attracted the eye of the Marquess of Clanricarde. We both know men such as he will not tolerate much in the way of scandal. Would it not be a shame if Olivia's mistake somehow altered Clanricarde's opinion of Emily?"

"So by my marrying Olivia, you will manage to closet the skeleton, so to speak."

"Precisely. And besides, the gal needs a husband. You're living proof of what can happen to a child who grows up fatherless."

Miles mentally struggled with the overwhelming need to drive his fist into Devonshire's pallid, sweating face. "I had a father," he reminded his host, "or I wouldn't be standing here now. Perhaps you simply meant a legitimate father, in which case I can hardly argue the point."

Devonshire moved away and dropped once again into his chair. "You should know that Olivia is headstrong and temperamental. Regardless of her error in judgment, she continues to be proud and stubborn to a fault. She might have made me a decent son had she been fortunate enough to be born a man." He picked up a silver bell from the desk and shook it. Immediately, a maidservant appeared at the door, her stiff black uniform adorned by a plain white apron. "Where is Olivia?" he asked.

"She's taking her afternoon stroll, sir. She should be back at any moment."

Devonshire sent her away with a wave of his hand. "Never mind. There will be time enough for all that later. Best to get on to the business at hand."

Miles moved around the desk. "I really don't feel that we have anything to discuss," he said.

Devonshire regarded him without speaking.

"I'm not in the least interested in your proposition, my lord. I need money, but not so desperately as to marry some woman I don't even know and take on the responsibility of raising her illegitimate child." He walked toward the door.

"Consider it," Devonshire said.

"There's nothing to consider." Miles paused and glanced back. "Once a whore always a whore." His voice sounded revealingly caustic.

"And once a bastard, always a bastard, eh?" Devonshire's eyes narrowed. "No matter whose name the bastard takes on, it won't change the fact that he was born out of wedlock."

Miles offered Devonshire an abrupt nod and quit the room. Best to leave before things got any uglier.

The child's cries pouring into the gallery from a nearby room stopped him short. Then Emily Devonshire appeared in the doorway, her beautiful young face pouting in displeasure as she demanded sharply, "For heaven's sake, Gertrude, do something about that appalling noise. It's giving me a dreadful headache!"

"I'm doing my best, Miss Emily. I fear young Bryan is in need of a nap."

"Then see that he gets one." Huffing in exasperation, Emily turned back to the gallery. Her blue eyes widened upon seeing Miles.

"Well, well," he said. "At last we meet again."

"What are *you* doing here?" she demanded.

"To see you, I thought. I fear your father had other ideas."

Emily glanced cautiously at the servant who had swept up the squirming lad in her arms and begun to pace around the room, reproaching the child's pugnaciousness firmly, but kindly, in the ensuing quiet. Emily closed the door and fixed Miles with a stare. "You have no right to be here," she told him. "The last time we spoke I said that I wished to never see you again."

He shrugged and allowed his mouth to form a lazy half-smile. "So I recalled. However, women have been known to change their minds."

Emily raised her chin and the long blond coils of hair against her shoulders reflected the light from the lamp on the wall. Her eyes were as cold as blue china. "I don't happen to be one of those wishy-washy females—"

"No?" He laughed without humor, bringing hot color to Emily's cheeks.

"Get out of here," she demanded, her voice quivering in anger; her small hands clenched and buried in the folds of her gown.

"What's wrong, sweetheart? Now that you've caught the eye of a marquess you've decided you're too good for us commoners? That's certainly not how you always felt. I don't think I'll ever again look out at a thunderstorm without recalling how your little face appeared with rain running down your cheeks."

"Ooh, you *are* vile, Miles Kemball!"

"Warwick," he replied in a soft, threatening tone. "In case you weren't aware, I had my name legally changed to my father's nearly a year ago."

She arched one thin eyebrow. "That doesn't change who you are, or, for that matter, *what* you are. I'm quite certain your half-brother is veritably trembling in vexation over the prospect of sharing the Warwick name with such a black-hearted reprobate."

"You're a viper," Miles replied in as flat a tone as his mounting fury would allow. "And furthermore, slandering my character is a little like the pot calling a kettle black, isn't it?"

Without speaking again, Miles turned his back on Emily and moved down the gallery hallway toward the massive double doors, barely hearing the sound of his footfalls echoing off the walls and the marble floor. A servant dashed from the shadows intending to open the door for him, but reaching the entryway before the round-eyed maid, Miles threw open the door with so much force that it crashed back against the wall.

The outside air felt frigid. Vaguely, he recalled that he hadn't bothered to retrieve his cloak—but it would be an even colder day in hell before he went back to fetch it. He couldn't believe he'd been so addled as to think the pretty little twit had actually wanted to see him, especially after their stormy relationship had ended with only a short note: *I must have been insane to become involved with a man like you!* He must have been out of his mind to come here; then again, the isolation of the Yorkshire moors could drive any normal red-blooded male to the point of desperation.

He trudged, head down, along the brick pathway, his eyes misting with cold and fog, his mind seething.

Damn his brother Damien. No doubt the good Earl Warwick had played a crucial part in this infuriating fiasco. Imagine Dame's believing he would stoop low enough to even consider marriage to some less-than-respectable spinster who'd had a child out of wedlock, and who'd danced with Gypsies—she had tattoos all over her body, for God's sake!

The cloaked and hooded figure materialized so suddenly that Miles could only pivot slightly on his boot heel, hoping to avoid colliding with the much smaller body. They hit anyway. The woman bounced off him, stumbled back, and as her heels hit an icy patch on the brick walk, her feet slid out from under her and she landed with a squeal on her backside.

"You idiotic buffoon!" she cried.

"You might try looking where you're going," he replied as harshly.

"Indeed!" Her pale face—or what he could see of it hidden within the bulky cowl—glared up at him. "I'm not accustomed to dodging strangers in my own home, sir." She extended her hand up to him. He ignored it. With a gasp of outrage and exasperation, she scrambled to her feet, sliding, slipping, and making a desperate grab for his arm.

Righting herself at last, she brought her gaze back to his; her eyes narrowed then widened as she appeared to recognize him at last. "You." It wasn't a question. Nor was it a comment. It sounded more like a vile insinuation.

"And you—" he said with equal condemnation, flipping back the cowl from her forehead with one finger, "must be Olivia. It seems the Devonshires all have the manners of Attila the Hun."

She backed away. Once again she pulled the hood into place, adequately hiding the upper portion of her face, but before she did Miles glimpsed the wave of rich, mahogany-brown hair that had apparently slid from her chignon. It had a disheveled look about it, as if, during her solitary walk, she might have removed the cowl and turned her face into the wind. The effect was somewhat startling. A few whisps of hair tousled about her forehead and temples made her big eyes appear all the wider—their blue-green hue intensified by the bright smudges of indignation on her cheeks—or perhaps it was only the cold that made her high cheekbones blaze so with color. A sudden realization hit him like a Scottish norther: if this truly was Olivia Devonshire, she was not ugly at all. Far from it.

"What are you doing here?" she demanded.

"Freezing," he replied, shoving his hands into his pockets.

"What are you doing here?" she repeated, her voice sounding strained.

"I was under the assumption that I came to see your sister. However—"

"And did you see her? Well? Did you? Answer me, damn you!" She stomped her foot.

Miles frowned, certain now that the smudges of hot color on her cheeks were *not* due to the cold. Her eyes snapped with fire, their irritation enhanced by brows that were black and swept up in arcs. He revised his earlier favorable opinion. Good God, it appeared as if the woman were as erratic and excitable as the rest of the family. "Yes," he snapped. "I saw her."

Her gloveless hands, pink with cold, clutched at her wrap; the color drained from her face. "The boy . . ." The words died on her lips but her gaze remained locked on him. Only the tiniest stream of vapor occasionally escaping her mouth lent life to her features.

Miles raised one eyebrow. "Ah, yes . . . the lad." He allowed her his most famous, or infamous, Warwick smile—cold, calculated, and condescending. "I saw him as well. Lungs as strong as a blacksmith's bellows. By judging I'd say he has the temperament of his mother. Or is it his father's . . . or do you know who the lad's father is, *Miss* Devonshire?"

The woman said nothing.

"Actually, now that I think about it, he does look somewhat like a Gypsy, all that dark hair and unrestrained personality—"

Not even a flinch. Yet as he stood there, toe to toe with the silent young woman, he sensed the fierce war raging within her. He'd seen that rigid set of her mouth, that same glazed, unblinking stare of disbelief and shock a thousand times before in his own mother's face. He knew that inside she was trembling.

At last, and with no parting words, she turned away. With spine straight, Miss Olivia Devonshire moved up the icy path with all the grace of a tightrope walker. Haughty little wench. Putting on airs as if she were better than him.

"Miss Devonshire!" he called, and she paused just long enough to look back with ill-concealed aggravation. "Just how many tattoos *do* you have?"

Her chin went up, her shoulders back. Red chilled fingers gripping her skirts, she skidded and lurched her way toward the house without so much as a muttered expletive in response. At the portico a shivering butler stood peering out at them, Miles's forgotten cloak extended in one hand. Olivia snatched it from him, regarded the garment a long moment, then slowly turned to face Miles again. She proffered him an indolent smile and declared, "A true gentleman would never concede to wearing a garment in such a deplorable state of disrepair. Your collar, sir, is frayed." Then she tossed the satin-lined mantle that had cost him ten pounds (a phenomenal amount six years ago) into a puddle of slush.

Olivia waited impatiently as the gray-haired major-domo removed her cloak and faintly heard him mutter under his breath that she would catch her death of cold if she continued carousing in the ghastly weather. She muttered back that he should mind his own business and that it was her prerogative if she wished to die in such a way. They exchanged brief smiles, then Jonah, with her cloak folded and smoothed neatly over his arm, shuffled off into the shadows of the immense house.

She dashed into the nearest drawing room, threw back

the velvet drape, and rubbed away a circle of condensation that had coated the windowpane. Miles Kemball
Warwick was just mounting his horse. He looked cold
and angry. The sodden cloak was thrown around his
shoulders.

He flashed a look toward the house.

Olivia thought him spectacular! His dark hair, having
been whipped by the sharp wind, framed his features that
were both uncompromising and ruthless in their strength.
His aristocracy was apparent in the high cut of his cheek
and noble brow. His mouth curled naturally in a manner
of cool disdain and challenge—as if he damned and
defied the world to condemn him.

Just then he wheeled his horse around and rode off
through the mist. Olivia stared after him long after he
had disappeared into the fog, a swift-rising sense of
excitement burning away the cold that had earlier made
her shiver. Imagine! She'd stood toe to toe with Miles
Warwick, and—

"Olivia!"

She spun around to find Emily in the doorway. The
younger girl pressed a delicate lace hankie to her temple
as she glared at Olivia. "That child hasn't stopped whim-
pering since you left. You simply must do something
about him before I'm forced to my bed again with a
headache."

Moving away from the window, Olivia regarded her
sister suspiciously. "What was *he* doing here, Emily?"

Emily hesitated. Her cheeks held high color, and
her eyes resembled a frightened deer's. "Who?" she
responded with bland reflection.

"Who? Oh, you know very well who I mean. I just
ploughed into him on the path."

"How should I know why Miles Kemball was here? *I* certainly didn't receive him."

Olivia narrowed her eyes.

Emily pouted. "Perhaps you should speak with Papa."

"What has Papa got to do with this?"

"He's the one who closeted himself up with that incorrigible oaf for over an hour." Fanning her face with her hankie, Emily allowed the barest hint of a smile to turn up the corners of her mouth. "I do believe the conversation had something to do with you."

Olivia didn't much care for the sound of that. By the look of smug satisfaction gleaming in her younger sister's eyes, she got the unnerving feeling that trouble was afoot.

She moved past her sister, who continued to regard her with the sliest of expressions. Without a final word, Olivia quit the room and hurried up the stairs to the nursery. Gertrude had gotten the lad to bed and was in the process of softly singing Olivia's son to sleep. Bryan Hamilton Chiswell (named after her mother's father and Olivia's favorite grandfather) Devonshire had the look of an angel and the temperament of a rapscallion. Emily attributed his mischievous nature to Olivia's spoiling him, but Olivia didn't think so. Bryan Hamilton Chiswell Devonshire had inherited his father's tremendous good looks, individualism, and whiplash disposition. Although his features were serene as an angel's in sleep, his face was a portrait of impishness.

Thank God for small favors.

The good-natured maid hushed Olivia with a finger pressed to her lips, then, certain the boy was fast asleep, tiptoed over to join her.

"He's been a bit restless," Gertrude whispered. "I

suspect he'll be fine once he's rested."

Olivia nodded, never taking her gaze from the boy. She felt winded and upended. The shock of seeing Miles Warwick sauntering down Devonswick's path, after all these years, had numbed her. "Miles Warwick was here," she said, glancing at last at the other woman.

Gertrude's eyebrows rose in surprise. "Was that who that was? Oh, my. So that's what a rounder looks like."

"Have you any idea why he was here?"

"No, ma'am." Gertrude shook her head. "I've been tending young Bryan since Bertrice was taken to bed with wind. Explicit instructions from your father to keep the lad hidden and quiet."

"Um. He would."

"I beg your pardon, miss?"

"Father, I mean. Wish to keep Bryan hidden and quiet. You know how Bryan's existence unnerves him."

"Now, don't you let such foolishness upset you, Miss Olivia. Regardless of the circumstances, your father's quite fond of the lad."

"Is he?" Olivia stepped from the room, closing the door gently behind her. Only then did she look at the rosy-cheeked maid and smile. "You're free for a while, Gertrude. Why don't you take the time for a cup of tea?"

"You're most kind, miss. I'd like that, I think."

Dismissing the woman with a nod of her head, Olivia watched her disappear down the stairwell, then headed to her own room adjacent to the nursery, stopping only long enough to peer in on Bertrice, her gray-haired nanny who had come to Devonswick twenty-seven years ago, soon after Olivia had been born. All her life she had cared for the girls, and now at age seventy, she lived in a foggy world. Apart from the four years Olivia had spent in Europe and Asia, Bertrice had been a constant companion and friend throughout her life. Now she cared for Olivia's son.

When Olivia was young Bertrice had held her in her arms and promised that someday she would discover her own Prince Charming.

But it hadn't worked out that way for Olivia. And why should it? She fell far short of what Society deemed as *de rigueur* in appearance. She was not delicate as the petal of a flower. Her skin wasn't pale as the proverbial porcelain. Her face wasn't fashionably oval and she didn't swoon at swear words.

Stepping into her own room, Olivia locked the door. She covered her face with her hands and stared through her fingers. "Stay calm," she told herself. "There is absolutely nothing to get excited about . . ."

But still she was excited. Hurrying to the west window, she threw back the drapes and stared out over the fog-drenched countryside. From this window she could normally see riders approaching Devonswick from half a mile away. But the weather wouldn't allow it today, which was just as well. She didn't need visible evidence to prove to her that Miles Kemball Warwick had confronted her face to face just moments before.

Time hadn't changed him, alas. He was still as arrogant and belligerent as always. And still as devastatingly handsome—like all the Warwicks. However, while other young ladies in the region had swooned and pondered over Randolf and Damien, she had always been fascinated with Miles—the outcast son who thrived on scandal. Olivia, an outcast herself, had always imagined that her caring and understanding would soothe the anger from Miles's soul.

On the other hand, Emily was the pretty one and pursuing Miles Warwick had been a game to prove to herself that she could capture any man—rakehell or angel—on whom she set her sights. But she'd gotten more than she'd bargained for with Miles. Instead of finding herself the user, for the first time Emily Devonshire had found herself used. So neither daughter had won him.

Allowing the drape to slide from her fingers, Olivia glanced about her room. A fire blazing in the small hearth cast a cozy glow to the comfortable chamber. The massive tester bed looked inviting with its plump goose-down mattress and pillows, but she couldn't sleep. Too restless. Her walk on the bluff had invigorated her. Then the shock of seeing Warwick . . .

What was he doing here? she wondered again. What possible business could her father have with a man like Miles Warwick? Everyone knew he'd made a complete failure out of his attempts to run his mines; the miners deplored him, indeed, the entire mining village of Gunnerside would have liked to string up Miles Warwick. And he didn't dare show his face again in London for fear that an unscrupulous gambling proprietor would take out the debts he owed them in blood.

Pacing, she tugged the combs from her hair, allowing the heavy dark tresses to spill down her back. Then she removed her damp dress and kicked it aside. She remembered a time when she'd danced in front of a campfire, dressed in far less than this shift. It seemed like another life. Standing before the fireplace, she watched the play of yellow and orange light on her skin, then thought again how Miles Kemball Warwick had looked with his loosely curling hair silvered with falling ice. His face had been pale from the cold, a striking contrast to his thick black hair. And his eyes . . . she'd always been mesmerized by his eyes. Despite the aura of danger and passion that whirled about Joseph Warwick's illegitimate son, his eyes—those fascinating eyes—were frighteningly lifeless. His moods were volatile and mercurial. And his sudden spates of violence in the past had left many a gentleman's club in ruin. Rumor was he once spent an entire fortnight incarcerated for breaking a chair over a policeman who had been summoned to remove him from the premises.

How very scandalous.

Intriguing.

Exciting.

Had she been fortunate enough to be born a man she liked to think that she would have rivaled his contumacious nature. After all, men needn't suffer beneath the burden of scandal; they effected scandal and relished in the consequences.

Thank God, the years hadn't tamed Warwick. To a Society that was suffocated by its own pomposity and sense of worth Miles was an invigorating breath of fresh air.

And now?

She frowned and stared harder into the fire. An uneasiness settled in her stomach. The last thing any of them needed was to become involved in any way with the man.

Olivia moved to the door leading from her room to the nursery. The vast chamber she had decorated with murals of nursery rhyme characters glowed rosy from a dwindling fire in the hearth. The lad lay among mounds of cozy comforters and goose-down pillows as he sleepily gazed at the ceiling. Hearing her enter the room, he turned his head and regarded her with big dark eyes.

"Here, now," she whispered, easing onto the bed beside him. "You're supposed to be napping, Master Bryan."

His pink, moist lips smiled as he reached for her. "Kiss, Mummy?" he said.

"Of course."

Olivia pressed her lips to the child's forehead, allowing herself to linger much longer than necessary as she closed her eyes and inhaled his familiar and much-loved scent of warm skin and talc, and perhaps just a mere touch of the orange marmalade he'd enjoyed for breakfast; she stroked his thick dark hair, and nestled him more snugly into the blankets, humming to him softly until his lids grew heavy and started to close. Still, he fought sleep, preferring instead to gaze adoringly up at Olivia, his tiny fingers toying with the satin ribbons on her chemise.

"Flower," he said, brushing her skin with the cool tips of his fingers.

"Rose," she explained as her gaze moved to the delicate, pale pink image of a rose tattoo that curved up the inside of her breast.

"Pretty," he whispered, and drifted off to sleep at last, leaving Olivia to watch his angelic features and smile wistfully. As a child he saw beauty in that which the world deemed unacceptable. At what point, she wondered, did humankind cease to look for the good in any object, and instead search out and dwell on the flaws?

With a last kiss on his forehead, Olivia returned to her room. She would have loved to cozy down into the comforter with her son and spend the remainder of the bleak afternoon napping with him. Alas, there was pressing business to attend.

Grabbing up a brush, she tugged it through her hair and tossed it on the dresser. With little effort, she coiled and twisted and plaited the tresses into a chignon and anchored it once again with her combs, then she dug through her wardrobe until she dragged out a severe gray dress that hugged her body from her chin to her toes.

Positioning her eyeglasses on her nose, she thought: *Lord Devonshire—dear, sweet,* manipulative *Father— has some answering to do.*

Oh! love is such a strange affair;
So strange to all.
It cometh from above
And lighteth like a dove
On some.
But some it never hits
Unless it give them fits.
Oh, hum.
—J. S. OGILVIE

CHAPTER TWO

OLIVIA STARED AT HER FATHER. "MARRIAGE," SHE repeated, fighting the stunned disbelief from her voice. "To Miles Warwick. I—I don't understand—"

" 'Tis simple enough, girl. You need a husband. The lad needs a father, and—"

"But Miles Warwick." She looked directly at her sister to determine if Emily had been aware of their father's plans. Emily's round blue eyes met hers in equal amazement, and shock. Her naturally pale cheeks bleached as white as flour.

"There, there," Lord Devonshire said. "There's no reason to look so forlorn—"

"How could you, Father? How *dare* you attempt to manipulate my life in such a despicable, underhanded manner? I'm hardly a child any longer—"

"Hardly," he grumbled.

"I deserve to be consulted about plans before you act on them."

He winced.

23

"I'm not a side of mutton to be bargained over!"

"As your father, I have that prerogative."

"Perhaps if I was some naïve child whose only education was that of coquetry, but Father, I'm twenty-seven years old—"

"With a four-year-old fatherless son." Planting his palms upon the desk, Lord Devonshire hefted himself from his chair and looked at Olivia without blinking. "We both know that I'm not well; I grow weaker every day, Olivia."

"Oh really, Father. Surely you didn't use such a lame excuse on Warwick. You've whined of afflictions every day for the past decade. We all know you're healthy as a horse."

Devonshire scowled and muttered, "Impertinent chit. Be that as it may, the promise you made your mother as she was dying wasn't meant to rob you of a life—"

"Don't!" Slamming her fist against the desk, Olivia shook her head. "Don't dare speak to me of promises. I've sacrificed years of my life to fulfill them. I vowed to my mother on her deathbed that I would watch over you and Emily the best that I was capable, and until this moment you've been perfectly content that I do so!"

"And you've done a damned impeccable job of it. Too much so, I'm afraid. My dependence on you has caused me to grow lazy—but most important, it's caused me to grow selfish. When your mother instructed you to take care of us, she never meant for you to 'sacrifice your life,' I'm certain. I regret that I cannot give you those years back; if I could then perhaps we could have avoided your . . . mistake." Devonshire shook his head, and the lines of weariness and regret deepened in his face. "Blast it, Olivia, had you only confessed your predicament before dashing off to Europe with Emily, this entire mess might have been remedied. Had you told me who the father was—"

"Never."

"Never." His face turned a slow burning red. "Should I ever learn who the bastard was who took advantage of you, I'll strangle him with my own hands. I'll have him quartered and hung from the gibbet—even that would be too good for him!" Glaring at her with the intensity of a cobra, he said, "Was he married?"

Olivia set her chin.

"Philandering cock," he muttered. "Castration would be too good for him."

"There's no need in discussing—"

"When did it happen? Will you tell me that? Here? In London? God forbid that it's one of my tenants—tell me which one it is or I'll line them all up in front of you and flog each one until—"

"You'll do no such thing! Just leave it alone, Father. What's done is done and no amount of swearing and flailing and threatening is going to remedy the situation. You have a beautiful grandson whom you should be proud of; he loves you deeply, Father, as do I."

Everett Devonshire huffed in exasperation, and shook his head. They'd had this argument too many times. He moved stiffly from behind the desk and walked to the window. "Perhaps if we had raised you differently," he said to the dark windowpanes. "Elizabeth and I always off in London. Ah me, it all seems so absurd now, when I think of how we left you here in the care of that addled old nanny. Then Emily was born, the very image of her mother—so small and delicate and pale as porcelain. By God, but I did so love your mother, Olivia."

Olivia looked at Emily; the younger girl hurried to her father's side and, in a playfully timid fashion, plucked at his coat sleeve. "And I remind you of Mama, don't I, Father?"

He regarded her a long, silent moment before turning again to Olivia. "There's no excuse for the indifference your mother and I showed you."

"I was your favorite," Emily blurted out, grabbing her father's arm more determinedly. "Wasn't I, Father? You told me a thousand times!"

Faint color rose in Olivia's cheeks; she turned her face away. The old, recognizable sting was back, settling in that familiar hollow pit in her stomach. "Of course you're his favorite, Emily," she replied in a soft, emotionless voice. "Tell her, Father. It's all right, you know. 'Tis nothing I haven't known, and heard, for the last twenty-two years of my life."

Still he refused to reply. Lord Devonshire's face had become a sallow shade of ash.

Olivia managed a tight smile. "Perhaps it would be best if you waited outside, Emily. I have a few things I'd like to say to Father in private."

"But—"

"Just for a few minutes, Emily." She nudged the reluctant girl out the door, and prepared to close it. Emily braced her shoulder against it and stared into Olivia's eyes. "I'll speak with you later," Olivia told her, then shut the door firmly between them.

She turned back to discover that her father had again taken his chair behind his desk, his composure regained. Olivia poured him a measure of brandy in a snifter and offered it to him.

"I apologize for your sister," he said.

"Please, Father—"

"We've spoiled her."

"Undeniably. But she loves you very much. She'd be crushed if she believed, even for a moment, that she had done anything to displease or hurt you."

Devonshire gazed into his brandy as he sat back in his chair. His voice was deeply weary when he at last spoke again. "I meant to speak to you on the matter of Warwick after I had discussed the situation with him."

"Let me guess," she said. "I imagine, knowing Miles's reputation, that he told you to take a flying leap off the Buttertubs." She held her breath, waiting for his reply.

Her father's silence spoke volumes.

"I see." A tendril of dark hair had escaped the chignon at the nape of her neck. Absently, she tucked it back into the thick, silky knot. She adjusted her glasses and tried to swallow. "Well," she barely managed, "what *did* he say?"

"Moronic buffoon," he grumbled, and took a drink. "Arrogant ne'er-do-well, as if he has any right to expect any better. I explained that you were gifted with a fine mind—"

"Men rarely consider a fine mind an asset in women, Father." She laughed tightly. "Please continue."

"Certainly, the issue of your unfortunate misalliance had to be approached; of course, I did so as delicately as possible, explaining that, considering Miles's background, he had little room to stand in judgment."

"Ah. And that didn't impress him? I can't imagine why. Tell me, Father, how much money did you offer him if he would agree to take me and my 'mistake' off your hands?"

"Here now," he blustered. "Watch how you speak!"

"Then have the decency to tell me just how much I'm worth."

"Didn't matter. He turned me down flat. Wasn't interested for any amount of money, he said. Bloody upstart. Always did believe he deserved something better; I reckon he should be thankful for what he can get . . ." The realization of what he'd just implied hit him with a jolt. Plunking the snifter onto the desk, he cursed and ran one hand through his thinning gray hair. "Dammit, Olivia, don't look at me that way. You know what I meant."

Olivia turned for the door.

"Where are you going?" he demanded.

Throwing open the door, she called for Jonah and directed him to bring up the coach. Then she started for the stairs, where Emily regarded her with a look of intense concern.

"I'm going out," Olivia told her.

"Out where?"

"To dance on the tabletops at King's Arms Tavern, of course."

Emily grabbed her arm. "You're going to see him."

Yanking her arm away, she proceeded up the stairs.

"But you can't! You mustn't! What are you going to say, Olivia?"

Spinning and grabbing the handrail, Olivia stared down at her sister's pale face. "I'm going to offer our father's humblest apologies, of course, for making an unmitigated ass of himself. For humiliating me, but most of all, for subjecting the darling child sleeping up those stairs to such an appalling degradation."

Olivia continued up the stairs. Her body burned. And shook. By the time she reached her chamber and slammed the door behind her she could hardly negotiate her way to the dressing table across the room.

Dropping into the chair, propping her elbows on the dresser, she buried her face in her hands. The tears were there; she couldn't help it.

"There, there," came the familiar, soothing voice of Bertrice Figmore. Olivia did her best to wipe away her tears as she watched the aged nanny's reflection approach in the dresser mirror. The old dear's silver hair stood out in cottonlike tufts all over her head. She waddled, rather than walked, but her smile was genuine and kind. "There, there," she repeated. "What's wrong with me girl? What has yer mummy and papa done to make Bertrice's lass so unhappy?"

Olivia blew her nose into a hankie. There was no point in explaining again that Olivia's mother had died twelve years ago; it would only distress and confuse Bertrice more.

"Don't tell me." Bertrice pursed her mouth in distaste. "That little terror has been at it again, ain't she? Naughty girl. But never mind."

"I fear it's not Emily's fault this time," Olivia replied. Turning partially in her chair, she gazed up into Bertrice's faded eyes and tried her best to dismiss the irregular racing of her heart. Her father had actually tried to marry her to Miles Warwick. It was like a fresh blow to realize the man she'd worshiped for years considered her a wayward frump. "It's Miles Kemball . . . *Warwick*. From Braithwaite. You remember him, don't you, Bertrice?"

Bertrice looked ponderous, then her face lit in recognition. "Ooh, aye! He's sweet on Emily, ain't that right?"

Olivia felt her face flush.

"You ain't still moonin' over the likes of him, are ya, lass?" Bertrice clucked her tongue. "He's a bad one, is that boy. He and yer sister deserve one another, if ya ask me."

Olivia stared into her friend's eyes for a long, silent minute. "That was five years ago," she said softly. "He wasn't interested in me then, and he isn't now. How could my father have embarrassed me in this fashion, and to *Miles Warwick*? Anyone but him, oh, *please* . . . !"

"Yer such a lovely little thing—so full of fire and promise. Any man would be proud to have ya . . ." Bertrice turned Olivia back toward the dresser, and her fingers began to pluck the pins from Olivia's hair. Deftly, she brushed out the dark brown strands so they shone like mink in the lantern light. "Never did care for yer sister's yellow hair. Looked like hay, if ya ask me."

"Miles told Emily that her hair was like silk sunlight."

"Ya took after yer father's side of the family, in looks and temperament."

"I overheard them once. I once feared she would marry him. I couldn't imagine having Miles Kemball as a brother-in-law . . . I used to imagine that one day he would notice me and forget all about her. He didn't, of course . . ."

"I told yer mother just last week that she'd someday come to regret how they ruined the lass with all their primpin' and fussin' over every little thing she does."

"The Marquess of Clanricarde is going to ask for her hand just any day," Olivia said, taking the brush from Bertrice's hand and placing it aside. She gathered the pins into a tidy pile, then began retying her hair at the nape of her neck.

The old nanny stooped so her round face was next to Olivia's in the mirror. "Why don't ya leave yer hair down, lass? It's ever so pretty curling down yer back, and makes ya look so much younger."

Jabbing the pins into her hair so tightly it tugged at her temples, Olivia focused on her own reflection and tried to disregard the disappointment in Bertrice's eyes. "Get me my coat," she ordered. "I'm going out."

By the time Miles reached his brother's house, a film of ice had settled upon his hair and face and shoulders. His fingers were stiff and he could no longer feel his toes.

The butler answered the door only after persistent pounding on Miles's part. Bright light and incredibly warm air spilled over the threshold as Stanley, upon recognizing Miles, placed himself as steadfast as a sentinel in the doorway.

"His Lordship," the butler announced, "is occupied with guests."

Hearing the guests' laughter, Miles stepped toward the door. The startled old butler quickly moved aside. The sudden rush of heat made Miles gasp for breath; his ears turned into what felt like white-hot flames. By the time he reached the dining hall water had started to drip from his tangled mass of dark, curly hair.

Upon Miles's unexpected entrance, Damien Warwick looked up from his chair at the end of the table. Indeed, the entirety of the room's visitants pinned Miles with incredulous stares.

"Hi ho!" cried Frederick Millhouse. "Everyone hide his valuables!"

"By Jove," added Claurence Newton, "and who said the devil resided in hell?"

A burst of laughter erupted from the half-dozen other guests. Bonnie, Damien's very pregnant wife, leapt from her chair next to Damien's, as if she were about to rush to Miles, but Damien stopped her with a firm hand about her wrist.

"Sit down," he told her firmly, and though her face turned a shocking pink with indignation, she did so.

A moment passed before the room fell into complete silence, every inquisitive stare fixed on Miles, whose gaze was locked on his brother.

"You're interrupting our meal," Damien told him, his voice coldly polite.

"I suppose my invitation was lost in the post," Miles returned, as chillingly polite.

Damien sat back in his chair. "What do you want, Miles?"

"What do you think I want?"

"A fight, by the looks of you."

"Hey ho!" Frederick cried. "My money's on Kemball!"

A wave of nervous laughter again rippled through the room, then silence once more.

"I was summoned to Devonswick today," Miles stated, his gaze going briefly to Bonnie's face. Her eyes were wide, their expression concerned.

Calmly, Damien placed his fine linen napkin on the table by his plate, and pushed back his chair. "Perhaps this is better discussed in private."

"Don't bother. Just thought I'd drop by and tell you to your face you can go to hell. I'll save Braithwaite myself—"

"And how do you intend to do that? You've already squandered your quarterly allowance, and—"

"I *won't* sell my soul to some trollop. Even I deserve better than that."

"Really? What gave you that idea?"

Philippe Fitzpatrick leapt from his chair as Miles lunged toward his brother. The fair-haired lord placed himself between the two, his hands planted firmly against Miles's shoulders. "Gentlemen! This is neither the time nor the place to discuss such a delicate matter."

"There's no discussion, Fitzpatrick," Miles replied. "I don't intend to marry the chit, Dame, and I resent the hell out of your attempts to manipulate my life."

"For your information," Damien snapped, "I had nothing to do with any so-called manipulation. Lord Devonshire approached me as head of the family on the matter last week, and I gave my approval."

"Just what the blazes gives you the almighty power over my personal life? You're not my father, Earl Warwick. You're my brother—oh, I do beg your pardon, m'lord—*half*-brother. My *younger* half-brother at that. You have no right—"

"The hell I don't." Kicking aside his chair, Damien moved around the table, resplendent in his finely tailored black velvet dinner jacket and snow-white cravat. Shoving Philippe Fitzpatrick out of the way, he stood toe to toe with Miles, the Warwick temper burning in his eyes, and his fists clenched. "I have every right, Kemball. Despite your inability to accept the stark, ugly realities of our situation, I am the head of this family. It is thanks only to my attempts to bring some sort of truce to our relationship that I have tolerated your ineptitude this long. You convinced me two years ago that if I would only give you the opportunity to prove that you could straighten out your life, you would accomplish grand things with both Braithwaite and the mines."

"Braithwaite should have been mine anyway, Dame. I was Joseph's firstborn—"

"Damn you, Miles! Why can't you get it through your thick head that as far as the prevailing laws in this country are concerned you don't exist."

Silence filled up the room. Even Freddy Millhouse had the good sense to remain quiet.

In a more restrained voice, Damien said, "As far as the mines are concerned, since you took control the miners are constantly going on strike. I understand it's due to unsafe conditions."

"There has to be money for renovations, m'lord. You know that. I've sunk every last shilling I own into those bloody pits. You expect me to work miracles, Damien. I'm doing my best—"

"Are you?"

"Yes, goddammit! I'm sick to my teeth of spending my days and nights negotiating with a lot of half-dead miners who seem to find some game in making my life a living hell."

"No game, Miles. They simply don't like you. And they sure as Hades don't trust you."

"That should bring you immeasurable pleasure."

Damien shook his head and said more softly, "No. It may surprise you to know that it doesn't please me at all. Believe it or not, Miles, I had hoped to see some spark of Warwick ambition in you. I had hoped that

I could take my family and move to America with the idea that I was leaving Braithwaite in worthy hands. The sad fact is, she's in worse shape now than when you took over residence. I simply thought marriage—and the accompanying settlement—would give you a new beginning."

Bonnie joined them then, and looked back and forth between them. "Please," she beseeched them. "Think of our guests, m'lord husband." Turning to Miles, she allowed him a warm but concerned smile. "I'll have Jewel set another place—"

He laughed dryly. "You're joking. Right?" Pivoting on his heels, he started for the door.

"Kemball!" Damien shouted, bringing Miles to an abrupt stop. "I understand Josiah Lubinsky has shown interest in buying the Warwick mine holdings."

"You can tell Lubinsky—and Devonshire—that they can both go to hell. I'm not selling."

Miles left the room. Bonnie hurried to follow while Damien remained at the table.

He sideswiped the butler on his way out and set the housemaid Jewel back on her heels. "Wait!" Bonnie cried, and grabbed his arm as he reached the front door. Her violet eyes were wide with distress. "You've got no call to be angry with Damien. He's done nothing to hurt you. I was there when Lord Devonshire broached the subject of his daughter—"

He tried to move around her. She blocked his way. "You've got yourself in trouble again, haven't you? I can always tell. You take out your anger and frustration on everyone but the one person who's the cause of it all. Namely you. When are you ever going to accept the responsibility of your own actions?"

Pinning her with his eyes, he snarled, "Spoken like a true friend."

"You've been gambling again, haven't you?" Frowning, she shook her head. "Damn your stupidity. How deeply in debt are you?"

He shrugged and looked away. "Ten thousand."

Bonnie's face turned white.

"I had hoped to win enough to invest it back into the house and business. So I wagered my entire quarterly allowance . . ."

"Oh my God. You know what's going to happen if Damien learns of this. He'll take it all back, Miles. Everything. Braithwaite. The businesses." She thumped his shoulder as hard as she could with her fist. "Bloody idiot, do you know how difficult it was to convince him to give you the chance to prove yourself? Do you?"

"Yes," he replied as he looked down into her big eyes. A monumental sense of guilt and regret pressed down on him. He might not give a flying leap about how the rest of the world saw him, but she was something else.

"I'm sorry," he told her. "I've let you down again. Not only am I a sorry example of a businessman, I'm a poor excuse for a friend." Nudging her aside, he opened the door and gazed out on the wet, freezing night. "Please extend my apologies to Damien and your guests—"

"Is there anything I can do to help?" she asked softly.

"I got myself into this mess, I'll get myself out . . . one way or another." He continued to stand there on the threshold, refusing to look at Bonnie again, his mind oddly blank and his body numbed of the earlier anger that had driven him to ride like a madman over the moor to his brother's house.

Bonnie touched his arm. "You might consider Lubinsky's offer."

"And sell my only chance to make something of myself?" He frowned at her and shook his head. "I'm going to prove that I'm a Warwick. I'm going to turn those mines around if it's the last thing I ever do, Bonnie."

"But Damien says there's not enough ore left in those mines to keep them going another year."

"That's a risk I'm willing to take. After all, I'm a gambler, right?"

"A very unsuccessful gambler," she pointed out.

"Ah ye of little faith." He smiled and touched her cheek with his hand, his gaze dropping briefly to her rounded belly before he looked again toward the rain-drenched countryside.

Finally, he pulled his sodden coat closed, and stepped out into the dark, cold, and drizzly night.

> "I have loved none but you. Unjust I may
> have been, weak and resentful I have been,
> but never inconstant . . . For you alone I
> think and plan. Have you not seen this?
> Can you fail to have understood my wishes?"
>
> —JANE AUSTIN,
> *Persuasion*

CHAPTER THREE

BY THE TIME OLIVIA LEFT DEVONSWICK THE FOG HAD grown dangerously thick, making the narrow winding road treacherous. Occasionally the driver's voice came to her as he tried to coax the shy horses onward as they became more and more confused in the stinging ice. While Bertrice continually nodded off, Olivia stared into the dark and asked herself repeatedly why she was risking their lives to confront Miles Warwick.

Her humiliation had somehow become tied up with anger. One moment she imagined throwing herself at his mercy and pleading with him to forgive her father's breach of good taste. The next she wanted simply to slap his indolent, handsome face for believing that he, of all people, was too good for her *or* Bryan.

Then she asked herself why she cared what he thought, of her *or* her father *or* Bryan. She'd long since turned a deaf ear to the slurs and gossip that occasionally reached her, laughing most of them off, or smiling with a sense of amusement at the ones that *were* true. Some time ago the thought had occurred to her that if the gossipmongers were going to accuse her of unprincipled living, why not relax and enjoy it. After all, a woman of her character needn't bother about rules and etiquette. Being charged with a crime without reaping the benefits of the experience seemed a shame.

Still, there was her father and sister to consider . . .

She sensed the moment they made the bend in the road that carried visitors to Braithwaite and away from Middleham. They had left her father's more hospitable country of wooded fields and plunged into the very heart of the moorland—vast, empty fields of heather and gorse where the galelike winds whined and moaned like souls crying in the night.

A peek from behind the window's velvet casing confirmed their location. The ancient stone fences and hedges that followed the roadway for nearly half a mile led to Braithwaite's impressive entry—a formidable gateway that had been restored soon after Miles took residence in the house . . . before he'd wasted his money on gambling and women. The towering wrought-iron bears, rearing on their back legs in challenge and guarding the entrance, had been the Warwick coat of arms for centuries—ever since the first Warwick "Kingmaker" had fought at King Richard's side.

At last they turned up the wide, sweeping drive that was pitted and boggy and rutted from years of neglect. A single light glowed in the distance, and the horses, sensing a warm stable might wait ahead, picked up their pace so the driver was forced to concern himself with stopping the pawing and snorting animals before they bypassed the house completely.

With her wrap clutched about her, more in dread than from cold, Olivia suspected, she waited until the driver opened the door and offered her his hand before debarking the coach. Leaving Bertrice to her sleep, Olivia descended into the cold night, briefly glancing up at the towering bulk of the immense house—a half-mansion half-castle configuration of sprawling wings and soaring rooflines, and black windows that stared blankly over their boundless domain like sightless eyes.

Olivia stood for some time on the manor's front steps, gazing up and up at the gray stone walls that disappeared into the low-lying mist. Vines did a passable job of filling in the widening cracks between the stones, but with the advent of freezing weather, the plants had turned brown and mostly barren. They rattled like dice in a cup as the chill wind whipped through them.

She took a slow, steady breath and knocked on the door.

Nothing.

She banged again, harder this time, and more determinedly with the butt of her hand. With a sinking realization she considered that possibly she had made a mistake in coming here. Actually, there was no *possibly* about it.

After what seemed like an unconscionably long time, the door opened abruptly.

Stepping back, Olivia focused on the unkempt servant who, with dirty white cap askew, her hair hanging in wisps demonstrating a vain attempt to hide ears that were abnormally big, regarded her with a look of incredulity. "I'm here to see Mr. Warwick," Olivia told her.

The thin woman stared and wiped her hands on her apron.

"I'm Olivia Devonshire," she stressed, "to see Mr. Warwick, if you please."

"Were he expectin' ya?" came the insolent demand.

"No, he wasn't. However—" The door began to close. Olivia braced herself against it. "Is Mr. Warwick in residence?"

"He ain't up to no visitors tonight." The woman shoved on the door.

Olivia shoved back. "Is he unwell?"

"Ya might say that."

"Perhaps I can be of assistance—"

"Can't nobody help him—"

"If you'll just tell him I'm here—"

"He's had a bad ni—"

"I've come a long way . . . it's imperative that I speak with . . . him . . ." Propping one shoulder against the door, the opposite hand on the doorjamb, Olivia declared, "If you won't tell him I'm here, I'll simply tell him myself!" Then she pushed her way in, sending the scruffy, belligerent servant back on her heels.

"Here now, just who the blazes do ya think ya are, come barrelin' into a man's home as if ya was a bloody queen's guard!"

Staring at the red-faced woman through her fogging spectacles, Olivia dug into her reticule and pulled out a calling card, handing it over as pleasantly as possible, considering the circumstances. "You may tell him I'm here."

The servant watched in disbelief as Bertrice waddled over the threshold with a flourish of woolen scarves that wrapped around her head and throat, all the way up to her nostrils.

"Kitty!" Bertrice sang aloud. "Here, kitty!" Turning to Olivia, she cried, "Oo, Lud, I've lost him!"

Olivia smiled into Bertrice's troubled eyes. "Dickens is at Devonswick, dear. We've come to Braithwaite to see Mr. Warwick. Remember?"

Bertrice gazed at her blankly.

There was a well-worn chair pushed against a nearby wall. Olivia, gently taking Bertrice by her shoulders, moved her to the chair and sat her in it. "Stay here," she ordered her quietly but firmly. "Don't leave this chair for an instant. Will you promise me? I shan't be long. In the meantime, perhaps this young woman will fetch you a cup of hot tea—"

"We ain't got no tea!" the servant snapped.

Doing her best to hide her exasperation, and nervousness, Olivia turned away and surveyed the cavernous gallery stretching off into the darkness.

So this was Braithwaite. The grand ol' dame of the moor. Once it had been the shining jewel of all Yorkshire. Its heritage alone put the smaller houses, such as her father's, to shame.

Oh, how she had dreamt of visiting this place—always on Miles's arm, of course. Together they might have lent each other enough dignity so they might have been able to hold their heads high with a semblance of self-respect as they confronted Society's resistance.

Dear heaven, it was just as beautiful as she had always imagined. The vast corridor stretched high, and in the dim shadows above her head she could make out the magnificent plaster ceilings, so intricately made and ornate they had been registered in the history logs as some of the most beautiful and inspired works in England. Gazing up at the pale, oval faces of dancing cherubs, she felt as if she were glimpsing a little bit of heaven.

And the staircase, a sweeping Jacobean masterpiece
garlanded with patterns of vines and animals that wound
up to two more levels of rooms that had once housed kings
and queens during their visits to Yorkshire. These very
walls had been constructed from the stones of Middleham
Castle, where knights in shining armor had wooed the
damsels of their choice.

Braithwaite.

It was everything she had imagined, and more. Yet, as
her childhood's imagination and fantasies subsided, and
reality reared its bleak head, the images took sharper focus
about her. She looked around in surprise. Upon these
expansive and impressive wainscoted walls one might
have expected to find priceless works of art, at the least
a family portrait or two. There was nothing but emptiness
and shadows that shivered as a draft whipped in from some
open doorway and flirted with the only illumination in the
foyer, that being a pair of branched candlesticks that were
dripping wax on the table where they rested.

"Do ya make a habit of trespassin' in other people's
homes?" the servant's low voice said behind her.

"Not normally," Olivia replied absently, her eyes still
searching out each detail of the house. "Where is he?"

"Ya act as if ya got some right to be here . . ."

A thin thread of dim light shone beneath a door down
the hall. Olivia moved toward it, ignoring the servant's
ever-increasing agitation.

She nudged the door open, just a little, enough to allow
her eyes to scan the room in a swift glance. A nice fire
roared in the fireplace. A high-backed chair sat before it.
Near the hearth, and to one side of the chair, had been
placed a heap of wood. On closer inspection, she realized
that the scraps were the legs and arms from a table and

chair. The upholstered seat and back had been discarded near the door.

A movement from behind the chair startled her; *his* arm came down then and he grasped the smoothly finished and delicately scrolled chair leg and tossed it into the fire, sending a flurry of crackling sparks up the chimney.

She moved cautiously into the room, her gaze fixed on the back of the chair, her step hesitating as the top of his head came into view at last, then his shoulders. With his elbows on his knees and his head down, he loosely held a whisky bottle in one hand. His clothes were sodden and muddied. The once fine linen shirt he wore clung almost transparently against his skin.

He looked up.

Her heart quit.

He showed no sign of surprise over her unannounced entry. His face appeared more haggard and sunken than it had that afternoon. Those wonderful eyes of changeable hazel that had earlier seemed so terrifying now seemed confused.

"Are you ill?" she asked. "Or just foxed?"

He looked back at the fire, and let go a groan. Without a moment's thought or hesitation, Olivia grabbed a chipped and cracked vase from the mantel and held it beneath his chin.

A moment later, she turned back to the round-eyed servant hovering near the door. "I suggest that you bring your master a blanket—he's obviously chilled—and some dry clothes as well, I suppose. Have you any bread?"

"That's about *all* we got," came the surly reply.

"Good. Bring Mr. Warwick a cup of boiling water and a plate of bread. Promptly, if you please," she stressed. Still, the servant dallied at the threshold a long minute before complying.

When the woman had departed, Olivia plucked the whisky bottle from Warwick's hand. She placed it and the vase on a table some distance away, where she remained as Warwick continued to hold his head in his hands.

Minutes trudged by. She began to wonder if he had forgotten her presence, or perhaps fallen asleep with his eyes open. He neither spoke nor moved, just continued to stare down at the floor between his booted feet while the room seemed to grow colder and the silence more strained.

Where was that bloody maid?

At last, his dark head came up and he regarded her once again. He studied her hard and dispassionately; she felt her face warm.

He appeared to be on the verge of speaking when the servant reentered the room, her arms loaded with rumpled clothes and a blanket. Bertrice trailed behind her, carrying the tray of bread and water.

The woman flung her bundle on the floor near Warwick's feet, turned on her heels, and quit the room. Bertrice, looking somewhat bewildered over what she should do with her burden, regarded Olivia with a sense of despair. Olivia hurried to take the tray and gently ordered the woman to return to her chair in the hall and not leave again for any purpose. Complying, Bertrice ambled toward the door, only to pause and say, "I ain't too addled to know he's cockeyed." Then drawing herself up, she wandered out.

Olivia turned to discover Miles regarding her again. She tried to smile. "She has a tendency to become somewhat confused," she found herself explaining.

"Kitty!" Bertrice's voice called out in the hallway. "Here, kitty!"

"You'll feel a great deal better once you have something to eat," Olivia said, feeling ridiculous as she attempted to drown out Bertrice who, obviously, was not prepared to sit quietly in the hallway.

"Here now!" Warwick's housemaid cried. "Ya can't go in there!"

Placing the tray on a table near his chair, Olivia did her best to ignore the fact that her face was flaming. She longed to remove her woolen cloak, then again, she had no plans to remain here any longer than necessary, especially since Warwick's scrutiny of her person had become frighteningly penetrating.

"The bread will absorb any whisky left in your stomach," she explained, and poured the hot water into a cup. "The hot water will help to dilute the liquor, as well as warm you." Meeting his intense gaze, she offered him the cup and saucer, thankful her hand didn't shake, causing them to clatter.

He ignored the cup and saucer.

Calmly, carefully, she replaced them on the tray and stood before him, hands clasped as casually as possible in the folds of her cloak, feeling as if a lightning bolt had replaced her backbone. Every nerve ending throughout her body felt electrified. Finally he spoke.

"Who the hell are you?" he demanded in a husky, slurred voice.

She had anticipated a great many ways in which he might have castigated her for her presence. This, obviously, was not one of them.

"I beg your pardon?" she replied uncertainly.

"I said, who the hell are you? And what are you doing in my house?"

"Olivia Devonshire. We met this—"

"You are *not* Olivia Devonshire," he interrupted. "I met Miss Devonshire earlier, and . . ." Frowning, his face growing paler, he glanced uncomfortably toward the vase and took a slow, steady breath. The moment passed, and he appeared to relax. Only then did his dark eyes look back at her. A wariness settled over his face. "You were much prettier this afternoon," he said matter-of-factly.

Feeling her spine turn hard as stone, she raised her chin slightly and struggled for composure. "And *you* were sober," she responded dryly.

Saying nothing, he sat back in the chair, long legs thrown wide and stretched out before him. His boots had dripped mud onto the once splendid carpet of intricate Turkish designs. Still, he had a presence about him, making her uncomfortable. "It's the glasses," he finally said. "Very unflattering, Miss Devonshire. They don't suit you at all."

Her first instinct was to grab the glasses from her nose. She kept her hands at her sides.

His face, in profile to the blazing fire in the hearth, remained immobile in its contemplation of her person. Was he intentionally prodding her to anger as he had that afternoon?

"If you've come here to plead your case—" he began.

She stared at him, speechless, as his meaning sank in.

"I don't wish to seem coldhearted, but I won't marry you. Now you can hurry home to your father and tell him—"

"Is that what you think, sir? That I came here to try and convince you to marry me? Oh, of course you would; your arrogance would have it no other way, I imagine." She laughed as lightheartedly as her immense hidden anger would allow. "I only came here to apologize for my father's behavior. Had I any inkling that he harbored the idea of our marrying, I would have disabused him of it immediately. The idea is ludicrous, of course. I'm quite content with my life. Beg *you* to marry *me,* sir? When it is *I* who live in a home that is warm and dry? When at my home there is bountiful food at hand? Not to mention servants who are clean, respectful, and helpful. Tell me why I would give all that up to marry some penniless drunk whom the entirety of England calls a moral degenerate and a debauched and unscrupulous villain?"

He shrugged. "To save face, I suppose. Why do women do anything that they do?"

His gaze drifted toward the fire, and for a long while Olivia watched the reflected flames dance in his eyes. She felt somewhat mesmerized, and oddly drained. There had been a thread of truth to his words. Her reasons for risking the journey to Braithwaite might have been masked as apologizing for her father, or even anger over Warwick's so blithely turning up his nose to her father's offer. In reality, she *had* hoped he would change his mind. Even if she then chose to spurn him.

"Well," she said with a sense of finality, "I've said what I came here to say. I'll leave you to your solitude."

"But why, Miss Devonshire? You've only just arrived." His handsome mouth smiled though his eyes did not. "I suspect that the last thing you want is to venture out into the weather again. Perhaps you'd care to join me in a drink before you go?"

Without giving her a chance to respond, he left the chair, his lithe, quick actions showing little evidence of his earlier weakness. He was once again the devil-may-care scoundrel.

Flinging the water from the teacup toward the fire, Miles filled the china piece with whisky and handed it to her.

Dare she?

"Why not?" he asked, as if reading her thoughts. "Your reputation could hardly suffer any more than it already has."

Reluctantly, she reached for the cup. Almost teasingly, he moved it away.

"One condition," he said. "Remove your cloak."

She shook her head. "I can't stay—"

"Briefly. Then you can have your drink and go."

"Very well." She removed the cloak. He took it from her and tossed it over the back of the overstuffed settee. She felt exposed suddenly. And vulnerable. She ran her hands self-consciously over her dark, severe hair and wondered if he were comparing her to Emily, whose hair was blond and full of sunshine. Of course he was. They all did. Men like Miles Warwick always preferred their women delicate and fair. Like Emily. Like her mother.

He made no comment as he stood before her, balancing the fragile cup in the palm of one big hand. His eyes, however, spoke volumes as they traveled in a leisurely fashion from the crown of her head to the tips of her toes. The silence lengthened and expanded, then filled ever so gradually with small sounds; the snapping of the flames in the hearth, the ticking of a clock, and the steady hiss of sleet scraping at the window.

At last, he offered her the drink. Perhaps a bit too eagerly, she accepted it.

"A toast," he said, raising the bottle between them. "To two misfits caught in a storm."

"Which storm?" she asked. "The one out there?" She motioned toward the window. "Or the one in here?"

He raised one eyebrow and something flashed in his eyes. Amusement? Surprise? Whatever, it made him smile, however briefly. Her fingers clutched the cup of whisky like a lifeline.

"Sit down," he told her, and pointed toward a straight-backed little chair near the fire. "Oh, I do beg your pardon," he hurried to add with a degree of sarcasm. "Won't you *please* sit down, m'lady? I beg you to forgive my breach of etiquette; I don't have visitors often. After a while one becomes overly accustomed to dealing only with belligerent servants."

"I should think any belligerence on a servant's part would call for immediate dismissal," she responded, glancing pointedly toward the door where the house-maid hovered outside the threshold. "*You* are master of Braithwaite."

He did not look at her, just laid his head back against the brocaded chair and stared off into space. "Master of this house? I beg to differ, Miss Devonshire. Braithwaite is mastered by no one. Besides, how does one master the monster of emptiness?"

"Do you mean emptiness or loneliness, Mr. Warwick?"

"Do I appear to be a lonely man, Miss Devonshire?"

"If I lived here alone I think I should come to fear for my sanity."

He made a soft sound in his throat then allowed his thoughts to dive again among the flames, where they remained for some time while Olivia took sip after sip of her drink and watched the light of the fire reflect from his granite-hewn features. At last, he looked up suddenly and found her staring at his face.

"What do you find so fascinating about me?" he asked. "Don't tell me you've never shared a cordial with a moral degenerate before."

"No," she replied. "I suppose I haven't."

"Ah. Just Gypsies and tattooists." He drank again and closed his eyes briefly. Then he motioned toward the chair near the fire and said, "Please sit down."

Reluctantly, she did so, and with some relief. How long she had stood there, as unmoving as a statue, she couldn't guess.

"So tell me, Miss Devonshire; is this your first visit to Braithwaite?"

"Yes."

"Is she what you expected?"

"Yes."

He brought his head up and regarded her with an expression of surprise. "How so?" he asked.

"She's very grand—"

"That goes without conjecture. Sheep could determine that from the next county. Tell me what you think of this." He flipped his hand toward the room. "Do you not find my companions lively?"

"They're dead," she replied, looking from one stuffed head to the other.

"And the rest of the house?"

"Cold and dark."

"Well, there you have it. Cold and dark and full of dead. What sort of being would subject himself to living in such an environment, I ask you?"

Turning the cup to her lips, she drank more deeply and considered. "I have it!" she declared, and offered him her cup to replenish. He did so, his dark eyes coming back to hers as he placed it in her hands. "A maggot," she replied with a set of her chin. "A bat. A *vampire* bat. That's even better. A slug. A beetle. A worm."

He held up one hand as if to deflect the words. "Enough! Maggot and worm? Good God. I suppose I should be thankful you didn't tick off fungi."

"But fungi have neither heart, mind, nor soul, sir."

He laughed, a deep and resonant sound. The music of it made her breathless. "No heart? No soul?" Warwick feigned a less than believable scowl that took nothing away from the twinkle in his dark eyes. "Considering I've been called a heartless and soulless creature for all of my life, Miss Devonshire, perhaps I would be more inclined toward fungi."

"But you live. And breathe. You even laugh. So you must have a heart."

"Admittedly, I've never seen fungi laugh."

"Nor a maggot nor a worm!"

"Carry on. Please do. I'm feeling better about myself every second."

"You walk upright—"

"Generally."

"And since I know no four-legged animal that prefers to reside alone and in chambers that are dark and cold and damp, that could leave only humans." She paused as if considering. "So that would make you either a monk or a hermit."

"A great many things I may be," he replied with a rakish lift of one eyebrow, "but a monk I ain't, dear heart."

She laughed. Or rather giggled. It was an odd sound coming from her, and she glanced with a degree of

bemusement at her emptied cup. Her face felt warm.
The fire at her back made her insides feel liquid. Or
perhaps it was the way Warwick sat in his chair, long
limbs so masculine but graceful as they stretched out
casually. His shirt had begun to dry nicely, but there
were still patches where the damp linen clung to his
skin, revealing the barest hint of flesh beneath. She
found herself staring at a dark, coin-shaped spot on his
chest, then realized it was his nipple.

Her gaze leapt back to his face, only to discover that he was watching her with an intensity that
caused a streak of reason to sluice like a spear
from her mind to her heart. What was she doing
sitting in Miles Warwick's company this hour of
the night, feeling as if someone had just twirled
her around a half-dozen times—thanks to the two
servings of whisky that she'd imbibed as if it were
lemonade.

And why was he looking at her like that? So curious?
So concentrated? All the insecurities she had temporarily
forgotten surged over her as the barest hint of a smile
appeared on his lips. Suddenly, she felt stone-cold sober;
she wanted to flee from the room.

"Don't bother," he said. "There isn't a hair out of
place."

Unaware that her hand had gone up to smooth back
her hair, Olivia paused.

"Your glasses are straight."

She adjusted them anyway.

"Why do you wear them?" he asked.

"Because I cannot see," she replied.

"The devil, you say. You weren't wearing them this
afternoon and you saw me perfectly well."

This afternoon? Sitting there with winter pecking at the window and a fire burning into her back, she thought that their meeting that afternoon had seemed like a fortnight ago.

"Take them off," he demanded. "I don't like them."

"I'm not inclined to care," she replied.

"They make your eyes look as if you're staring at me from inside a fishbowl."

"I need them to read."

"But you aren't reading now."

"No." She shook her head. "I shan't remove them."

"Very well, then. Tell me why you wear your hair that way."

"I beg your pardon?"

"It's ugly."

"I—"

"And that dress you're wearing. It's bloody atrocious. Gray doesn't suit you. You look as if you're in mourning. *Are* you in mourning, Miss Devonshire?"

"I don't think, sir, that you have the right to insult me when you, yourself, sit there in dirty boots, wet clothes, with a suspicious stain on the front of your shirt."

Silently he regarded her. To Olivia's mortification she felt her eyes well with tears. She really had had a lot to drink. If she blinked they would spill, but she'd learned long ago that if she continued to stare straight ahead—no movement at all of her head—and *didn't* blink, she could adequately hide her emotions. If she hurried to excuse herself she might even make it as far as the coach before completely losing her composure.

"Won't you come into the garden?
I would like my roses to see you."
—Rose Henniker Heaton

CHAPTER FOUR

WARWICK LEFT HIS CHAIR AND PROCEEDED TO MOVE around the room, nudging this and toeing that. He walked to the door and stood there with his hands in his pockets and his back to Olivia. "There was a time," he said to the shadows, "when no matter what wing of the house you were in, there was always noise. From the help, mostly, but that didn't matter. I was always guaranteed that if I raised enough hell, someone somewhere would come along."

Glancing back at her, he said, "My greatest dream was to have Braithwaite for my own. She obsessed my every waking hour. I would lie in my bed at night and fantasize walking through these halls surveying all around me, and I tried to imagine the pride I would feel—the sense of accomplishment or worth; the overwhelming sense of belonging to something at last . . ."

His voice faded, but he didn't move. Neither did Olivia. Nor did she breathe. The hurt and embarrassment

she'd experienced seconds before was forgotten as she
stared at Warwick's broad back and the dark, drying hair
that spilled in loose rich curls over his shirt collar. An
odd sort of thrill hummed in her veins as she realized
that she was witnessing a Miles Warwick that few people
ever had. No doubt it was the liquor talking—she was
certainly no stranger to the effect it could have on a
man, or woman's, better judgment—but she also knew
that herein lay the truth.

Still, he didn't talk like an inebriated man. The words
weren't so slurred.

He spoke again. "Then my father died and everything
passed to Randolf. When Randolf died from a shooting accident I hoped—prayed—that somehow the house
would pass to me. Damien, after all, had established
himself in Mississippi and didn't give a damn about
Braithwaite. But of course he returned and took control
and suddenly I wasn't even welcome in the house in
which I had grown up. Mind you, Miss Devonshire,
I couldn't really blame Damien. I had never been the
most ideal brother."

Turning to face her, he leaned against the doorjamb
and ran one hand through his hair. He did not look at
her, but allowed his gaze to slide, unseeing, from one
mounted beast-head to another. "No doubt you've heard
the rumors that I tried to kill him. Well," he said with a
touch of defiance in his weary voice, "they're true."

He looked at her directly at last, a breathtaking god
momentarily lost in a bleak abysm of contrition. "What,
Miss Devonshire? Not even a gasp? Not a feminine cry
for hartshorn? Perhaps the rumors I've heard about you
are true as well."

"Perhaps," she stated simply, and adjusted the spectacles more comfortably on her nose. "Do continue, Mr. Warwick."

"My, but you are a singular young woman, Miss Devonshire. Very well. I did attempt to murder him twice. Once on a hunting expedition I tried to shoot him, pretending, of course, that the gun misfired. Another time I cut the girth on his saddle; he wound up with a broken bone and nothing more. Still not swooning in horror, Miss Devonshire?"

"I think that you would like me to. After all, have you not built your reputation on shocking people? Or perhaps you're simply attempting to frighten me, thinking I'll flee into the night, never to be seen at Braithwaite again. Really, sir. You needn't go to such extremes, I assure you." She raised one eyebrow and smiled. "Besides, I'm not easily shocked. How could I be, considering my own reputation?"

"Indeed." He regarded her thoughtfully. "Then perhaps if I tell you that I'm the cause of Damien's traipsing off to that godforsaken, mosquito-ridden country called Mississippi, you'll change your mind. You see, I slept with his fiancée the night before their wedding, and he discovered us. Mind you, I hadn't set out with such intentions. It was fully the young woman's doing—she simply didn't want to marry Dame. Still, I suppose it worked out all right in the end. When Dame returned to England after five years he met Bonnie."

A look crossed his face that caused an uneasy stirring in Olivia's breast. She'd heard the rumors about Bonnie as well—how Miles was secretly in love with the young woman.

He moved from the door then and walked to a window. "Come here, Miss Devonshire."

The stern directive caught her off guard. She'd been

too busy considering the disturbing upheaval of emotions he'd brought on by mentioning another woman's name. Ironic, she thought, considering his attempts to shock her (if that was truly what he had intended) hadn't succeeded in causing so much as a skip in her heartbeat.

"Come here," he repeated.

Putting her cup and saucer aside, Olivia forced herself to stand. Her knees were jelly. Preposterous. She had never been some weak-hearted ninny.

"Miss Devonshire?" he said.

She moved to join him, being careful, of course, to keep a respectable distance between them as she gazed out at a vast garden of brown, shriveled rosebushes.

"Once upon a time," he began, "in the summer this garden would be a vibrant, shimmering rainbow of colors. My God, it was beautiful. My bedroom overlooked the garden, and during those months that the roses bloomed I would wake up in the morning and the fragrance would be so heady in the air I'd become dizzy."

Olivia did her best to imagine the lifeless garden in bloom. Instead, her eyes continued to focus on Warwick's reflection on the dark, rain-speckled glass. For an instant she thought she caught a glimpse of the youth's eyes that had looked out upon a garden of sweet-smelling roses and found pleasure.

"I would sit in the window and watch Dame's mother work with the flowers; I'd watch her hands, how gently she caressed the tiny buds; she touched her children with the same tenderness, and I'd catch myself wishing . . ." Frowning, he pressed one finger to a single droplet of condensation on the glass and rubbed it vigorously, as if doing his best to scrub away the mental imagery that had wormed its way from his memory.

"If the roses bring you such pleasure," she ventured, "why do you allow them to die?"

"They were dead by the time I took residence."

"Are you certain?"

He looked at her at last, and though she refused to meet his gaze directly, she continued to regard his reflection in the window. "Is there a way to the garden from this room?" she asked.

He pointed to a single French door near the corner of the room. Olivia moved to the door, and finding it unlocked, opened it and stepped out onto the veranda. Here, the driving wind was blocked by two sprawling wings of the house, and though the icy drizzle continued to fall from the black sky, the cold did not seem so unbearable.

The light from the house enabled her to make out the brick walkways that divided the garden into neat sections. Stepping from the veranda and into the damp semidarkness, she searched out the nearest rosebush and stooped beside it. Weeds and brown leaves, having grown sodden and dense through years of neglect, had piled thickly around the base of the bush. With some effort, Olivia raked them away from the prickly stalk, and locating a solitary thorn, snapped it from the stem.

"Mr. Warwick!" she called. Getting no reply, she glanced over her shoulder to find his tall frame silhouetted against the light. "Come here," she beseeched him. "Make haste, if you please. I don't intend to catch my death of cold while you continue to stand there and brood."

With some reluctance, he joined her, going down to one knee beside her. Pointing one shivering finger at the stalk, she said, "There's life yet. Do you see it? There.

Where I broke away the thorn. I wager, sir, that if you were to cut away all the undesirable refuse, you'd find that there's hope for your garden."

"Do you think so?" His voice sounded uncharacteristically soft and hopeful, and so very near.

"Of course." Her voice didn't fluctuate, but kept the indifferent monotone that she had perfected over the years. "Once the bad is cleared away, and that which has been buried is given sunlight once more, I'm certain you'd discover a rebirth of the bushes. Nothing good can come of complete darkness, after all."

He neither moved nor spoke as the cold drizzle whispered amid the dead leaves blanketing the ground. At last, unable to refrain, she allowed her gaze to drift to his face, unnerved to discover that he was regarding her, and not the plant. She stared at him through the beads of moisture on her glasses, and didn't breathe, wishing to all the saints in heaven that she *had* removed her glasses as he'd asked her to minutes before. And she wished that she'd worn another dress, one that wasn't so atrocious—but then again, she didn't own anything prettier. To spend money on fashionable attire for herself had always seemed wasteful.

Standing, she did her best to slap the mud from her hands, then hurried back to the house and to the fireplace, where she closed her eyes and allowed the heat to thaw her. A moment passed before the door closed behind her. Now he would tell her to leave and remind her that she was an unwelcome and uninvited intruder. And that she had no business digging about in his garden of dead roses, and—

"You'll catch your death," came the quiet words. A blanket slid around her shoulders. Clutching it to her and staring into the fire, she tried to say thank you, mortified because she could accomplish nothing more than a soundless twitch of her lips.

They stood there, both silent, both staring into the fire while the chair arms and legs snapped and crackled and slowly turned to char-red embers.

"That was a very nice chair," she told him.

"Yes, it was."

"Have you no money for fuel?"

"No."

"What will you do now?"

"Torch the settee, I suppose."

She laughed and looked up at him. His face was lit from the golden firelight, and for the first time since she'd arrived at Braithwaite she noticed the tiny lines etched into the skin at each outside corner of his eyes. There were two small vertical indentations between his brows as well. And he needed to shave. And he smelled slightly of whisky and bay rum. And rain.

Very slowly, he reached for her glasses and removed them with utmost care. "That's better," he said. "I rather like your eyes when they aren't distorted. You have very nice eyes, Miss Devonshire."

They stood there for several moments, locked in mutual bewilderment by the sudden bursting forth of sentiments that danced between them as vividly as the fire flickering in the hearth.

Could he really find her, even in the remotest sense, attractive? Olivia wondered. Or was this just another ploy to scandalize her? To send her running from the house, never to darken his door again?

Good God, he thought. Either he'd been too long without a woman, or Olivia Devonshire was far more

attractive than he'd imagined, with her rain-kissed face
and moisture clinging to her silky black lashes. The
curve of her breasts owed nothing to the artifices so
often employed by women, and for a startling moment
he imagined releasing them into his hands, perhaps burying his face into their lushness . . . while her long legs
easily spread to afford him a gentle entry. Or perhaps
she preferred it rough, wild, and abandoned; she was,
after all, a paradox: a woman in an old maid's guise
with the heart and soul of a harlot. Perchance she hadn't
come here to wrangle him into marriage. Possibly she
had nothing more in mind than a fast and furious tumble
in the sheets. In that case . . .

"Tell me," he said. "Why did you really come here,
Miss Devonshire?"

She glanced longingly at the spectacles hanging by
the end piece from his index finger. "I told you. To
apologize—"

"Come, come. I've been more than honest with you.
I think you owe me the same consideration."

Folding her glasses, he slid them into a pocket in
his trousers, his eyes never leaving her. Her eyes were
wide and growing wider by the second. Yet, as he eased
one hand around her nape, he felt her start, and trem-
ble, and for an instant she looked frightened enough
to flee.

But she didn't. Just remained stock-still while her
breathing quickened and her soft pink lips parted to
release a small sound of surprise. Or perhaps it was
simply desire.

He stepped against her, his body pressing against hers
as his fingers gently tightened upon her nape, drifting
upward and into the knot of hair that, with slight pres-

sure, tumbled from its anchoring of pins and spilled over her shoulders and down her back. She stretched out a hand in a feeble show of resistance, causing him to smile his satyr's smile that made even the most innocent maidens yield.

"Don't," she managed to whisper. "You mustn't. You're only trying to shock me again, and . . ."

"Is that what I'm doing, dear heart?" He laughed softly, wondering himself. Perhaps in the beginning, but now . . . ?

Sliding his arm around her, he held her hard and close, and for a brief moment she resisted frantically, her body rigid, and her green eyes fearful as they stared up into his. How she had changed in the space of an instant, with the thick, soft waves of her hair framing her face and her head fallen back, partially exposing the smooth curve of her throat. Oh yes. He could imagine this woman tempting an entire tribe of Gypsies. Or perhaps one of her father's tenants. Or even some less than noble aristocrat—such as himself—who found himself drowning in the whirlpool of her eyes. If he was smart he'd send her scrambling back to her father with a message that Miles Kemball Warwick was nobody's fool when it came to women, he couldn't possibly be seduced into marriage; but he wasn't feeling so smart at that moment. Far from it. And he'd been a hell of a long time without a woman . . .

He breathed in her ear.

She gasped.

He nuzzled the soft, fragrant skin along the underside of her jaw.

She melted against him.

He kissed her, tentatively at first, a brush of his mouth

on the corner of hers, then a slow, easy glide of his lips
onto hers that were trembling and far softer than he'd
imagined. And he touched his tongue to hers. And buried
his hand into her hair, fondling the curve of her head and
holding it closely, possessively while the nerve endings
in his body expanded to minute pinpoints of pleasure
and pain.

Olivia groaned with the ecstasy of it, the drugging
wonder of it that momentarily deprived her of all power
of thought, movement, or denial. The arousing warmth
and wetness of his mouth was intoxicating, overwhelming. Never had she imagined it would feel like this.
Taste like this. She'd waited a lifetime to experience
this moment with him.

Don't stop! her mind cried, and her body responded
hungrily by pressing closer, by parting her lips eagerly
to allow the plunge of his tongue against hers, where he
thrust and withdrew and thrust again in a rhythm that
made her body turn liquid and quivering and helpless.
With only a slight hesitation, she slid her arms around
his neck and buried one hand in his glorious hair, as
she had dreamt of doing for most of her life, and kissed
him back with an abandonment that would have shocked
even herself just moments before.

He pulled away. Suddenly. Breathing hard. His eyes
burning.

Reality crashed in on her.

Miles backed away. They stood facing one another in
clumsy silence for several moments.

At last, Miles backed away and moved across the
room. He propped himself against the desk and crossed
his arms over his chest as he focused hard on her face,
his own disquietude obvious.

"Who was he?" he demanded in a husky voice. "Or rather, who is he?"

She frowned and glanced desperately at the hairpins scattered over the floor. She couldn't think.

"Don't pretend to be daft. You know who I mean. The boy's father. Who is he?"

This sudden turn of topics left Olivia even more rattled, if that were possible. The fact that he had approached the subject of her son so straightforwardly caused the room to turn unbearably warm. "That is none of your business," she finally managed.

"Your father made it my business."

"You rejected my father's offer, therefore it is not."

"Did you love him?"

Where was her cloak? On the settee. She'd be forced to walk directly by him to fetch it. She wasn't certain she could, not with her knees feeling like aspic and her heart jumping like a March hare in her breast. How foolish to think she could confront a man as undisciplined as Miles Warwick and expect to come out of it unscathed.

She did her best to focus her thoughts on escape.

"Do I know him?" came his voice.

"I really must be going." She started for the sofa.

"Is he local?"

"I shouldn't have come here. It was silly really . . ."

"Does he know about the boy?"

"The boy's name is Bryan."

"Does he help support the boy?"

"*Bryan.* His name is *Bryan,*" she stressed with a growing sense of frustration.

"Is he married? Obviously, or he would've married you. Are you still lovers?" Moving before her, he blocked her way to the settee, bringing her to stop short. Still, she

refused to meet his look directly, and proceeded to walk
around him. He stopped her again by stepping sideward.
"I've politely asked you a question," he said.

"As politely, I have told you that my affairs are of no
concern to you."

"You must have loved him very much since you continue to protect his name and reputation, while yours has
been blown to perdition."

"I really must be going. If you please—"

"I have it. You thought by getting into this fix that you
would trap the scoundrel into marrying you, therefore
saving you from frittering your life away in the company
of your father and sister. Ah! I must be close. Your eyes
flashed. Your cheeks are growing warm with color."

"This vein of conversation is entirely objectionable—"

"No, mademoiselle, your reputation is objectionable.
Your coming here in the middle of the night is objectionable. Your manner of dressing is objectionable. Your
deportment is objectionable. Your attempts to seduce me
into marrying you are objectionable. Shall I continue?

"Your father told me you made your mother a vow
to take care of your father and sister. When it became
obvious that your opportunity to marry and escape
Devonswick was passing you by, you had a love affair,
thinking a pregnancy would offer you a life beyond your
sister's shadow and your father's domination."

"Have you finished?" she demanded.

"I'm not sure. Let me think on it a few minutes. In
the meanwhile, take your chair again and pour yourself
another drink."

"I would rather die of thirst and freeze of cold than to
sit in that chair in front of that fire and share a whisky
with you again." She stepped around him; this time,

he didn't stop her. Grabbing up her cloak, she moved toward the door while pulling the garment about her shoulders.

Where was Bertrice? Pausing, she looked one way, then the other, discovering nothing but shadows looming in the distance. "Damn," she said quietly. "Where has she got to?"

"Looking for her cat, no doubt," Warwick said behind her. "Won't you come back in here where it's warm, Miss Devonshire? I'll even toss another chair on the fire."

"Bertrice!" she called.

"You know this house has a way of devouring people."

"Bertrice!"

"Up here!" the voice cried from above. The housemaid appeared at the top of the stairs, cap slid down over her brow. "The daft woman is up here," she explained in a voice vibrating with aggravation.

Olivia hurried up the stairs, trying her best to ignore the fact that Miles was behind her, taking two steps to her every one, and his housemaid was before her, babbling furiously.

To Olivia's dismay, she was led to a large bedchamber and quickly discovered Bertrice had retired. In Miles's bedroom. In his bed. She lay peacefully with her silver-haired head on his pillow and the bedcovers pulled up to her chin.

"I suppose she didn't find her cat," Miles said from the doorway.

Standing at the foot of the massive tester, Olivia gazed down at her old nanny, wondering if she should explain to her host that Dickens the cat had expired six years ago.

Mortification consumed her. The sudden realization that she was standing in Warwick's bedroom didn't help. Nor did the cat-that-ate-the-canary smile on his face.

"I do beg your pardon," she said stiffly. "It seems Bertrice has made herself at home."

"So it seems."

"If you'll lend me a hand, I'll get her up."

"Don't bother."

"But you don't understand; Bertrice is quite fond of sleeping. Once she's out, she'll sleep right through the night."

"Generally, that's how it's done."

Frustration mounting, Olivia shot him a hot look. He only shrugged. "Seems you'll have to stay a while longer after all."

"And allow you to abuse my sensibilities again? I think not. Bertrice? Bertrice! Wake up."

"If I promise to be nice—"

"I doubt seriously if the word exists in your vocabulary, Mr. Warwick."

"Very well then. If I simply promise not to bring up the subject of your lovers—"

She shook the woman vehemently; Bertrice only mumbled in her sleep.

Miles moved up behind Olivia and gently yet firmly took hold of her arm. "Let her sleep," he repeated.

"Take your hand from my person this—"

"I'll send her home in the morning. Good God, you're a fiery little thing when you get your back up."

"Then you should try harder not to get my back up." She yanked her arm away and started for the door, forgetting all about Bertrice or the fact that he still had her glasses.

The surly housemaid jumped aside as Olivia left the room, only realizing *after* she'd walked a far distance that she was headed the wrong direction. With a silent groan of frustration, she turned back to discover Warwick at the top of the stairs, glasses suspended from his little finger. Insufferable buffoon.

"So tell me," he said as she rejoined him. "Are you angry because I said you look better without these?" He made a face at the spectacles. "Or because I asked you about the boy's father? I don't think it's because I kissed you since you apparently enjoyed it. Or could it be . . ." His voice lowered and his features took on a serious look. "You were thinking of *him* when I kissed you."

"Don't be daft." She made a quick grab for the glasses. As quickly he snatched them away.

With a lift of her chin, Olivia turned down the stairs. "Very well," she said with a gladiatorial air. "You can keep the bloody things for all I care."

Miles reached the bottom of the stairs before her and stood blocking her way. He looked like a pirate with his clothes so carelessly worn and his dark hair windblown and still damp from his ride through the rain. There was a mood of recklessness about him, a wildness that flashed in his eyes and momentarily left her disturbingly mesmerized. She realized despairingly that if he attempted to kiss her again she would probably let him.

"Don't go," he finally said. "I'll have Sally cook up a mix of something—"

"We ain't got nothin' to mix," came the tart reply from up the stairs.

"So we'll have bread and water."

"I—I think not, considering the circumstances."

"If you're meaning the kiss, not to worry. It didn't mean anything. Unless you want it to."

"And what is that supposed to mean?"

He shrugged. "You're welcome to stay the night, if you're so disposed."

"Sir, are you implying what I think you are?" Her eyes widened as he grinned.

Her attempt to dart around him was impaired as he threw out his arm, blocking her path like a barrier. "Very well," he said, as she turned her eyes full of mounting irritation and distress on him. His face was very near hers. The light from the candelabra made his hair shine like copper. "I acquiesce, Miss Devonshire," he continued quietly, and without emotion. "I confess to allowing my selfishness to get the better of me. Before you arrived I was caught in the doldrums; perhaps feeling much too sorry for myself. This isn't the Braithwaite I ached for with my every fiber. I suppose the old adage is true: one must be careful what one wishes for."

"Perhaps it wasn't, or isn't, the *house* that you've always wanted," she replied.

He made no comment and Olivia was aware of a queer sense of electricity that hummed in the air. His expression was both perplexed and angry.

"I fear I've kept you overly long, Miss Devonshire. May I bid you good night?"

Love has been compared to debt: both
keep their captives awake at night,
and in a perpetual state of unrest
during the day.
—FREDERICK SAUNDERS

CHAPTER FIVE

THE MORNING DAWNED WET AND COLD AND GRAY WITH
fog. It had snowed during the night; long ice crystals
clung to the scattering of trees around Devonswick, causing their heavy bare branches to appear like enchanted
weeping willows.

Olivia awoke with an enormous headache. She'd slept
little. She relived her hours with Miles Warwick, her
dreams changing their encounter into strange variations.
At half past four she finally rolled out of bed and proceeded to the kitchen where the tweeny made her a strong
hot pot of tea and located a plate of leftover scones.
Olivia ate every one as she sat before the hearth and
mentally castigated herself for journeying to Braithwaite
to confront Warwick.

Silly, idiotic ninny. She'd done many a foolish thing
in her life, but none she so adamantly wished she could
take back. No doubt he'd spent the entirety of the night
laughing at her; imagine his coming right out and accus-
ing her of attempting to coerce him into marriage. And

then to so blatantly address the matter of Bryan! To top
that off she'd allowed him liberties. She felt shamed.

Alas, she could not take it back. Neither could she
forget the thrill of his kiss, the breathtaking pleasure
of his mouth on hers that shattered the self-imposed
gyves that had adequately shielded her sensibilities the
last years.

As her strict routine dictated, she bathed and dressed
by seven and adjourned to her father's office where she
opened and read the correspondence that had arrived the
afternoon before . . . or tried to. It wasn't easy without
her glasses.

She'd been halfway back from Braithwaite last night
before realizing that she'd forgotten her eyeglasses. Her
only hope was that Warwick would send the spectacles
home with Bertrice. Until then, any attempt to read
was virtually impossible. Still, she did her best. No
matter how bad the strain on her eyes it was better than
visualizing her making a fool of herself with Warwick.

Warwick! Dear God, why could she not put him from
her mind? Sitting there, staring at row upon row of
numbers until her head throbbed, the all-encompassing
thought in her mind throughout the morning was how
firm and hot and wet his mouth had been on hers and
the smell of his skin as he stood near her before the fire
had made her entire body feel as if it were slowly turning
inside out.

At a quarter of eleven the door was flung open
and Emily entered. Her arms full of dresses, she
swept through the room like a spring breeze, her
ivory face flushed with enthusiasm. She had pulled
her blond hair straight back and confined it in a net
of pale pink silk that perfectly matched her morning

frock. Her tiny feet were encased in supple leather slippers.

Placing her pen and paper aside, Olivia laced her fingers together and tried her best to ignore her throbbing temples long enough to smile. "And good morning to you, too, sister. What have you there?"

"Dresses of course," Emily replied with a lilting laugh. "I simply must have your opinion, Oli. The Marquess is due to call today. Which dress suits me more, do you think?" She flung several in the vicinity of a wing chair. They landed instead in a heap on the floor. Taking no notice, Emily held another up to her chin and pirouetted before Olivia. "Isn't this divine, Oli? Do you think Lord Willowby will like it?"

"He's certain to love you in anything, Em, unless he's blind or a fool."

The dress sailed away and Emily swept up another. "What about this one? I understand that the blond ruching and the tiny primroses along the décolletage are *de rigueur* in Paris this season."

Leaving her chair, Olivia moved to the scattering of dresses on the floor and proceeded to gather them up. There was a yellow gown with a satin bodice and an overskirt of striped gauze trimmed with gold lace, an exquisite creation that Emily had pleaded for—indeed, threatened to expire for—a few months before. As far as Olivia knew, her sister had never so much as tried it on since it arrived from Paris wrapped in mounds of tissue and ribbons.

"I'm positively certain that Lord Willowby will speak to Father today," Emily said. "Why else would he venture out in this despicable weather? Oli, dear, what do you think you're doing?"

Olivia was holding an Italian-made gown up against herself. She met her sister's incredulous eyes, and felt her face grow warm.

"Don't be a ninny," Emily said, and grabbed the dress away. "You're much too old to wear a dress like this; the color doesn't suit you at all, not with that awful olive tone to your skin. Besides, where on earth would you wear a gown like this? To fidget with Father's ledgers? Or perhaps"—she lowered her voice to a whisper, and her eyes became cold as glass—"to visit Miles Warwick."

Olivia returned to her chair and took up her pen.

"What could you be thinking to go like that to Braithwaite? I mean, it was enough of a shock to learn that Papa had attempted to bribe the incorrigible man to marry you. Can you imagine Miles Warwick as a member of this family—"

"Considering he turned Papa's offer down, Em, I hardly think you or I have anything to worry about. Now please, I have work to finish and my head is killing me. If you wish to take up the subject of Miles again, do so with Father."

There came a knock on the door, and Jonah entered. He regarded Emily with one lifted eyebrow, then smiled at Olivia. "Miss, young Bryan is ready for his outing."

Relieved to have a graceful exit, Olivia put aside her pen and sat back in her chair. "Thank you, Jonah. Will you have Deets bring up the coach? And would you mind terribly to get my wrap?"

Her face clouding, Emily frowned. "Surely you aren't going out in this cold, Olivia."

"A little cold never hurt anyone, Emily, and besides, Bryan looks forward to his outings. A child needs fresh air and exercise if he's to maintain good health and a proper attitude. Or perhaps, being the doting, loving, and concerned *aunt* that you are, you would rather entertain him for the remainder of the afternoon?"

Emily's face flushed a brilliant red, and she averted her eyes. Olivia allowed herself the pleasure of smiling, if only slightly. It wasn't often that Emily had the good grace to show her discomfiture.

Jonah cleared his throat, and Olivia looked around. "Is there something else?" she asked.

"Yes, miss. There's a guest waiting."

"Oh?"

"Miles Warwick."

Warwick.

"Warwick?" she repeated.

"Yes, miss."

"I . . . see. Well, simply tell him that my father—"

"He's not here to see your father, miss."

Olivia glanced at Emily. Emily's blue eyes were round and her pink lips were forming an O of surprise that, in a fraction of a second, melted into a moue of displeasure. With a toss of her blond curls, she announced, "I refuse to see him. Tell him to go away, Jonah, I—"

"I beg your pardon, Miss Emily, but he isn't here to see you. He's here to speak with Miss Olivia."

A bubble of something that felt suspiciously close to excitement centered in Olivia's stomach. And this after spending the entire night convincing herself that Miles Warwick wasn't worth the effort it took to worry about his opinion of her. Setting her shoulders, she took a much-needed breath and said, "Tell him I'm unable to receive him. Bryan is waiting, after all, and . . . well . . . just tell him, if you please."

Jonah nodded and quit the room.

Stepping over the heap of dresses at her feet, Emily planted herself before the desk, and leaning toward Olivia, demanded in an urgent voice, "What is he doing here?"

"He's brought Bertrice home. I'm sure that's it. Calm down, Em, you look as if you've seen a banshee rise out of a fog."

"You're not looking so well yourself," she snapped. "Or perhaps that flush on your cheeks stems from excitement instead of anxiety."

"Don't be daft."

Wringing her hands, Emily cast a frantic glance toward the door. "Oh, God, what if he were to meet Lord Willowby? Knowing Miles, he'd take grand pleasure in telling His Lordship every disgusting detail of our relationship. Get rid of him, Oli, before he destroys my entire future!"

Olivia moved toward the door just as Bryan's laughter rang out in the hallway, along with the sound of running feet. Then the child was there, flinging himself into her arms, his green eyes dancing with merriment.

"Mummy," he cried, "Cook prepared me pudding!"

Olivia sank to one knee and hugged the warmly bundled boy tightly. His breath smelled of orange marmalade, and there was a mustache of milk over his lip that felt moist as he kissed her cheek. She laughed and kissed him back, momentarily forgetting Warwick . . . until Jonah's weak voice called out:

"Here now, my good man, Miss Olivia cannot be disturbed!"

She turned her head, and there he stood, legs slightly spread and his cloak hanging loosely from his shoulders to his shins. Jonah, not far behind him, looked helplessly at Olivia. She sent him away with a nod of her head, and slowly stood up.

"Do you commonly walk into a woman's home under protest?" she asked Warwick.

"If the occasion suits. Do you always show up on a man's doorstep after dark and uninvited?"

Olivia forced herself to take a slow, deep breath. "*Touché*. I assume you've returned Bertrice?"

He nodded and a dark strand of hair spilled over his forehead.

"Well . . . please accept my gratitude, Mr. Warwick. As well as my apologies for the loss of your bed. Now, if you'll excuse us—"

"I'd like to speak with you," he interrupted.

"That won't be possible, alas. I was preparing to leave, you see. With my son."

She watched Warwick's gaze drop to the child, who was clinging to her leg and partially burying his little face in her skirt as he peered up at the tall, dark stranger.

"It's routine," Olivia hurried to add, bringing Warwick's attention back to her. "I take him out every morning."

"How very touching." The words were drolly spoken, yet his features didn't change. His eyes were hard, his expression uncompromising, giving Olivia the impression that he was going to say what he wanted, regardless.

Seeing that he wouldn't be easily dissuaded, she said, "Perhaps you would care to join us."

Emily, who had remained in the study, gasped softly. In truth, Olivia was more than a little shocked at her offer as well. She had put her foot in it again. Still, she would rather that he say what was on his mind in private.

Silence ensued for a long moment as Warwick's gaze shifted from her to the boy, then back to her again. "Very well," he finally replied.

Miles had only meant to escort Bertrice home. He'd never intended to confront Olivia. Certainly not after last night—when he'd made a total idiot out of himself. First by drinking too much, then by prattling about his personal woes.

And there was, of course, the little matter of that kiss.

Couldn't quite shake the idea that he'd enjoyed it.

Very much.

Fact is, he'd walked the house the better part of the night thinking about it.

The coach hit a bump in the road, jarring Miles's discomforting thoughts back to the present. He sat directly across from Olivia, who was wrapped in a cloak with a fox collar. Beside her sat the boy, apple-cheeked with cold, a blanket tucked snuggly over his lap. The lad's green eyes were wide and staring at him. His small but pudgy fingers were laced very properly on his lap.

"Well?" came Olivia's voice, drawing Miles's attention back to her. In the shadowed quarters, and hidden partially by her cowl—as it had been yesterday—her face looked the color of velvety cream; her eyes were large, perhaps enhanced by the darkness and length of her thick lashes. "What did you wish to say, Mr. Warwick?"

He thought hard for a moment, then reached into his pocket, withdrawing her eyeglasses. Tapping them on his knee, he glanced again at the boy, then tossed them onto Olivia's lap.

"That's it?" She didn't smile. "You could have returned the eyeglasses with Bertrice, or left them with Jonah."

He shrugged and crossed one leg over the other, bumping hers in the process.

"If you have something to say, sir, then say it. You needn't worry about Bryan, unless, of course, you wish to dwell again on his parentage—a subject that I don't intend to discuss."

He watched her gloved fingers toy with the stems of her glasses; she did not, however, put them on. "Perhaps I was simply in the mood for a bit of conversation," he said.

"I doubt it. You don't strike me as the kind of man who trifles with chitchat."

"You're a very straightforward young woman, Miss Devonshire."

"I'm hardly young, sir, and therefore am not often entertained by my own coquetry. I've grown too old for games, and have come to appreciate honesty above all else."

"Honesty is often unkind and can cut more painfully than a lie. It's been my experience that people prefer lies, Miss Devonshire."

"Yourself included, Mr. Warwick?"

He smiled a little. "I have a reputation for being blatantly honest, I fear. In that respect my repute is often held in less than admirable esteem."

The coach rocked; a horse whinnied. Deets, the driver, cracked a whip and encouraged the animals on with a sharp whistle.

They sat in stilted silence while Bryan played with his fingers and continually stared at Miles, who returned the

lad's interest with a lifted eyebrow. No doubt the child
had inherited many of the Devonshire traits. Miles found
himself looking from the boy to his mother, comparing
their eyes, nose, mouth. Very similar. The hair, however,
must have been inherited from his father. No one in the
Devonshire family could boast of such a thick crop of
curly black-brown hair.

Frowning, Miles forced himself to look out the window and did his best to dispel the image of Olivia
Devonshire dancing naked with a lot of Gypsies.

Margrove Bluff, a long gray claw of sheer flint that
thrust itself above the meandering river Ure, was the
highest point on the Colsterdale Moor. Grooved into
the surrounding hillside were the remnants of hushes
produced hundreds of years ago as early miners dammed
streams in order to uncover veins of lead. That had been
the ancient way, of course, before shafts and levels—
before the miners gave up hope of discovering ore riches
in the vicinity and moved off to Gunnerside Gill.

The centuries and weather hadn't totally decimated the
relics of those days, however, because scattered over the
surrounding hills and dales were the debris of stone ruins
and heaps of tippings. Folk in the area swore that on
cold winter nights they could hear the ghosts of miners
singing—as the men always did when they trooped to
and from their dangerous job.

From the bluff's peak one could see all the way
to Middleham on a clear day, across the wild country, the empty rolling miles of browns and greens and
yellows. As it was, the wind had scattered the fog just
enough to reveal the high-pitched gables of what was
once Caldbergh Workhouse, and beyond that, the rooftop

and chimneys of Braithwaite Manor.

With his hands in his pockets and his back to the wind, Miles regarded the panorama and wondered what the blazes he was doing here, surprised he was out here with Olivia and her boy. The ground was crunchy with frost and the wind sharp enough to blister his face. His fingers and toes and nose were turning numb, yet the lad seemed hardly to notice. With a scarf wrapped around his head, and mittens covering his hands, Bryan went scooting down a long, sloping hill on his little backside while his mother stood rigidly at the top of the rise, hands at her sides, looking like some ice doll who would shatter with the least pressure.

No doubt about it, Olivia Devonshire was a stuffy little thing. Intense. Unfriendly . . . unless she'd quaffed two portions of whisky, of course, as she had the previous night. He had to hand it to her, most ladies would have passed out with a mere whiff of the stuff.

He watched as she cupped her hands around her mouth and called out for her son to come away from the Ure's icy shoal. Immediately, he scampered away, skidded and plunked hard on his bottom, only to scramble to his feet and dash off again, his breath puffing from his mouth like a steam locomotive. Miles reflected, for a moment, on the times he had come here—always alone—to sit atop the bluff and contemplate life and love; at least until he had grown old enough to realize that life could be experienced without living—"existing" seemed to be a more appropriate verb. And love? There had never been that, as far as he could remember. Standing there now, with the wind moaning over the moor, he tried to recall if his own mother had ever played with him in some frozen Parisian fields.

Not likely. She would have been too busy entertaining her latest paramour.

Olivia turned to look at him. A wind rounded the bluff in that moment and belled the cloak around her ankles and stirred the strands of brown grass that peaked over the snow like ripples on a calm pond. Then she walked toward him, never once taking her eyes from his—no pretense at helplessness common with most females who gave the impression they might swoon if they soiled their shoes or the hem of their dress. It struck him in that moment that Olivia Devonshire was not beautiful, in any conventional sense, yet there was something noble in her features. Her skin seemed almost ruddy with cold; she had a strong nose and a stubborn jaw; her lips were tinged slightly blue.

Stopping an arm's length from him, she said nothing, just fixed him with a steadfast look as if waiting for him to spark the conversation. "I was only thinking," he found himself stating. "Wondering, I suppose, what you would be doing if I wasn't here."

"What do you think?" she asked.

He shrugged. "I can imagine you removing your cowl and turning your face into the wind. Perhaps you might even let down your hair. I'm quite certain you would be sliding down the hill on your backside, just like the boy."

"And no doubt you would find such behavior scandalous and unacceptable."

"I'm hardly in a position to judge."

"True."

He pulled his cloak tighter and turned the collar up around his ears. The need to stomp his feet against the ground to warm them seemed tempting, but he resisted.

She, after all, appeared to be unbothered by the cold.

"Why are you here?" she asked, never faltering in her penetrating gaze.

"I don't know, Miss Devonshire; I was asking myself the same; I'm bloody freezing and it's obvious you're more inclined to keep company with your son."

"Bryan is the most important person in my life."

"He is the *only* person in your life, aside from your father and sister, of course. Both of whom are hardly the most stimulating company."

"You certainly didn't think that way four years ago, when you were courting my sister."

"Courting? A misnomer, I'm sure."

"I'm sure."

"She doesn't appear to have suffered for it."

"I fear Emily doesn't have the depth of character to suffer overly much about anything. While I love her deeply I'm not so fond that I cannot recognize her shortcomings."

"Like your father, for instance?"

"Emily has a way of blinding men."

"Hardly a phenomenon where women are concerned. I've always had the impression that females come into this world with a chameleonlike ability to transform into whatever is necessary to attract the desired mate."

"You do us an injustice, I think. We don't all live and breathe for the love of a man. Nor would we sacrifice our dignity to trap some unsuspecting fool into matrimony," she said pointedly. "Besides, I cannot imagine loving a man long who did not love me in return. It seems a dreadful waste of time."

"Ah. I begin to understand."

Her brow knit slightly in contemplation.

"Perhaps we've all unjustly accused the boy's father. Perhaps his only crime, aside from seduction, was his lack of heartfelt affection. Perhaps he was willing to marry you after all, but you weren't about to settle for anything less than a love match. My dear Miss Devonshire, do you know how many marriages would not have taken place if either party waited for Cupid's arrow to strike him, or her? Good God, I fear the human race would have grown extinct a very long time ago."

"Do you deny that marriages of love exist?"

"Quite the contrary. Take my brother and his wife, for instance. They are more than a little fond of one another."

"As were my parents. Then again, my mother was an incredible beauty. Every man who ever met her fell in love immediately. Emily is the very image of her in every way."

At last her features changed, albeit subtly. It was in the eyes. They became distant and somehow tragic; a sea-green well of sorrow that made him temporarily forget about the icy wind. In that space of time—no more than three or four seconds—she said nothing, just looked away over the moor; then she resumed her study of him, all emotion washed from her features, but there was a difference. Her shoulders did not seem quite so rigid. In truth, they appeared burdened by some colossal invisible weight. He saw it all, the reality. It sang in the air like wind whipping around a kite string—all the reasons why Olivia Devonshire had so meekly accepted her reputation of spinster, and worse.

Precisely then a cry rang out. A curlew, perhaps, or a jackdaw. Yet the sky showed no hint of birds, and a cursory look over the frosty landscape revealed

no human or animal shape. Then the realization struck
him . . .

"Bryan?" Olivia called. "Where is he? Bryan!"

Frowning, Miles directed his gaze toward the river.
There was nothing there but the ice-covered water, with
an occasional clump of spiky weeds thrusting up through
the frozen mire.

"Bryan!" Olivia called more loudly, turning and turning in a frantic effort to locate her suddenly missing son.
She ran toward the bluff's precipice, her cloak flying
out behind her, her ankles twisting as her shoes tangled
in her skirt and the dense sodden overgrowth blanketing
the moor.

"Miss Devonshire!" Miles shouted, as he watched
her stumble. He moved swiftly up the incline, reaching
Olivia as she struggled to her feet.

"Let me go," she demanded as he grabbed her shoulders and held her. "My son is missing—"

"You're sure as hell not going to help him if you go
plunging headfirst off this precipice. Listen to me!" He
shook her.

The cry came again. Olivia shoved Miles away and
ran to the crown of the cliff, crying aloud as a covey
of brown birds exploded from their hiding place amid a
snarl of briars. Cursing, Miles grabbed her from behind
and pinned her against him as he searched the rock-
studded face and floor of the bluff for any sign that the
lad had toppled over the ledge.

Nothing.

Olivia squirmed from his arms and stumbled back
down the hill, crying Bryan's name and calling for Deets
who, having heard her cries, came rushing toward them.
Breathing hard, Miles searched the undulating ground,

his mind scrambling for any plausible way the lad could simply disappear without a trace. He, himself, had played here as a youth; as far as he could remember, aside from the sheer drop of the bluff itself, there had been no hazards . . . except for . . .

He struck out running, half sliding down the steep incline, tearing off his cloak and flinging it away in an effort to move more swiftly, while his eyes frantically scanned the terrain and his ears strained to detect the boy's cries.

There!

He almost stumbled into the sinkhole before locating the black pit with his eyes. Bryan's terrified wails were muffled by the depth of the cavity, and the dense coverage of vegetation hadn't helped. Falling to his knees, he focused hard on the darkness and called Bryan's name.

The lad responded with a terrified sob.

"Don't move, Bryan," Miles said as calmly as possible. "Your Mummy and I will have you out of there in a wink."

Silence for a moment. A sniffle. Then a quaking: "Promise?"

He grinned. "Promise."

Miles stood as Olivia ran toward him, Deets close on her heels. Her face white and eyes glassy with fear, she did her best to push past him while he held her fiercely and did his best to push her back. "Listen to me," he told her, and shook her until her hair spilled down her back and her body turned rigid. "Hysteria won't help your son, Miss Devonshire. He's safe enough where he is as long as he doesn't try to move."

"Is it a well of some sort?" Deets asked, peering concernedly over the lip of the pit.

"A sinkhole. These bluffs are full of them. Some of them are simply caused by the roofs of underground caves falling in."

"How deep is it?" Olivia demanded as she gripped his shirt in her fists.

"I can't tell, but he seems to be well enough so far." Looking at Deets, he said, "I'll need a rope."

"I'll be needin' to return to Devonswick for that," the driver replied.

"There isn't time for that!" Olivia cried.

Stepping around her, Miles stared down into the black void as he removed his suit coat and began rolling up his shirtsleeves. Then he dropped to his knees.

Deets did likewise, and as Miles eased over the ledge of the pit, the driver grabbed his ankles.

Hanging upside down, the jagged edges of flint scraping his face, arms, and chest, Miles stretched his hands toward the child's blurry form huddled against the earthen wall. "Give me your hand," he ordered quietly. When the lad refused, he repeated the directive more forcefully and stretched harder. There came a mutter, a curse, a frantic scramble from above just as Miles felt himself sliding farther into the hole. He made a desperate grab for something, *anything,* to stop the inevitable fall, only to find himself plummeting headfirst into the cold, rank-smelling morass a dozen feet below.

Far above him Olivia cried out in alarm. Deets, forgetting himself, yelled an explicit curse and profuse apologies for his clumsiness, while just above his head Bryan wailed in fear. Miles floundered in the slime and mire, and dragged himself up on the ledge where Bryan perched. They each sat there on the narrow lip, shivering, staring at the other's dim features in the dark.

Finally, Miles raised a hand to him, and the boy scrambled onto his lap, buried his face in Miles's chest and sobbed.

"There, there," Miles said, blinking grit from his eyes. Hesitantly, he wrapped one arm around the little form and gazed up at the spherical gray sky overhead.

"Mr. Warwick!" Olivia called. "Can you hear me?"

He nodded.

"Mr. Warwick!"

"I can hear you, dammit!"

"Is Bryan all right?"

"Faring better than I," he muttered. "At least he's dry."

After much manipulation, Miles managed to extricate the boy by first standing the lad on his shoulders, then gripping his ankles and hefting him up far enough so Olivia and Deets could grab his hands. There came a chorus of relieved cries that gradually diminished into silence while Miles stood weaving on the narrow ledge, shivered with cold, and waited his turn.

And waited.

"Ah . . ." He cleared his throat. "Hello!" he shouted. "What about me? Hello, is anyone there?"

More silence while there came a splashing in the muck below him.

At last, Deets stuck his head over the ledge and called out, "Right then. Would ya like a hand, sir?"

With great difficulty, Miles managed to locate sufficient toeholds amid the jagged rocks to claw his way far enough up to grab Deets's outstretched hand. Flung out on the frozen ground, Miles momentarily stared at the sky while the wind drove through him as piercingly as an icicle.

Removing his coat, Deets tossed it around Miles's shoulders and helped him to stand. Far below, Olivia, with Bryan wrapped in Miles's cloak in her arms, was just boarding the coach.

The interior of the coach brought relief from the cold. As Deets whipped the horses into a dash for Devonswick, Olivia held her son in her lap and briskly rubbed his hands and feet; the boy slowly regained his color, and his shivering subsided. Still, she gripped him fiercely to her, kissing his small head time and again, her eyes only occasionally, reluctantly, drawn to Miles's.

Finally, he said, "I suppose it's a good thing that I came along after all."

"Had you not come along," she retorted, "this wouldn't have happened."

His eyebrows went up.

"As it was," she continued in a more level voice, "you diverted my attention—"

"I'm sitting here freezing in clothes that are wet through and you're blaming me for this? Look at me," he added, brandishing his scraped hands. His shirt was raggedly torn in a half-dozen places.

Bryan squirmed into a sitting position then looked straight at Miles, and held out his arms.

Silence. The coach swayed. Miles frowned.

Without a word, Bryan slid off his mother's lap and climbed onto Miles's. With his small, damp head pressed to Miles's chest, he proceeded to gaze up at him with big, gray-green eyes.

"Good God," Miles muttered, vaguely aware of an unsettling shift of something in the vicinity of his heart.

Fear, no doubt. He'd never so much as spoken to a child, much less held one. Or perhaps it was simply distaste. For him children had always been a necessary nuisance, essential mainly for continuing a bloodline, an entity foreign to a man of his dubious origins.

Olivia said nothing, yet her body tensed. She watched him with an intensity that bordered on panic. Yet, there was something else there too. An awakening of sorts.

She withdrew the child from his lap just as the coach stopped at Devonswick's front door. Deets, having flung open the coach door and dropped the steps, assisted Olivia and her son to the ground, then escorted them at a brisk pace into the house. Miles took his time stepping into the cold. He told himself that he should leave; his business, whatever that had been, was finished. And he was wet through. Then the sound of excited voices reached him. Obviously the help were scurrying to see to the boy's needs.

He stepped into the foyer in time to see Emily join her sister and nephew at the foot of the stairs. She might have just stepped off some Paris fashion plate, adorned as she was in a pearl-colored silk gown trimmed with cerise edged with black lace. Quite a contrast to Olivia's plain brown frock.

"What on earth are you doing?" Emily demanded.

"Bryan fell into some horrible pit, and—"

"You've left mud all over the floor, Oli! Look at the mess, and Lord Willowby is due to arrive just any minute."

Holding Bryan in her arms, Olivia stood up to her sister. "Didn't you hear what I said, Emily? Bryan could have been killed. Have you no sense of compassion? No modicum of concern for this child? Dear heavens, Emily, occasionally I truly question both your sense of morality and conscience."

With that, Olivia swept the child up the stairs. Only then did Emily turn to discover Miles standing inside the door. She looked shocked.

"I don't recall having invited you in," she said, recovering herself.

"You wouldn't," he replied indifferently, his mouth curved in a hard smile.

She hurried toward him, stopping short and covering her nose with her hankie. Emily's blue eyes slid down his person, noting his damp, mud-encrusted clothes and boots. She said nothing about them; however, she lifted her gaze back to his and hissed, "Get out of this house. Do you hear me? Get out!"

"What's wrong, sweetheart? Afraid my being here is going to somehow upset old Lord Willowby?" He laughed and anger glittered in her eyes. "Have you beguiled him with your innocence? As I recall, you were quite good at that."

She gasped. "Get out," she demanded.

"And if I don't?"

"Then I'll have you thrown out."

"And what's to stop me from riding over the hill and waiting for Willowby? Perhaps informing him that his angel-faced sweetheart has a heart-shaped mole on the inside of her left thigh, and that she's particularly sensitive to the touch of a tongue on her—"

"Blackmailer!" she whispered furiously. "What will it take to make you leave here and never come back?" She looked thoughtful, then her eyes narrowed. Moving nearer in a suggestive manner, she forced a shaky smile.

"Don't bother," he replied to her shocked eyes. "I'm completely uninterested."

"I hate you," Emily sneered.

He winked and adjusted the sleeves of his soiled suit coat and decided his cloak could wait. He'd had about enough of the Devonshire women for one day.

"Mr. Warwick."

Looking around, he found Olivia standing at the foot of the stairs. Again, she wore her eyeglasses. Her hair, however, still spilled becomingly around her face.

Twirling, Emily stomped toward her, pausing only long enough to say, "Get him out of here, Oli, before His Lordship arrives or I'll never forgive you." Then she fled the foyer through a nearby threshold, slamming the door behind her.

A moment passed before Olivia turned her eyes back to Miles's. "Your cloak," she stated evenly, and approached him, the article folded neatly over one of her arms. The idea occurred to him that she was probably one of those women who were fanatics about tidiness; no doubt if he was to march up those stairs and stroll to her room he would discover that every filmy object in her wardrobe drawers would be fastidiously neat and arranged by color. Then again, judging by the way she dressed, she probably owned no filmy undergarments.

"Your cloak," she repeated as she stopped before him, her eyes holding his. He knew in an instant that she was fully aware of what had just taken place between him and her sister. Olivia Devonshire might have been a great number of things, but she wasn't a fool.

He took the cloak.

Olivia stepped back and clasped her hands before her. "I fear I was remiss in showing my appreciation.

You saved Bryan's life. My only excuse for my sorry behavior was that I allowed my fear of losing him to overcome my sense of decency."

"An apology isn't necessary, Miss Devonshire. Neither is your gratitude. I have a feeling you would have handled the situation equally as well without me. The only difference is, I'm the one who fell in the hole instead of you."

A look of amusement lit her eyes and toyed with her lips. Damn, she had fine lips. Pleasant to look at, full and pink and soft. He wondered how many men had kissed them as fervently as he had last night.

"Your clothes," those lips said, then smiled. "I totally forgot about them. If you'd care to send them back, I'll see that they're properly mended and laundered and your boots cleaned."

Miles looked down his legs, to his boots, to the muddy footprints he'd left on the floor, and shook his head. "No, thank you."

Without another word, he turned on his heels and quit the house, stood shivering on the porch steps (the idea of putting on his cloak never occurring to him) while his driver brought up the coach. Once inside, he sank into the leather seat, nudged back the maroon velvet shade with one finger, and found Olivia still standing in the doorway, gazing off down the drive.

She had removed her eyeglasses.

"I am now forty-one years old," he went on. "I may
have been called a confirmed bachelor, and I was
a confirmed bachelor. I had never any views of myself as
a husband in my earlier days, nor have I made any
calculation on the subject since I have been older.
But we all change, and my change, in this matter, came
with seeing you. I have felt lately, more and more,
that my present way of living is bad in every respect.
Beyond all things, I want you as my wife."

—THOMAS HARDY,
Far from the Madding Crowd

CHAPTER SIX

MILES HAD REMAINED A BACHELOR THESE THIRTY-
nine years because he'd imagined himself waiting for a
paragon. She, of course, would be breathtakingly beautiful, as well as highly intelligent.

How did Olivia Devonshire fare on these counts?
First, he realized Miss Devonshire was far from unat-
tractive. In fact with the proper clothes and arrangement
of her hair he suspected she could rival her sister.

Intelligence?

That was probably an unfair requirement. Most wom-
en weren't particularly well educated in anything except
deceit and flirtation—Olivia Devonshire being the exception, of course. According to her father she could probably teach his professors at Cambridge a thing or two
about economics . . . And he could certainly use some
help in that area.

Miles lay back in his tub of tepid water and smoked
his Cuban cigar. He frowned.

Certainly his wife would have to possess a wonderful

sense of humor. Olivia Devonshire didn't have one iota of humor in her entire stiff-as-a-poker little body. No doubt the woman's face would crack if she attempted to laugh . . .

Then again, he supposed that she really didn't have a great deal to laugh about. Someone needed to teach her not to take life so seriously . . . which could prove to be an interesting and pleasant task . . .

Any woman he would even consider marrying would come from a well-respected family. Her impeccable reputation and position in Society would afford him the respect and ultimate success that had slipped through his fingers all of his life, due to his own sorry heritage. Certainly, that in itself was the problem. No woman of such stature would afford him a minute of her time, much less her dowry.

And there was the little matter of love . . .

He believed in the institution of marriage. And while he could prattle all day to Olivia Devonshire about the many marriages that were loveless, he had always imagined himself loving the woman with whom he would spend the rest of his life. He'd never been able to envisage himself being forced to share the routine of living with a companion who displeased him. For that reason, his love affairs had been a series of short, unemotional dalliances.

Undoubtedly he was more like his mother than he cared to admit. Although Alyson Kemball had taken many lovers, and had had the opportunity to marry numerous times, she had loved only one man, and that had been Joseph Warwick. Because she could not have Joseph she had opted for no marriage at all.

Which brought his mind back to Olivia Devonshire. And her son.

He glanced at the pile of discarded and ruined clothes on the floor and recalled the discomfort he'd experienced under the lad's intense scrutiny during the ride to Margrave Bluff. Might have been watching a moment from his own past—a fatherless boy sitting at his mother's side and wondering about the man sitting across from him. Was he his father? Would he be his father in the future? Just where the blazes was his father?

Poor lad. Deserved better. Seemed bright enough. Handsome little tyke. Certainly affectionate—not to mention brave. He'd held up as well, if not better, than Miles as they waited for help in the bottom of that pit. An admirable quality, that. His father should feel proud.

Miles put out his cigar in the water then stepped from the tub, waiting as Sally wrapped a towel around his waist. The room was cold, the windows frosty. Sally hurried to grab up his dressing gown, a silk magenta wrap that tied at the waist with a wide sash, and helped him slide his arms into the loose, flowing sleeves. Then she handed him a silver chalice of warm wine.

"Will there be aught else?" she asked, drying her hands on her apron.

He smiled and regarded her eyes, acknowledging the spark of interest there. Another time he might have obliged her.

"No," he replied, "thank you."

She shrugged and quit the room.

Miles stared at the door and considered calling her back. But something stopped him.

He drank the warm liquid and moved across the room, to the foot of his tester bed. Months had passed since he'd last entertained at Braithwaite, and then his guests had been nothing more than a dozen acquaintances with their pockets full of currency and their sleeves full of aces. By the time they'd returned to London he'd been glad to get shut of them, even relished the quiet and solitude.

But last night had been hell.

He drank again.

For some odd reason, the moment Olivia Devonshire had closed Braithwaite's door behind her, emptiness had roared up like a gale from every dark hallway, stairwell, and threshold. And while Bertrice had snored in his bed, he'd tossed and turned in another room, doing his best to forget how good Olivia had felt in his arms.

Must be getting desperate, old man, he thought. No doubt he'd imagined and exaggerated her responsiveness. Then again, with a woman with so disreputable a past, why should he be surprised?

Frowning and again thinking of Olivia's son, Miles quaffed the remainder of his wine and plunked the cup on a table strewn with playing cards. Too bad about the boy. Had Olivia been a plain-as-a-mouse little spinster who was desperate to marry simply so she would not wither away like some flower on a vine, then he might have considered marriage, with the understanding that their union would be strictly for convenience; they would each be free to live their lives independent of the other, each free to take their lovers as they so desired.

But the lad was a monstrous responsibility . . . and an unnerving reminder of his mother's sordid past.

Not that the lad should, in any way, be held accountable for his mother's poor judgment . . . . as Miles himself had been.

He dressed for tea. Always did. Habits were hard to break, and besides, there was nothing else to do. He thought of riding over to Damien's, give his brother's guests something fresh to gossip about, but the tumble into the sinkhole had left him stiff and sore.

Adjourning to his study, Miles paced the room with no very clear purpose, tossed the arm from a seventeenth-century French fauteuil in the fire and watched sparks scatter up the chimney, then taking his chair behind the desk, he sifted through the stacks of correspondence, most of which he hadn't bothered to open since they'd arrived weeks, perhaps months, before. There were several from Gunnerside complaining of the mining conditions; nothing new there, the same old threats of striking, demands for pay increases, and complaints about factors that made working the pits dangerous if not lethal.

There was also a letter from Josiah Lubinsky, which he tossed in the waste bin without so much as opening the envelope. Miles was uninterested in selling the mines. Not yet. Not until he was positive beyond all doubt that the damn pits were played out.

Tugging loose his cravat, Miles flipped through the dozen or so letters containing demand notices from creditors that had lain forgotten for weeks, was about to send them the way of Lubinsky's when the simple and discreet return address on an envelope buried among others caught his eye.

"J. P. Mathews & Assoc. London, England."

Miles closed his eyes briefly. How long had the letter lain there unnoticed? He broke the seal and flipped open the envelope, doing his best to regulate his breathing and regretting that he had thrown that chair leg into the fire.

The air in the room felt unbearably hot.

"Dear Mr. Warwick: As you recall from previous correspondence, there has been a problem of monies owed . . ."

Miles rubbed his eyes and stared at the ceiling a long while before forcing his attention back to the missive.

"Therefore, it is with deepest regret that we must terminate the association . . ."

Damn. Oh, damn.

"Unless this office hears from you by 1 November in the matter of monies owed, you may expect my colleagues, and their charge, to arrive at Braithwaite by 15 November at the latest. With deepest and most sincere apologies for whatever inconvenience this may cause you . . ."

Olivia fell asleep with her glasses on. She hadn't meant to doze, but the strain of the afternoon had left her limp.

Drifting in and out of sleep, she tried her best to forget the previous hours, especially the moment, at the top of the stairs, when she had looked down into the foyer to find Miles and Emily standing toe to toe and conversing in heated whispers.

"Olivia? Olivia, wake up!"

Olivia opened her eyes with effort. But for one burning oil lamp on a distant table, the room was dark.

Her eyeglasses had slid off her nose and lay lopsidedly on her cheek. Righting the spectacles, she did her best to make out the silhouette looming over her in the shadows.

"Emily?" Coming up on her elbows, Olivia searched her sister's distraught features, experiencing a sense of panic. "Oh, God, it's Bryan, isn't it? Something's happened—"

"He's come back, Oli."

"Who?"

"Miles. He's been holed up in Papa's office for the past two hours."

Olivia tried to push aside her sleepish confusion. "What does he want?"

Her fists clenched, her blue eyes round, Emily cried, "What do you think he wants, you idiot? You!"

Shocked at first, then agitated, Olivia threw back the counterpane and swung her feet from the bed. "Don't be absurd, Emily."

"Absurd, am I? Then why are he and Papa carrying on together in that room, laughing and drinking like comrades-in-arms? And why," she added, thrusting her face at Olivia's, "did Papa just send me word that I was to get you up, dressed in your prettiest frock, and down to the office in the next ten minutes?"

Olivia didn't so much as blink; it might have, in some way, revealed the upheaval of anxiety inside her.

Anxiety? she wondered. Or excitement?

Please, God, don't let it be hope. She had given up on that a very long time ago.

Her mind still groggy with sleep, she stumbled to the lantern and turned up the light, then hurried about the room, lighting the globe fixtures atop claw-footed tables until the room shimmered from the fire-yellow illumination. The ashes in the fireplace had dulled to a glowing pewter-gray. Olivia shifted them around with a poker until the flames gasped for life, then she tossed in a shovel of coal, adding a portion of peat for good measure.

"You can't be serious," Emily said. "You're not really going down there?"

"I don't normally defy Father. And why should I?" Throwing open the wardrobe door, Olivia studied her meager selection of gowns, or attempted to. Her thoughts were scattering in a thousand directions, but always coming back to the one vibrating question: *What if?*

Choosing a white blouse and brown skirt, Olivia dressed as Emily proceeded to pace around the room.

"How dare he?" Emily whined. "And today of all days, just hours after Lord Willowby asked for my hand in marriage."

Grabbing up a brush, Olivia dragged it through her hair, frowning as it sprang wildly around her face and over her shoulders, fumbling in her attempt to style the heavy mane into a chignon.

Emily flopped into a chair and covered her face with her hands. "What will Lord Willowby think if you marry that dreadful man? Oh God, he's bound to find out about Miles!"

"You're jumping to conclusions, Em. For all we know Father invited Warwick over to show his appreciation for Miles's fishing Bryan out of that pit this morning."

"Well, it would have been better for everyone if he had simply let the boy remain there!"

Olivia flew across the room, and before Emily could so much as form an O of surprise with her lips, grabbed her arms tightly and shook her hard. When her sister cried out in pain, Olivia froze. Emily stared up at her, too stunned at first to even cry.

Olivia, too, was stunned at herself. Mortified. For years she had been her sister's biggest supporter. Hiding her mistakes from her father, and especially Emily's highly regarded social world, indulging all of her sister's selfish whims, because somehow Olivia had ignorantly believed that by doing so she would endear herself to her father.

But Emily's wishing Bryan dead—even if it had been said in the heat of the moment . . . dear God, it was simply too much to bear . . .

Emily burst into tears, and leaping from the chair, ran from the room. Olivia stared after her, her heart breaking . . . whether for Emily, or herself, or for Bryan . . . she couldn't tell.

Olivia stood before her father's desk feeling as if she were some child caught stealing apples from an orchard. His face looked very stern, yet there was a certain sadness in his eyes; when he smiled, the gesture did nothing to soften his visage.

"Marriage?" Olivia repeated, feeling her knees grow as wobbly as clotted cream. She refused to look at Miles Warwick, who had planted himself near the fireplace, one elbow casually perched upon the mantel, his observation of her unwavering.

"Yes," her father replied. "Marriage. Warwick has returned to Devonswick to ask my permission to take you as wife. I've of course given him my blessings. You must make the final decision."

"To marry Miles Warwick."

Her father nodded.

At last, she forced her gaze to Warwick's. How could he stand there proposing marriage with no more emotion than if he had offered for a cow? "I beg your pardon," she managed, "I'm just a little taken aback. Just yesterday—"

"Understandably," Warwick said, then turned his attention back to her father. "Perhaps if I could speak with Olivia alone."

"Certainly! Of course." Her father left his chair and quit the room, easing the door closed behind him. Silence then stretched out between her and Warwick. For eternal moments she waited for him to speak, to break the uncompanionable quiet. Yet, he only stood there, dressed in a dark gray suit so smartly tailored that it accentuated his broad shoulders, slender waist, and narrow hips. His eyes looked very dark and perfectly matched his vest of forest-green Chinese silk, embroidered with butterflies in gold thread.

"Well," she finally said in a voice that sounded too obviously nervous. "Dare I ask if you've dipped a little too deeply into your whisky again? Or perhaps my father simply upped the ante, proffering you an offer only a man as wealthy as Prince Edward would turn down."

"No," he replied simply.

"Oh? Surely you don't expect me to believe that you've come here on some pretense of fondness—"

"No."

She looked away. "Well, you didn't exaggerate your honesty."

"I'm sorry if I injured your feelings."

"My feelings are not easily injured, sir."

From the corner of her eye, she saw him move. He walked to the window behind her father's desk and looked out. His dark hair curled thick and rich over his back collar, and the light reflected in red-gold swatches amid the luxurious strands. *Oh . . . she could not breathe!* She was forced to press her fingers to the desktop to steady herself.

"Your father speaks highly of your business sense," he said without turning. "You manage this house admirably." He slowly pivoted to face her and all she could think of was how the whiteness of his expertly tied cravat accentuated the bronze tone of his skin. Miles Warwick loved the sun—she knew that much. Years ago she'd watched him ride wildly across the moor on the Arabians he so loved. She also knew that he had been forced to sell most of the remaining stable in order to meet his debts. "You need a husband," he said, and added almost wearily, "and I need a wife."

"You need a dowry, sir."

"I can hardly deny that."

"Surely there are younger and prettier women whose fathers would be equally as generous—"

"I doubt it."

Her eyes met his in surprise.

"Their fathers would never approve of me as a son-in-law."

She nudged her eyeglasses, just enough so they lay more comfortably on the bridge of her nose.

"Ours would not be the first loveless marriage," he explained.

She nodded.

"And there's the boy to consider . . ."

"I'm well aware of my responsibilities. So I must ask you to keep him out of this. If we're to be totally honest, I must say that, if circumstances were different, I would search out a better respected subject to help raise Bryan."

Miles leaned back against the windowsill, noting that Olivia's cheeks had flushed with the first mention of her son. Odd how her normally stoic façade was blown to

Hades when he mentioned the lad. "True. Neither of us can be choosy. In short, were I not such a poor catch I would search out a woman who was chaste, who wasn't known for frolicking with Gypsies and Asian tattooists." Her chin went up slightly, her shoulders back. Her eyes turned that vivid shade of green that he'd witnessed when they'd plowed into one another on the walk. "Although when I look at you I cannot believe the restrained woman standing before me is the same woman who has inspired so many wild stories. So tell me, dear heart," he added with a lopsided smile, "is it true?"

"What?" she snapped.

"Have you danced with Gypsies? Subjected yourself to the tortures of a tattooist?"

"Would it matter if I had?"

"Perhaps it would be better if we entered into the blissful state of matrimony with full disclosures, so to speak."

"You seem to have taken for granted that I accept your offer of marriage, sir."

"Don't you?"

"I don't know. There's a great deal to consider."

"Such as?"

"You, for one. 'Tis well known you're a womanizer. A gambler who's been known to cheat. You have a chip on your shoulder the size of Wales when concerning your family. Are those stories true?"

"All but one."

She looked at him, surprised.

"I don't cheat at cards." His sudden move toward her made her flinch. He watched her sidle a short way along the desk before she apparently caught herself and set her heels to the carpet. That stubborn and defiant tilt to her jaw returned, and she regarded him as warily as a cornered fox: *Should she flee for escape or face the big bad wolf and take her chances?* Pausing at the corner of the desk, he said, "Now it's your turn, Miss Devonshire."

She glared at him through her spectacles, her hair pulled back so tightly at the temples that the outside tips of her eyes looked slanted. It was obvious that she'd dressed her hair hurriedly; the chignon on the back of her head that was normally fastidiously neat now looked more like a ruffled hedgehog. There was a pin working its way out of the fuzzy coil. The temptation to flick the perilously placed object away and allow her hair to tumble where it may, as it had the evening before, was almost impossible to resist.

"I'm waiting," he prodded.

"It's true. All of it." She took a deep, shaky breath, yet her gaze never wavered from his. "I did dance with Gypsies—"

"Naked?"

She hesitated as hot color crept up her throat from under her high-collared blouse. Her hip leaned a little harder against the desk. "A slight exaggeration. I . . . was gowned in scarves and veils. As for the tattooist . . . true as well."

"Ah."

"Are you repulsed, sir?"

"That depends. How big is the tattoo? Or how many do you have? Or rather, where are they? For that matter, *what* are they?"

"What difference does it make? There's no undoing what's been done."

"I'd like to be prepared for the eventuality of witnessing my wife displaying a flesh canvas of fire-breathing dragons or skulls and crossbones."

"In your circumstances I imagine you should be grateful for whatever you can get."

"In your circumstances, I imagine you should feel the same."

"There you have it, sir. What sort of happiness can two such lost souls find with one another?"

"Companionship."

"But I have companionship here, with my father, sister, and son. Not to mention Bertrice."

"A father who would sacrifice you to a ne'er-do-well like me just to guarantee his younger daughter's station. A sister who would remind you every day of your life that you were put on this earth to leap at her every beck and call. A senile old nanny who keeps company with an invisible cat, and a son whose life you would doom, for the rest of his life, branded as the son of a fallen woman."

"While you keep company with ghosts from your past, and cobwebs, and furnishings used as fuel!" she replied hotly. "While you find fellowship with belligerent servants and bottles of whisky. I'm no naïve ninny, sir. 'Tis not companionship you seek, but a means to end your poverty, to buy back your good credit, to rebuild your dreams for Braithwaite, and at it, to establish yourself solidly in the gentry that was denied you because *you,* sir, are the offspring of a 'fallen woman.'"

He said nothing for a long while; gradually, the quiet was replaced by the harmony of falling rain against the windowpane and the subtle humming of flames in the hearth. At last, he offered her a tight smile. "There's little doubt, that should we decide to enter into this . . . venture, for lack of a better word, we'll do so with little hypocrisy between us. True, I don't love you. I often wonder if I'm capable of loving any woman."

"So tell me. If this union is to be one strictly of convenience, are you to be given the freedom to do as you please in regard to outside relationships?"

He studied her expressionless features and the thin gold rim of her eyeglasses where they balanced on her nose. "If I so desire," he finally replied in a hard, surprisingly defensive voice.

Olivia just raised one arched brow in a show of mild aggressiveness, and crossed her slender arms over her breasts. "I presume I'll be offered the same freedom," she said.

He stared into her steadfast eyes a blind moment, her features obliterated by his mind's image of Olivia Devonshire . . . *Warwick* sneaking away in the dead of night to some clandestine meeting with a lover. The idea was laughable, really, then again, he reminded himself that while the gal might look like someone's prudish spinster aunt on the surface, the fact was very clear that beneath that puritanical veneer was a very enticing woman—and somewhere out there was at least one man whom she had cared about enough to sacrifice her reputation. How moronic of him to continue to forget.

Olivia watched Warwick's face turn dark, and the smug, self-satisfied expression on his features melt like wax from a flame. "Well?" she demanded. "What? No reply? Surely you aren't having second thoughts; it stands to reason that the fact that you've returned to Devonswick with marriage on your mind means you've suddenly grown more desperate for money—perhaps a few of your more unsavory creditors have made threats? But that is neither here nor there. I only wonder why would you care if I indulged in my amours as long as I didn't flaunt them?"

He turned away and moved along the wall of books, pausing occasionally as if to study a particular title. When coming to a table lined with liquor-filled decanters, he hesitated, ran one long finger up and down the neck of a glittering crystal bottle, then said, "It seems I have a habit of forgetting about your situation. I believe you mentioned the man's name last evening . . . ?"

"No. I didn't."

"Certainly you did." He partially turned his head and gave her an inquisitive appraisal. "I'm sure of it. Just as you finished your second cup of whisky—"

"No, I didn't."

"I think it's only fair that I know the identity of the boy's father."

" 'Twould serve no purpose, I tell you."

Facing her again, his hands on his hips so his coat caught behind his wrists, he regarded her fiercely. "Blast it then, will you at least tell me if you loved him?"

"Would it make a difference?"

"Just tell me, dammit."

"Yes. I loved him."

"I see. And do you still love him?"

"Do I love Bryan's father? Is that what you are asking, Mr. Warwick?"

He nodded.

"I admit to experiencing moments of extreme fondness for Bryan's father. Too, there are times, when I reflect on the type of character that he is, that I feel a certain disappointment, if not outright disgust."

"And what sort of character is he?"

"A man without scruples, certainly, or he would never

have taken advantage of an unmarried young woman of family, no matter how weak she was."

"So he's charming, is he?"

"Undoubtedly, but only when the occasion suits." Propping her derriere on the desk edge, she leveled him with a look as intense as his own. Yet her knees, beneath her brown muslin skirt, were once more turning to jelly as she realized that she just might have stuck her foot in it again. But then, perhaps it was all for the best. He had not proposed marriage for any of the right reasons, and she wasn't about to surrender what little dignity she'd retained. The matter of Bryan's future and happiness was far too important.

Warwick moved toward the door, and Olivia came upright so quickly the objects on the desktop, along with the desk, danced in place.

He paused at the threshold, and without looking back, declared, "If you're the least bit interested in my proposal, Miss Devonshire, let me know. I'll hear from you, 'yea' or 'nay,' by this time tomorrow or you can forget I was ever here." Then he was gone.

She stared at the empty doorway, her heart hammering in her chest and her lungs constricting severely enough that she could hardly breathe. Then she dashed to the door opening to find him poised in the foyer, taking his coat from Jonah.

"Mr. Warwick," she called, bringing Miles's head and shoulders around. "If you don't mind my saying, sir, your manners leave a great deal to be desired. One does not simply walk into a woman's home like some cave dweller and issue her ultimatums, especially when it concerns a matter of some importance, such as marriage."

Jonah's bushy eyebrows shot up. "Marriage!" he cried,

then calling to a watchful housemaid with eyes round as an owl's who was loitering near the foot of the stairs, he said, "Glory day, Miss Olivia is betrothed!"

"I'm no such thing!" she argued in a panic.

"Miss Olivia is betrothed!" a voice called out somewhere down the gallery.

Lowering her head slightly, she charged up the foyer to confront Warwick toe to toe. He, on the other hand, didn't budge, just regarded her with narrowed eyes.

"For your information," she said to no one in particular and to everyone at once, "I have not agreed to marry this man."

"What's got you so upset?" Warwick drawled. "Could it be that I didn't present you with flowers and candy and go to one knee to propose?"

"Don't be absurd, sir. I haven't got the slightest desire for such feminine trivialities."

"No? Then perhaps you're simply unaccustomed to dealing with people you can't, or who won't, bend to your will. Or perhaps you're just afraid."

"Of you!" It wasn't a question.

"Of the world outside those doors, Miss Devonshire. You know what I think? I think you lied about it all. There weren't any Gypsies or any tattooist. You made them up right here." He tapped her temple with one finger. She gasped and her face turned ten shades of red. She could feel it as vividly as she could sense her self-control evaporating under the heat of her mounting indignation. "As a matter of fact," he added with a deliberate pause. "You're such a prig I wouldn't be surprised if you even lied about Bryan's conception."

Her mouth opened and closed without speaking. Her pulse felt as if it were climbing up her throat, a certain sign of panic—each individual hair on her scalp felt as if it had stood straight up on end.

Lowering his head toward hers, and curving his sensual mouth in a sarcastic half-smile that accentuated the prominence of one cheekbone, he said, "I'd stake my life on the possibility that he was begot by immaculate conception."

Tension slid from her shoulder blades; she almost collapsed. Had her body not been shaking still from her momentary upset she might have laughed. As it was, she only managed to afford him a smug smile, and slowly, deliberately, she plucked open the tiny pearl buttons on her blouse, starting at the collar and moving down, while Warwick's eyes narrowed and his chiseled features took on the appearance of granite as the fine blouse spilled open to expose her throat, then her collarbone, and finally the lacy edge of the chemise covering her breasts.

As his dark eyes slowly returned to hers, she stared into their shockingly intense depths, and said softly, "Just so there's no misunderstanding, sir . . ." Catching the filmy chemise with the tip of one finger, she tugged it down, just enough to expose the subtly colored and expertly drawn tattoo of a pale pink rose that curved gracefully up the inside swell of her breast. "I assure you, Mr. Warwick, that I'm everything rumors have made me out to be. And possibly more."

His gaze dropped again to her breast, and remained there while the silence stretched out and Olivia felt the first flush of discomfiture and chagrin turn her flesh to fire.

At last, Warwick's lips curved, and causing Olivia to catch her breath, he lightly pressed one fingertip to the rose stem and slowly drew his finger up, up to the pink bloom where he hesitated, bringing his eyes back to hers. "Very nice. If I cry encore will you remove something else?"

She clutched her blouse shut at her throat.

"You'll learn soon enough that I'm not easily shocked, Miss Devonshire. Not nearly so easily as you."

"Meaning?"

"Meaning that your face turned a magnificent shade of crimson the moment I touched your breast. I wonder how deeply it would blush if I stroked your—"

"Good evening, Mr. Warwick."

Olivia turned her back on Warwick, and with spine rigid, made for the stairs.

Her father, his robust face the color of a turnip, exited an adjoining doorway, arms thrown wide and his round body bouncing in anticipation. "So a wedding it will be! By Jove, what a day when both of my daughters are betrothed!"

"Miss Devonshire!" Warwick called.

She slowed.

"Those godawful spectacles fog up when you get angry. Just thought you'd appreciate knowing."

"Go to hell!" she snapped, bringing her father to an abrupt stop.

"Right," Warwick retorted. "I'll see you there."

Then the front door slammed, then another and another, up and down the hallway and throughout the house as the eavesdropping servants suddenly discovered the fracas had ended. Olivia stood simmering at the foot of the stairs, as angry at herself for allowing her emotions to get out of control as she was at Warwick for . . . for . . . every reason imaginable.

For not going down on one knee and proposing.

For not holding her in the slightest esteem, or even pretending to.

For being honest.

For being arrogant.

For being so devastatingly handsome, and lonely, and hurting so passionately over his past—just as she was over hers—that she would throw caution and care to the wind and agree to marry him no matter how loudly the voice in her head screamed that she shouldn't.

She moved toward the front door, stiffly at first, then faster.

"Olivia!" Emily flew down the stairs, one hand gripping the rail, the other grappling with her skirts. "Don't do it! You mustn't! You know what it'll mean! Olivia! I'll never speak to you again!" Emily caught up to Olivia as she reached the door, and grabbing her arm, dragged her around.

"He doesn't love you!" Emily cried.

Olivia reached for the door.

"He's marrying you for only one reason. Your dowry. He'll spend your money on his scores of mistresses and gambling and horses and that crumbling relic of a house, and when he's used that up he'll toss you away like old tea draff."

"Get out of my way, Emily."

"For the love of God," their father bellowed. "Come away, Em, and leave the gal be."

"Tell her, Papa! Tell her not to marry him! I beg you!"

Staring in disbelief at her sister's tear-swollen eyes, Olivia shook her head. "Would you refuse me this one, and possibly only, chance for freedom, Emily?"

"He's detestable!"

"You didn't think so once."

"Think of Bryan."

"That's exactly who I'm thinking of."

"Come, come, Emily." Devonshire took his daughter by her shoulders and did his best to pull her aside. "Gads, gel, you act as if you're caught in some jealous fit—"

"Jealous!" Emily laughed and cried at once, and beat his hands away. "Jealous of her? Of him? Surely you jest, Papa. Why, it's me he loves. He's only trying to pay me back because . . ."

"Because what?" he demanded.

Emily turned her burning eyes on Olivia again, and thrusting her face near Olivia's ear, whispered harshly, "How could you live with the idea that your husband and sister have been lovers—that when he's bedding you he's no doubt thinking of me."

"What in God's name have I ever done to you to make you hate me so?" Olivia asked softly, her sadness closing off her throat like a fist. "I've raised you and loved you like a mother. I've sacrificed everything I hold dear so that you might glide through life without a care, that you might marry a man with great power and position like Lord Willowby, yet you begrudge me this one opportunity."

"But Bryan deserves—"

"Don't you dare even mutter his name; you aren't worthy. Save your hypocritical show of concern over *my* son for someone it'll impress. Now . . . get out of my way."

Slipping past her sister, Olivia flung open the door, gasping and stepping back as the first brace of cold air rushed over her. Gripping her skirts, she ran down the brick steps and onto the drive, squinting to make out the disappearing shape of Warwick's coach.

"Wait!" she cried, walking, then running down the drive, certain the driver would not hear her over the clattering of hooves and the jangle of harnesses. Yet she called out again anyway, running gingerly on the rain-slick surface.

Olivia practically ran headlong into the back of the coach before she realized the conveyance had been brought to a halt. Suddenly the driver was there, and the coach door swung open, and Warwick's hazy form gracefully stepped to the ground.

She was breathless from the sprint down the drive and now that she'd achieved her goal she was suddenly swamped by a sense of regret for acting so desperate.

"Damn," she muttered, and as Warwick walked toward her, she closed her eyes in mortification. Dear God, she must surely look the imbecile, she thought, as she realized that her feet and shins and skirt hem were doused liberally with muddy water, and her hair had spilled over her shoulders, and her blouse was gaping open and clinging damply to her body.

"Miss Devonshire."

She turned her head sharply toward the sound of Warwick's voice. His form seemed very hazy.

He reached for her glasses and gently removed them from her face. The world instantly regained its clarity. Warwick was regarding her with one raised eyebrow while his hands cleaned the condensation from the spectacle lenses with the lapel of his coat.

"You wished to tell me something," he said.

She stared at the swagging fob of a pocket watch that was tucked into a vent in his waistcoat. Odd that she hadn't noticed it before; it glimmered now. "Yes," she finally managed to respond. "I . . ." She swallowed and tried to breathe, finding the effort difficult when paralyzed by discomposure.

Warwick tipped her eyeglasses up toward the sky and, squinting, regarded the lenses intently. Satisfied, he carefully put them back on Olivia's nose, and eased the wire end pieces around her ears. His fingers trailed through the fine hair at her temples, and slid along the rim of her ear. "I told you those eyeglasses fog up when you get angry. Didn't I, Miss Devonshire?"

She nodded.

He proceeded to button her blouse while she stood like a statue and watched the fading light heighten each angle of his face. Her heart pounded double time as his fingers brushed her breasts. "I still believe that you can see better without those bloody things," he said, "but never mind. You didn't haul down my coach to discuss your eyesight. I take it that you've experienced a rather sudden and drastic change of heart considering my proposal."

She nodded.

"And I assume that you've decided that a union between us would serve to ameliorate our circumstances."

She nodded.

"And would you agree that the sooner we can bring this about the better for us both?"

She nodded.

"Very well. I'll speak to the Superintendent Registrar. Normally, I believe it's customary to post banns three weeks before a marriage, but I happen to know Registrar Hargreaves, with an adequate enough incentive, is willing to overlook the normal procedures. Can we agree that the ceremony will take place one week from today at the Registrar's office?"

"One week?"

"I realize that doesn't leave you much time to prepare, then again a regular ceremony isn't necessary considering our circumstances."

She nodded.

He stood watching her in silence for a long moment. She had begun to shiver; whether from the cold, or from the shock of realizing that she had just agreed to marry Miles Warwick (in one week, no less, and without having said a word), Olivia couldn't tell. Her teeth had begun to chatter and the damp was crawling its way up her stockings to her knees.

Removing his cloak, Miles swung the wrap around her shoulders and pulled it closed around her throat. The warmth of his body still permeated the expensive wool and the shabby satin lining of the coat. She could detect, too, the vague scent of his bay rum cologne. "Thank you," she told him.

He smiled briefly and appeared thoughtful before bending slightly, and brushing her lips lightly with his. "You're welcome," he whispered.

He turned back to the coach, and as the driver waited by the steps, he swung up through the door with the grace of an acrobat. "Good night, Miss Devonshire," came his voice from within. "You'll be hearing from me."

The driver slammed the door and scrambled up to his chair. "Good night," she said, and watched as the coach rolled underway, and disappeared into the dark.

You did not come,
And marching Time drew on, and wore
me numb.—
Yet less for loss of your dear presence there
Than that I thus found lacking in your make
That high compassion which can overbear
Reluctance for pure lovingkindness' sake
Grieved I, when, as the hope-hour stroked
its sum
You did not come.

—THOMAS HARDY

CHAPTER SEVEN

"I'M CERTAIN YOU CAN APPRECIATE MY REASONS FOR this, Warwick. I don't wish to appear callous to your feelings—by Jove, we *are* men, and being men who pride themselves in controlling their own destinies I'm certain such conditions as those I've laid out for you will initially be hard to accept. However . . ." Devonshire cleared his throat and fixed Miles with a penetrating look, while outside the wind howled and pounded frigid fists against the windowpanes. "I'm sure you can understand the reasoning behind my motives. First and foremost, I must consider Olivia's future. In doing so, of course, I must look closely at your history. Obviously, you have a weakness for the sport of gambling. You have no business sense. Mind you," he hurried to add, "you cannot be faulted for that, considering your upbringing . . . Are you listening to me, Warwick?"

"Of course." Miles's voice was caustic but controlled. Olivia thought she had never witnessed such contained fury in a man's being.

"Thus I have put before you the conditions of this dowry. Olivia is to have complete control of the finances. She, of course, will be fair and considerate of your specific needs."

"What you're saying," he directed to Olivia, "is that I'll be forced to beg money from you."

She swallowed.

" 'Beg' is such a harsh word," Devonshire said. "Please do try to keep this all in perspective. Considering your record—"

"This isn't the way it's done. Wives don't keep their husbands on an allowance. It's the other way around."

Devonshire moved between Olivia and Miles, and smiled down into his face. "Surely you understand my concern. Why, stories abound of rounders who squander their wives' dowries, then the poor lass is forced to live in less than pleasant conditions for the remainder of her days. Obviously, this is hardly a love match. It would be a crime if Olivia woke up one morning to find herself, and her son, cast aside for another woman."

Devonshire's eyes hardened and his smile became brittle. "Take your own mother and father, for instance. The Warwicks' history of fidelity leaves a great deal to be desired."

The conversation droned on. Olivia barely listened. Instead, she stared into the face of her future husband and watched his features go from stupefied, to angry, to frightfully furious. A tiny voice in her mind whispered that she should be finding some pleasure in the scene— after all, his reasons for marrying her were far from chivalrous—so why wasn't she? Why did she feel as if she wanted to jump up and scream at her father that the idea of her totally controlling the fortune she would bring to this marriage was ludicrous? Miles's pride had been wounded enough, being forced, as he was, into marriage. He had every right to withdraw his proposal, just on principle. But would he? Just how desperate was he? she wondered.

Olivia recalled the previous night of tossing and turning and dreading this meeting, fearing Warwick's reaction when the contracts were laid before him and the ugly reality of his situation was spelled out in legal jargon.

She had dreamt throughout the night that he refused the conditions of the dowry and stormed from the house.

She dreamt, too, that he'd dropped to his knees and professed his undying devotion, and because he loved her so intensely, he would agree to anything—anything—just so he could have her as his wife.

So far, neither had happened.

"Tell me, Warwick. Are you agreeable to these terms?" Devonshire asked.

Miles sat in a straight-backed chair, appearing for all the world as if he were relaxed and unbothered by this shocking turn of events. How very composed and arrogant he looked, dressed in his finest navy blue broadcloth jacket with gold buttons, leather breeches, and highly polished Hessians. Yet, it was his eyes that gave away his immense anger. They were like a forest burning—gray-green with a frightening light. As she waited for his response, a clock in the hallway ticked the seconds into silence, and the sound of each swing of the pendulum grew louder and louder in the stillness.

"It seems I have little choice," he finally replied.

Devonswick smiled and offered his hand. Miles ignored it.

The smile fading, Olivia's father said, "There is one other matter."

"You don't say. Let me guess. I'm to slit my wrist and sign those contracts in blood."

"Nothing so radical, my good man. Actually, it concerns the boy." He shuffled through the papers. "If by chance the marriage between you should be dissolved, his mother will retain custody."

Miles laughed softly, his only response. Then he left his chair. To Olivia, he said, "I've spoken with the proper officials at the Registry office. I'll leave the rest up to you, since you appear to be inclined toward controlling the situation."

He turned on his heels and quit the room without so much as an adieu. Olivia hurried after him. "What time—" she called out.

"Noon," came the short response.

She followed him to the foyer, where Jonah stood with Miles's cloak and gloves. The old butler helped him into the cloak before opening the door. "Mr. Warwick," she called.

Pausing in the threshold, Miles looked back, obviously furious. She considered informing him that the shocking conditions of her dowry contract had been her father's idea, but what good would it do?

"I . . . understand how you must be feeling," she said.

"Really?" He raised his eyebrows in feigned amusement as he slid one hand into a kid-leather riding glove. "Tell me, Miss Devonshire, how am I feeling?"

"Emasculated."

"Ah." He flashed her a cold smile. "Well put, love."

"No one will hold a gun to your head and force you to go through with it."

"That is a matter of opinion."

Olivia took a deep breath. "You must be very desperate, sir."

He shrugged and tugged on the other glove. "No more than you, I suppose."

She frowned and her eyes grew larger as Warwick walked slowly toward her, the wind through the open door buffeting his shoulders and hair. Only it wasn't the wind that caused his cheeks to blaze with hot color, and his eyes to glitter like fire.

"Indeed you will have to be exceedingly desperate to marry me, Miss Devonshire," he said in a chillingly unemotional tone. "Because I'm not a man who concedes his dignity willingly. Chance a glance at my rather notorious history and you'll understand my meaning. Those who have sought to trip me up usually have found themselves tripped facedown in their own stupidity."

"Is that a threat?" she demanded, sounding far braver than she felt.

"I don't threaten, Miss Devonshire. I'm not like an American rattlesnake that shakes his tail to warn some hapless little creature that he's about to strike. I'm much more subtle." Olivia stiffened as he lightly placed one finger upon her breast, precisely where the tattoo lay hidden beneath her blouse, then drew his finger up, up, slowly to her throat and around the back of her neck until his big hand cradled her nape and his gloved fingers buried into her hair. His head lowered over hers, and her heartbeat quickened. She couldn't think. Or move. His eyes were hypnotic and she vaguely wondered if it was fear or thrill that made her knees feel as if they would give beneath her at any moment.

"Oh, I'm much more subtle than that," he said softly.

"I'm more like an asp, Miss Devonshire. I slither into your bed and coil up between the sheets. I wait until you're most vulnerable before I strike."

"If you're trying to frighten me—"

"Hardly. Just a friendly warning among friends. We are friends, aren't we, Miss Devonshire?"

She tried to nod. Impossible.

Behind her, her father left his office and stood rooted to the floor at the sight of Olivia and Miles. "Here now," came his concerned voice. "What's this?"

His eyes not leaving hers, Miles said, "Just a kiss before I go. I think I have that right, my lord. Don't you? After all, what sort of fiancé would I be not to show my one and only love my heartfelt affection?"

Olivia watched him, a tinge of fear reflected in her features. Oh, yes, she was frightened; he had succeeded at that most impressively. And she was uncertain, yet without the hostility he might have expected from a weaker woman.

She held him with her inscrutable eyes for what felt like an eternity longer, until his anger at her and her wily old father turned in on itself.

He bent and kissed her fully on her mouth—as he had before—opening his lips as she opened hers and tasting the spicy flavor of her tongue.

His breath caught.

He pulled away.

Turning on his heels, Miles left the house.

On Saturday morning Olivia awoke with a queasy feeling in the pit of her stomach. It was her wedding day and she'd heard not a word from her fiancé since he'd stormed from the house five days ago.

The night before she had lain out her wedding attire, as humble as it was: a home-stitched gown void of the lace that normally adorned a bride's dress. There were her usual stockings—not the fine silk embroidered ones with flowers on the ankles. The maid had managed to shine her shoes well enough and replaced the soiled lace-up ribbons with new ones. Once or twice as the morning rolled on she'd been tempted to ask Emily if she might borrow one of the two dozen pairs of shoes from her impressive Parisian collection, but she hadn't. Such a request would only upset Emily. As it was, her sister had taken to her bed pleading a sick headache. She simply couldn't go through with the awful ordeal of standing as Olivia's witness in the ceremony, therefore Olivia had asked Bertrice.

Olivia spent the early hours of morning with her son. They took their traditional walk around the estate pathways, strolled down to a garden pond. As they huddled together on a marble bench, Olivia did her best to explain to her son just what was about to take place in their lives.

"Will we be happier there?" he asked.

"Yes," she replied. "We'll be very happy."

"I'll have a papa?"

"Very definitely."

"Do he love you?"

Olivia smiled and watched a rabbit scurry through the snow.

Bryan took her face in his small hands. His eyes were large and searching and far wiser than they should have been at his age. "Do he love you, Mummy?"

"Yes, he does."

"Do he love me?"

"Of course. He loves us both or . . . he wouldn't care to marry us, would he?"

Those words followed her throughout the morning, as she bathed and donned her gown. Sitting before her dressing table, she gazed at her reflection in the mirror while Bertrice brushed and plaited her hair. Her cheeks were as pale as ash, her eyes startlingly glassy.

As if reading her thoughts, Bertrice offered her a reassuring hug. " 'Tis only natural, lass. It's called preweddin' jitters. It isn't as if you're havin' second thoughts about marrying Warwick, is it?"

"Of course not. It's just . . ." Olivia shrugged and looked away. "I suppose I'm only feeling a little sorry for myself."

Taking Olivia's hand, Bertrice pulled her over to the bed where they sat side by side. Today was one of Bertrice's more lucid days. "Tell Bertrice what's wrong, lass."

Olivia didn't want to elaborate, and Bertrice would have forgotten within the hour anyway. "How very ironic that things have turned out as they have," she said thoughtfully, and with a faint smile on her lips. "And yet . . ." She turned back to face Bertrice, who continued to watch her from the shadow of the tester bed. "Yet, when once I would have chosen marriage to Miles under any circumstances, now I feel as if . . ."

"As if what, love? Tell Bertrice what's botherin' you."

Olivia sighed. "I would rather that he loved me."

Having been shown to a private chamber by the Superintendent Registrar, Olivia sat in a chair and stared at a china clock shaped like bells. The room had been decorated for weddings. The window, door, and paintings of loving couples on the walls were all framed with wreaths of leaves tied with long white ribbons. A table dressed in white lace and linen took up one wall. Normally wedding favors would be placed there until they were moved into the vestry for the guests. Not knowing if Miles had invited anyone as a witness, Olivia had only made a dozen favors that consisted of white ribbon, lace, flowers, and silver leaves. As it was, by a quarter to twelve only one guest had arrived, that being Miles's brother, Earl Warwick, who congratulated her with a smile and an apology on his wife's behalf. The Countess Warwick was expecting their third child just any day.

The ceremony was to have begun at straight up noon. Bryan had perched himself on a cushion near the window and assured her that he would announce the moment his new "Papa" arrived. Yet, as the clock struck noon, the wedding party, seated expectantly in the Marriage Room, waited for the arrival of the groom, and the groom did not appear.

At twelve-fifteen Olivia sat calmly on the lip of her chair and occasionally toyed with her gown sleeves, and still Miles did not show.

Twelve-thirty and Bryan continued to stare out onto the street, squirm on his seat, and ask repeatedly, "Mummy, is he comin' yet?"

"Soon," she replied staunchly.

"Soon," she replied, worried.

"Soon," she replied in a voice that made her throat ache and her chest hurt so badly she couldn't catch her breath.

"Mummy?" Bryan asked, wrapping his little fingers around her hand. "Are you cryin', Mummy?"

*   *   *

The Hound and Hearth tavern was unusually packed for so early in the day. Men pressed close to the bar and tipped up their pints to an occasional hardy cheer and a facetious toast to the bride and groom at Braithwaite.

"Here's to that bastard Kemball who never saw a decent day's work in his worthless life. May he and his wife forever enjoy the fruits of his labor!"

"Ol' Kemball knows how to pick 'em, don't he?"

They burst out in ribald laughter again.

"I ain't seen that Devonshire woman in years, but I hear she's plain as a post."

"And she's got that brat some says was fathered by a Romanian Gypsy."

"Word is she's got a pair of dragons tattooed on her fanny. One on each cheek. When she walks they look as if they're trippin' an Irish jig."

Laughter again, shaking the walls of the smoke-filled tavern.

Little by little the laughter dwindled as heads turned, one by one, toward the doorway where Earl Warwick stood, resplendent in an exquisite, finely tailored gray dress coat and pleated trousers. His peach-colored cravat was slightly lopsided, however, and his black hair an unruly mess.

Silence fell like a stone as Damien shifted his malevolent gaze from the revelers' chagrined faces to Miles's, where he sat in the dark in the back of the room, slumped in his chair, his fingers wrapped around the neck of a whisky bottle.

There came a smattering of comments: "Why didn't nobody tell me he was here?" and "I didn't know myself." Miles rewarded the gaping patrons with a thin smile and a lift of his bottle in a salute. Then he watched his brother move like a tempered storm toward him, stopping at the opposite edge of the table.

"Well, well, look who's here," Miles said. "What took you, Dame?"

"I'm certain you're well aware of the time."

He tugged his pocket watch from his waistcoat and flipped it open. "Twelve-thirty."

"Aren't you forgetting something?"

He poured himself another drink and shoved the bottle aside. "As a matter of fact, my lord, I've been sitting here remembering a great many things."

Damien started to speak; Miles waved it away and shifted in his chair, glancing at the open-faced watch he had placed on the table near the whisky bottle. "Admittedly, I didn't make the wisest of choices when I was young. Now that I'm not so young I can look back on my mistakes with a modicum of understanding and tell myself that I won't make such errors again . . . if given another chance."

"What has any of this got to do with Olivia?" Damien asked.

Miles ran one hand through his hair and wearily rubbed his eyes.

Leaning onto the table, Damien looked hard into Miles's face. "I think I know. You believe she isn't good enough. Now that you're working so damn hard to become respectable, perhaps you feel that, considering her past, she would be a reminder of yours. That's it, isn't it, Kemball? How can a man become respected when burdened by a wife whose past is as sordid as his? Undoubtedly, she would prove to be a constant reminder that you've been forced to accept scraps again."

Miles frowned.

Damien dragged back a chair and dropped into it. "Do you mind?" he asked, and grabbed up the whisky bottle and turned it up to his mouth. "Perhaps you're right, Kemball. I mean, I really couldn't imagine the two of you together."

"No?"

Damien shook his head. "No. Who wants a wife who's danced naked with a bunch of Gypsies?"

"She wasn't naked," Miles snapped.

"But—"

"She wore scarves."

"Ah. Well, there's the little matter of her tattoos . . ."

"They don't show so what the hell difference does it make?"

Sitting back in his chair, Damien shrugged. "She's not very pretty—"

"Quite the contrary. There are times when she's more than a little presentable."

"Really? When?"

"When she removes her spectacles. When her hair is slightly windblown. When anger or embarrassment—or spirits—has brought color to her cheeks . . . and when she dabbles in the garden with roses."

"Huh. Pretty, is she?"

"Every bit as pretty as her addled sister."

Damien watched as Miles quaffed his measure of whisky, then he refilled the glass. "Of course, there's the little matter of her reputation."

"What of it?"

"There's the lad."

"His name is Bryan."

"It's anyone's guess who sired the boy."

"Bryan. His name is Bryan."

"Forever you would be faced with the responsibility of raising another man's son. I could imagine that such a prospect would certainly be a cross to bear—"

"What the hell are you insinuating?"

"Well . . . he *is* a bastard."

Miles slowly came out of his chair. "Don't call him that."

"Illegitimate, then. Face it, Kemball, he was born out of wedlock, and—"

Miles easily bent over the table and, twisting his fists into Damien's coat, yanked him out of his chair and partially over the table, scattering bottles and glasses and sending the pocket watch spinning to the floor. "Are you insinuating that due to his mother's and father's carelessness Bryan is any less worthy of understanding and love than any other child? I happen to know that Bryan, aside from being an exceptionally beautiful lad, is extremely well behaved and would make any man proud to call him son."

Damien didn't so much as blink as he stared into Miles's red-rimmed eyes. "Seems you're awfully touchy about Miss Devonshire and her son. I wonder why, Kemball, especially in light of the fact that it appears you've stood them both up at the altar."

Gradually, Miles released his grip on Damien's coat. Around them, the patrons stood rooted to the sawdust floor, some staring into their pints and pretending they hadn't heard the exchange between the brothers. Others watched with furrowed brows and mustaches damp with their dark, tepid ale. Regardless, there wasn't a sound to be heard but for the slight creak of wood under Miles's and Damien's weight.

"Damn you, Dame," Miles said under his breath.

Damien only shrugged and tugged loose from his grip. He said, "Are you sober enough to make it to the Registry Office?"

"I . . . don't know."

"If we hurry we might arrive before the bride flees in total disgrace."

"Let's get something straight."

"Fine."

"I'm marrying the gal for no other reason than to get my hands on her dowry."

"I believe you, Kemball."

"The name is Warwick."

Damien shifted his broad shoulders and smoothed his lapels. "Funny thing about that name, Warwick. Not since the first Warwick fought at King Richard's side has a Warwick ever married a woman whom he didn't love with all his heart. Call it tradition."

Miles glared at Damien a long, hard minute, then stalked from the tavern, leaving it in silence.

The Registry official spoke solemnly and quickly as Olivia and Miles stood side by side trying hard to concentrate on his words and doing their best to ignore the tension electrifying the air between them.

Olivia's throat felt raw, but she had learned long ago that there was a time and place for everything. Losing one's temper in public would only serve to lower her esteem in the eyes of those who already questioned her character.

Dear God, it was obvious that Miles had spent the last hours in a tavern. He smelled of stale ale and whisky and smoke. He hadn't even bothered to change into his suit, but wore a riding jacket (with a patched elbow), leather breeches, and Hessians that were mud-spattered. He stood there, weaving slightly from side to side and mumbling his vows so no one, aside from himself, could possibly hear.

So why was she going through with this charade?

Miles did his best to focus on the somber official and concentrate on his words; his eyes, however, kept drifting down to the woman at his left. Olivia had not so much as offered him a solitary look while he, apparently, couldn't seem to take his gaze from her. Where was the plain-as-a-post little spinster who hid behind thick-lensed spectacles?

He had rehearsed an apology, certain that she would reject it, and him. But she had refused to see him when he arrived at the office, replying only to her father, "Let's get on with it."

Fine. Then be that way. Don't allow him the opportunity to lie and feel good about the ass he'd made of himself.

He'd worked up his sarcasm and ire, but the moment he'd looked up to see her walking into the room in her simple but pretty wedding gown the prepared defenses fled. Her hair was an array of cascading mahogany coils and curls that framed her smooth-as-porcelain features. And she walked hand in hand with her son who now stood at her side and gazed around his mother up at him, a world of confusion and hope in his wide green eyes.

"Mr. Warwick."

He forced his eyes up to the Superintendent Registrar, who had raised his eyebrows in question.

"I said, sir, do you take this woman—"

"Of course I do or I wouldn't be standing here."

Damien cleared his throat.

Olivia stared straight ahead, stone-faced.

Sir Hargreaves pursed his lips and looked back and forth between the two. "Miss Devonshire, do you take this man as your lawfully wedded husband?"

Silence.

Silence.

Someone cleared his throat again—Dame, no doubt, attempting to hold back his laughter as the seconds trudged by and it became more and more obvious that Olivia was considering her decision.

Ah, so here it comes, Miles thought. Of course. He should have guessed. He'd humiliated her by not showing up at the appointed time, now it was her turn. She would announce to the meager gathering of increasingly uncomfortable guests and beleaguered official that it would be a cold day in hell before she exchanged vows with the bastard of Braithwaite.

Bryan looked up at his mother, then tugged on her skirt. "Please, Mummy," he whispered.

"Yes," she said softly and without emotion. "I do."

Closing his eyes, Miles released his breath, aware only in that instant that he had been holding it.

There were more words spoken in monotone followed by a discomforting moment when the official asked for the bride's ring.

"I . . ." Feeling his face turn cold then scalding hot, he ran his hands over his waistcoat and into the pockets of his jacket before dropping his hands to his sides and clenching his fists. "I don't have one," he confessed.

"I see . . . Then I pronounce you man and wife. Mr. Warwick, you may kiss your bride."

Miles stared at the man and didn't move.

"Sir, you can at least do that," the official stressed with an obvious degree of pique and disapproval.

He woodenly turned to face her, and she did the same, choosing, however, to stare at his shirtfront instead of meeting his discomfited gaze. He took her shoulders lightly, clumsily, in his hands and looked down at her features. She did not turn her mouth up to his or even offer the slightest encouragement.

"Olivia," he said quietly, perhaps a touch unsteady with the use of her name for the first time. Then, gently catching her chin with the end of one finger, he tipped her face up to his. "I'm sorry," he whispered to her cold eyes, and as he bent his head to lightly touch his lips to hers, she tilted her face so he kissed her cheek.

It was done.

I desire a return of affection.
FAREWELL.
—Verse from a nineteenth-century
calling card

CHAPTER EIGHT

OLIVIA AND MILES WAITED TOGETHER IN THE SUPER-
intendent's office; she stood at the window gazing up at
the spires of an old church, while Miles paced the floor
like a caged cat.

"It's bloody freezing in here," Miles said.

Olivia shivered, but it had little to do with the frigid
chamber. In truth, she envied the village folk who moved
up and down the cobblestone street wrapped in woolen
scarves and cloaks, pausing occasionally to speak to a
friend or acquaintance then to wave their good-byes.
She envied their lives. Their friends. The very routine
of their existences. A pressure had centered in her chest,
and though she attempted to breathe deeply it simply
wouldn't go away.

Miles lightly touched her shoulder.

Olivia jumped and turned. Their eyes remained on
each other's, as if hypnotized.

"It's freezing out there," he said, then attempted to

reach past her to close the window. "You'll catch your death of cold."

She stepped away. "Then you'll be a very wealthy widower, won't you, Mr. Warwick?"

"I believe we're beyond the mister and missus stage, don't you?"

"How dare you?" she said through her teeth. "How dare you pretend that everything is fine?"

"That wasn't my intention—"

"I suppose it means nothing to you that you humiliated me."

"There will be plenty of time to discuss this late—"

"I don't want to discuss it later! I want to discuss it now!"

"For God's sake, you're being hysterical," he snapped.

Stepping forcefully up against him, so her breasts were pressed to his chest and her head was thrown back, she stated coldly, "It's my wedding day, sir. I have every right to be hysterical. I also have every right to know the joy and thrill of beginning a new life for myself and my son. I have the right to enjoy bouquets and candy and love poems on my wedding night. I have the right to surround myself with loving family and friends who join hands and wish me a fairy-tale life. But most of all I deserve a husband who cares for me." Her voice breaking, she cried, "If you haven't noticed, damn you to hell, I haven't experienced a solitary one, and I hate you for that. Do you understand me? I hate you!"

"Fine!" he shouted back, focusing on his wife's white, furious features. "In case it hasn't sunk in yet, *Mrs.* Warwick, I don't give a fig what you feel for me. That was the understanding, if you'll recall. This so-called marriage was agreed upon for two reasons: to alleviate my money woes and to help restore your reputation that got blown to hell when you spread your legs for Bryan's father!"

She gasped. Stumbled back. Stared at him as if he'd shot her. Then her hand swung with the ferocity of a striking snake and struck him across the cheek so hard the world turned red.

Someone cleared their throat.

Olivia blinked as reality crashed in around her.

Miles, his face furious and his cheek throbbing like fire, turned away.

Superintendent Hargreaves closed the door, and looking more than a little discomfited, moved to his desk where the Register lay open, waiting to be signed by the bride and groom. Removing a pair of spectacles from his pocket, he placed them on his nose and appeared to study the page. Finally, he looked up at Olivia. "I feel I must explain to you that should you decide not to sign this register, the previous ceremony will be declared null and void."

Laughter sounded in the hallway—couples waiting to be married—a wealth of congratulations from their guests. Miles stood at the desk edge, his fingers pressed against it as he stared over the Superintendent's shoulder at a framed oil painting of Queen Victoria. He could see Olivia's reflection in the glass. Her color was high, her features defiant. A tickling of disconcertion centered in his chest.

"Well?" Hargreaves said, his features somber as an undertaker's. "Miss Devonshire?"

Olivia flashed one last look at Miles, then bent to sign her name with a flourish in the book.

*   *   *

They joined their guests in the crowded hallway—
Lord Devonshire, Bertrice, and Earl Warwick. Bryan
threw himself into Olivia's arms and kissed her on the
cheek.

Lord Devonshire pulled Miles aside and quietly
explained that duty called him back to Devonswick.

"It's Emily. I worry about her. She's so frail, and since
the death of my wife . . . Well, you understand."

Miles stared down into his father-in-law's countenance and said nothing. Devonshire's was a fat face,
sallow and puffy. The man was completely selfish, Miles
realized, entrusting his loyal daughter's life to a malfea-
sant like him—all for the sake of Emily's happiness.

"I'll be off then," Devonshire announced and turned
for the door.

"What?" Miles said, bringing Devonshire to an abrupt
stop and a slow rotation toward him. The old man stood
where he was, swaying a little and breathing heavily.
Miles continued. "No intense and private instruction
from a father on how a man such as myself should
treat his daughter? No politely muttered threats on what
might happen to me should I abuse her sensibilities?"

"Well, I—"

"Not even a word of good-bye to her? No assurances
that if her life with me should become hell on earth that
she has a place to which she can go for support? I think a
simple affectionate peck on the cheek would suffice."

"You have little room to criticize, sir, considering your
deplorable behavior today, for the last week, for that
matter. I'm surprised that the gel went through with it at
all. You know what they say, Kemball. He who lives in
glass houses shouldn't throw stones." Devonshire hitched
up his trousers then, and with a jut of his jaw, quit the
building.

"The old bastard should be tied up and horsewhipped," Damien said behind Miles.

He glanced at Damien over his shoulder. The unnerving realization struck him in that moment that Olivia's own family showed little caring about her feelings and welfare, while Damien, despite Miles's illegitimacy and all the trouble he had caused the Warwicks through the years, had come today in a show of support.

"You're wanting to put your fist through his teeth, aren't you?" Damien said.

"Why would I want to do that, Dame? The sonofabitch is about to make me a very wealthy man."

"Because rattling around in that vast but empty cavity of your chest is the stirrings of a human heart. I've often suspected that it's been there—even denied it to myself because I don't particularly like you. The rather abhorrent fact is, you're a lot like me, you know. When I returned from America I was the most cold, calculating, distant bastard I had ever known. But that was before I met Bonnie. Do you feel guilty?"

"Yes."

"Good. That means there's hope, or there should be if Olivia will forgive you. I suspect that she will. She really doesn't strike me as a vindictive, petty woman. If she were, I suspect Bryan's father would have long since felt the bite of the courts. Who knows, perhaps you'll end up happy."

A force hit Miles's leg in that moment, and squeezed. He looked down to find Bryan gazing up, green eyes round and cheeks blooming with color.

Damien laughed. "What's wrong, Papa? You look as if you've never been fallen upon by a child before."

"I haven't. And don't call me that. I'm not his papa,"

he added for Earl Warwick's ears alone.

Damien's smile didn't waver. "I would wager that he doesn't bite."

"Are you certain? Correct me if I'm wrong, but isn't that drool at the corners of his lips?"

"He seems fond of you, Kemball. What are you afraid of?"

"I've heard rumors of children's unpredictability."

"Having never grown up yourself, I imagine you could relate rather well."

Miles lifted one eyebrow in Damien's direction. Damien only laughed.

Going to one knee, Miles mustered a smile for the curious child. What did one say to a four-year-old? How did one say it? The sudden realization that he would be staring into the child's face every day for several years to come made his stomach feel strange. Not exactly as if he wanted to jump and run, but close to it.

Bryan mumbled something, then looked at his feet.

Miles bent lower and focused hard on Bryan's little face. "I didn't hear you," he said.

The boy timidly tucked in his chin a little more and whispered, "You made Mummy cry."

"I'm sorry. I didn't mean to."

"But you did."

Taking a deep breath, Miles glanced up at Damien, who regarded him and the boy intensely. His look said, *Get yourself out of this one gracefully.*

"Bryan," he began, "I'm very certain that we're all going to be very happy at Braithwaite." He tipped up the lad's face with one finger. "Perhaps we'll go riding sometime. Or maybe I'll show you a few of the secret places where I used to hide and play when I was a little boy."

Bryan's eyes sparkled with interest. "Secret places?"

"Hidden rooms and hallways where I would pretend that I was a king of a castle surrounded by my knights in shining armor."

"My mummy used to say that one day a knight in shinin' armor was goin' to come and take us away from Grandpapa and Aunt Emily." Wrinkling his little nose and screwing his pink mouth to one side, he whispered, "They don't like me very much."

Damien stopped smiling.

Miles laid his hand on the lad's shoulder and felt some emotion unfurl inside him. Anger. Not just anger, but fury. Heartbreak. Embarrassment for the boy. Empathy all wrapped up in a painful ribbon of understanding.

Suddenly Bryan's eyes grew rounder and greener as excitement lit up his face. " 'Cept we got somethin' better than a knight in shinin' armor, didn't we, sir? We got a king instead!"

Bryan then dashed down the hallway as if on wings.

"Very nice," Earl Warwick said. "Wouldn't it be a shock to discover that children actually like you? Or, even more surprising, that you actually like children."

"Children like me? Surely you jest, Damien. We both know that I'm the sort from whom children run for the sake of their lives."

"He was running all right. But it wasn't from fear. I do believe you've made Master Bryan very, very happy. I suspect that tonight he'll be dreaming of dragon slaying and rescuing damsels in distress."

Miles stood; he straightened his jacket and wondered at the odd expression on Damien's face. Earl Warwick regarded him with an unwavering display of curiosity, and something else Miles couldn't quite place.

"Tell me," Earl Warwick said quietly, looking again toward the door through which Bryan had escaped. "Did you say that you had known Olivia some years ago?"

"Yes."

"How well did you know her?"

"I was infatuated by her sister at the time and took no notice of her at all."

"Emily?" Earl Warwick affected a shudder. "Good God, what any man sees in that ill-natured little witch I'll never know. For the life of me I can't understand what Clanricarde finds remotely appealing in the fair-haired little brat."

"You wouldn't. You have eyes only for Bonnie." He grinned.

"How long did you spend with Emily?"

He shrugged in an offhand manner. "Can't say as I recall. Or care. Might have been a few weeks, or months. It's been so long ago—"

"How long?"

"Five years, give or take a few months."

"Obviously, just before she and Olivia left for Europe."

Miles frowned and glanced around for his wife.

His wife.

Odd that he should think of her that way so quickly. Especially since he'd spent the entire morning doing his best to evade her.

His hands in his pockets, he moved down the corridor to the Marriage Room, which was now occupied by another couple and their guests—all village folk, their features lined by hardship and weather. The bride, however, looked radiant, the groom a trifle uncertain but happy. Amid them stood Olivia, pinning her own favors to their attire, bringing even greater pleasure to their faces, flashing them a smile as they congratulated her in return.

When she joined him at last, he said, "What were you doing in there?"

"I had made too many favors," she replied. "I thought it would be a shame for them to go to waste."

Then she left him standing in the hallway looking after her.

The journey home seemed to take an eternity. The ride was grueling, with little to see along the Rash roadside but vast stretches of brown grass and craggy hills. But Olivia kept her face averted, pretending to find pleasure in the monotonous countryside while her stomach was knotted up like a fist.

Miles had instructed Bryan and Bertrice to take another coach to Braithwaite, pointing out, with a somewhat cryptic smile, that this was their wedding day. Newlyweds had a right to their privacy, after all. As the driver opened the coach door and offered his hand to Olivia, she carefully stepped down and glanced back for her son's coach.

"They'll be along later," Warwick said behind her.

As usual, Sally met them at the door, red hair in strings, uniform unkempt, her disposition surly. She took Olivia's cloak, then turned to Miles as he removed his.

"I've made meat pies and tea for supper. I s'pose there will be enough for the two of ya. I hope ya like meat pies," she said to Olivia, " 'cause I don't know how to cook much else. Don't really like to cook, and besides, that wasn't what I was hired to do."

"I'm certain meat pies will be fine, Miss . . . ?"

"Pinney," Sally replied.

"Miss Pinney. And you needn't worry about there being enough for the two of us. I'm not very hungry."

"Suit yerself."

Sally turned away. "Miss Pinney," Olivia called.

"What?" Sally replied without glancing over her shoulder as she headed out of the vestibule.

"Miss Pinney."

Sally stopped and looked back, frowning.

"You haven't been dismissed," Olivia pointed out.

Amusement and disbelief flashed across the servant's features. Warwick regarded them both with his arms crossed over his chest and one eyebrow raised.

"Until I can find a full-time cook, you'll please check with me from now on regarding the day's menu. I'm certain I shouldn't have great difficulty in finding a cook. I understand there's a wonderful French chef who's just resigned his position at an estate in Scrafton. I'll pen him a letter tomorrow."

"Right," Sally grumbled. "Will that be all?" she added somewhat sarcastically.

Olivia nodded and the maid trundled off, muttering under her breath and dragging Miles's coat on the floor.

"I see you and Sally will get along famously." Warwick stood in semidarkness, the light from the sconce on the wall making shadows on his hair and shoulders. In truth, the entire vestibule seemed immensely gloomy and cold.

"I fear your staff has grown fat and lazy, sir."

"Sally is my staff, for the most part."

"Then I shall endeavor to remedy that situation as soon as possible."

His eyes appeared to narrow. His mouth curled. Olivia wondered briefly if she had overstepped her position, then decided not.

"Well, I think this calls for a drink. Come along, and I'll buy you a brandy, Olivia."

She followed Miles down the gallery to a small, glass-fronted room that faced the west horizon. "Please sit down," Miles told her, as he opened a cabinet of liquors and proceeded to pour them a small measure of brandy into two snifters. Olivia did her best to focus her attention on the moor beyond Braithwaite's overgrown gardens, and not on her husband.

Her husband.

Dear God, to think only a week ago she had imagined her life as beginning and ending at Devonswick. Now she was married.

"Olivia?"

She looked around to find Miles next to her chair, brandy extended. She took it but didn't drink.

Miles eased into a chair near hers and swirled the brandy round and round in the glass. "Do you like this room?" he asked.

"It's very pretty."

"It's feminine. Damien's mother used to come here. She'd sit for hours in that chair, reading to her children."

"And where were you?"

"Outside listening."

"Were you never invited to join them?"

"Frequently."

"But you didn't."

"I never allowed myself to believe they really wanted me here."

"That was very foolish."

"I was only a child. Besides, I wanted my own mother to read to me."

Olivia put her drink down. "You're very angry with your mother."

No response. Miles stood abruptly and moved around the room, crossing to a table covered with a fine film of gray dust. A book lay there, dusty as well. He flipped open the cover, then as quickly shut it. "You're very straightforward," he finally said without looking at her.

"Does that bother you?"

He shrugged and a look of anger crossed his features. "I didn't bring you here to discuss Alyson Kemball."

"Really? As I recall, you brought up the matter. Not I. However, perhaps you wish to talk about business. Very well. We can begin with the books—"

"Olivia."

Miles put down his snifter and regarded his wife's profile as she gazed out on the darkening panorama. He felt . . . disturbed. Strangely nervous. Perplexed by his awkwardness. "We have the rest of our lives to deal with Braithwaite business. For now, I feel we should discuss us."

He wondered if she had heard him as she continued to focus on some distant object. Then, by a little upward movement of her head she showed that she was waiting for him to continue.

"This is our wedding day, is it not?"

"How very ironic that you should be reminding me."

"There are certain aspects of this arrangement that should be discussed."

Color crept into her cheeks. She reached for the snifter she had earlier discarded. "I was under the impression that our union was little more than a business arrangement—a marriage of convenience only."

The dry finality of her voice puzzled him a moment. "Then perhaps I didn't make myself very clear."

"You made yourself perfectly clear. I was to allow you to take lovers, while you weren't inclined to return the liberties. You aren't fond of me, therefore you have no desire to bed me."

"Since when did fondness for one another become crucial for a man and woman to enjoy sex together?"

"I can't imagine it otherwise."

Her frankness left him momentarily speechless. Finally, he said, "What about desire for desire's sake?"

"Desire?" Her dark brows drew together. "How does one desire a person they don't like?"

"I never said that I don't like you."

"You never said you liked me either."

"I don't know you."

"Yet you married me."

"Am I to be crucified for that? After all, you married me as well, and you don't know me."

"I know you. I've known you for years. We met fifteen years ago, when I was twelve. You were, perhaps, twenty-four or -five. I came upon you at Margrave Bluff. You were standing upon the summit looking out toward Braithwaite. You became angry when you found me watching you from behind the stump of an old rowan tree." She finally looked at him. "You said, 'Who the deuce are you and what are you doing hiding behind that tree?'"

Intrigued, Miles asked, "And what did you say?"

"I fear I was too stricken to say anything."

"Stricken by what? Fear? Was I so formidable?"

"For a country-bred and -raised girl who had yet to make her first sojourn to London you were very formidable. Aloof. Sophisticated. So very aristocratic. I thought for certain you must be some gallant knight. After all, you rode that beautiful black stallion—"

"Gdansk."

"I thought he suited you tremendously."

"We had the same disposition. Wild and belligerent." He smiled with the memory.

Olivia stared into the amber liquid. "You embodied my every fantasy," she said softly, sounding oddly vulnerable—more vulnerable than he would have ever imagined her being. "You were beautiful and defiant. Free. I would ride to Margrave every day with the hopes of seeing you. Sometimes I would even ride bareback and drive my little mare as fast as I could across the moor and pretend that I was you and that she was a black stallion with wings on his hooves."

Raising the glass to her mouth, she slightly moistened her lips with the drink and breathed deeply, as if finding some puissance in the bouquet. "Then you left Braithwaite for a number of years, returning infrequently. Every time I rode to Margrave, I thought of you and imagined the life you must be living abroad. Perhaps I even hoped that, if I continued to ride to Margrave, I would eventually see you again. So you see, sir, you are hardly a stranger to me."

Gently, Miles put his drink down and walked over to Olivia. He stooped beside her chair, and being slightly lower than she, looked up into her face. "Why did you marry me, Olivia, if you knew me so well? Were my foibles, my heritage, my reputation and demeanor not repugnant to you?"

Turning her face away, she cast down her eyes, briefly—so briefly a stranger would not have noticed. "Because," she replied in a resolute voice, "I feel in my innermost heart that you are worth saving."

"I do not love thee!—no! I do not love thee!
And yet when thou art absent I am sad;
And envy even the bright blue sky above thee,
Whose quiet stars may see thee and be glad."
—CAROLINE NORTON

CHAPTER NINE

HE LAID HIS HAND ON HER KNEE. OLIVIA LOOKED DOWN
into his face, his eyes—those eyes that had brought her
so many sleepless nights. What did she see there? Disbelief? Confusion? Would he suddenly see through her
motives and recognize the fact that she, in fact, was in
love with him and had been since that moment he had
found her spying on him from behind the old rowan tree
so many years ago?

"I am worth saving?" he said softly, thoughtfully, his
expression one of bemusement, if not amazement. Yet,
the smile that curved his lips was cynical. "Do you think
so, Olivia?"

Suddenly, feeling immensely embarrassed, she turned
her face away. She had revealed too much. No doubt he
would laugh at her, perhaps scorn her for her naïveté,
and for her childish romanticism.

Why did he continue to stare at her?

"Look at me," he commanded, and when she refused,
he caught her chin with his finger. His eyes gleamed

strangely. "Why?" he asked simply.

"Why not? You are my husband. Is it not my place?"

"Your place or your obligation? You felt obligated to please your father and sister, therefore you married me. You felt obligated to better your son's circumstances, therefore you married me. Yet you sit there and make me believe that you entered this marriage in order to save me—as if you truly care for me." A bitterness crept into his voice as he continued in a lower tone, "No one has ever believed that I am worth saving, dear heart. Why should I, even for a moment, believe that you do? You, who are a stranger to me no matter that we met briefly half a lifetime ago."

She had no answer for that, except for the truth, and the truth in itself seemed absurd even to her. Therefore she remained silent, her gaze drifting to the hand he had placed on her knee, the singular feel of it warming her body like the sun.

The moment ended as Sally stepped into the room. Bryan burst through the threshold behind the servant, setting her back on her heels with a little squeal.

"Mummy!" the lad cried and squirmed into Olivia's lap. Wrapping her arms around him, she turned her eyes to Miles as he stood and regarded the scene rather stiffly.

Bertrice wandered in, looking somewhat baffled. Bryan giggled. "She's havin' another one of her spells again," he said. "She made Deets stop by the road and look for kitty."

"Good God," Miles mumbled and returned to the table where he had put his drink.

"I can't imagine where he's got off to," Bertrice murmured sadly.

Turning his attention to Olivia, Miles declared, "You failed to mention that she would be moving in with you."

"It should go without saying, sir. She's my son's nanny."

"Is she safe?"

"Very trustworthy, I assure you."

"I'm hungry," Bryan informed them.

"Miss Pinney has prepared meat pies and tea for supper."

"I don't like meat pies."

Sally huffed and left the room.

"Perhaps you can make an exception today."

"This house is cold and dark and smells funny. Is it haunted?"

"I think not."

"I want to see my room."

Olivia glanced at Miles. "Have you prepared him a room, sir?"

"It didn't occur to me."

"Then I shall do so. Where would you have him stay?"

Plunking his snifter on the table, he snapped, "There are twenty-five bedrooms in this house—give or take. Take your pick."

Gathering the child in her arms, Olivia walked to the door, hesitating briefly as she looked somewhat cautiously, and curiously, at her husband's dark face. "Come along, Bertrice," she said, and quit the room.

Miles did not take supper with the others. Instead, he chose to barricade himself in his office and stand at the window overlooking the pitiful rose garden. The beast of responsibility loomed over him with gargantuan presence. It was one thing to take a wife—especially a woman as strong and independent as Olivia. But a child still in knickers and a crazy old woman?

He groaned. Children, it seemed, had an unnerving way of looking beyond one's façade to see the truth behind a person's motives.

Imagine the little brat wondering if the house was haunted.

Miles grinned then frowned as he suddenly recalled the evening he'd first arrived at Braithwaite. He'd been eight years old. Alone. Having never set eyes on his father before. With a grubby note clutched in his hand, he'd stood alone in the foyer staring up the massive staircase. At that moment he'd thought for certain that the ghost of King Richard would come careening at him down the balustrade. No apparition appeared, of course. Only his father, whose stern and furious demeanor had caused him more consternation than a dozen disembodied souls.

With his hands in his pockets, Miles left the office and wandered to the dining hall, only to discover the old table cluttered with dirty dishes. No doubt Olivia was accustomed to servants clearing away after her meals.

Sally entered the room behind him, her face as red as her hair. "I ain't ever been so insulted." She snatched up a china cup and saucer, sloshing cold tea down the front of her apron. "I reckon I ought to quit and see who the blazes sees to her bloody bath then."

Miles raised one eyebrow as she plunked the china onto the table again and propped her fists on her ample hips, squaring him with a look of immense indignation. "I ain't got to take that treatment from her, have I?"

"What treatment?"

"Acts like she's the bloody Queen, she does. Tellin' me to fetch up a tub of hot water. What do I look like, a bleedin' draft horse? And if that weren't enough she proceeds to tell me that from now on I ain't to show meself to her unless I'm clean. Clean! She says I smell!"

"Ah."

"She says I look like somethin's been rollin' with the damned pigs. What sort of stuff is that to be sayin' to a loyal laborin' servant, I ask ya? 'Specially as hard as I work 'round here. Says me appearance is an insult to her sensibilities and asked when I was last deloused. She's got a nerve. If that weren't enough she's told me to cut me hair or start wearin' it back in a net. Says it ain't sanitary. Might drop in her food or some such nonsense. If that ain't bad enough, that cheeky little mouse of a lad said me meat pies taste like pig fodder."

The cheeky little mouse of a lad was right, Miles thought, but he dared not say so. In truth, it was all he could do not to smile.

"Have they settled into their rooms?" he asked.

Sally nodded and proceeded to clear the table again, slinging this and slamming that and muttering under her breath about uppity aristocrats. With her arms full of plates, cups, and saucers, she traipsed to the door before pausing long enough to look back and say, "She wants crumpets for breakfast. I says even if I knew how to make crumpets it would take me half the night—but since I don't know how she'll have to do with toast. Know what she said?"

He shook his head.

"That she'd be glad to show me how to cook crumpets if I'd care to learn. I told her I ain't goin' to be

bothered—'specially since she's goin' to be employin'
some fancy French chef. She says she wants crumpets
anyhow so I'll just have to do the best I can. And
she requests orange marmalade. I says there ain't been
orange marmalade in this house in five years. So she
suggested that I ride over to Devonswick and fetch a
pot. As if I ain't got enough to do, boilin' her bloody
bathwater and delousin' meself and preparing crumpets
when I don't know how. When's a girl supposed to sleep,
I ask ya? And to top that off, that crazy old woman has
asked for a saucer of warm milk for her bleedin' cat."

"Then I suggest that you get a saucer of warm milk
to Bertrice's room as soon as possible."

Sally glared at him as if he had sprouted a forked tail.
"Yer crazy as the rest of 'em," she muttered, then hurried
from the room.

He dallied a moment, for the lack of anything else to
do. Then leaving the dining hall, Miles moved into the
gallery and stood at the foot of the staircase, staring up
into the shadows, listening. For what?

Then it came. A hint of a sound. A voice swallowed
by the vastness of the ancient house.

He closed his eyes.

A child's laughter.

He took a breath.

A mother's patient but persistent plea for equanim-
ity.

Then mother and child together. Laughter like the
tinkling of two merry bells.

He left the house without his cloak, preferring to feel
the vicious cold. Olivia's laughter. That he had never
heard his wife laugh before seemed preposterous. That
the music of it would affect him in such an unexpected

manner seemed equally as preposterous.

The stables had once been a magnificent stone structure with glistening panes in the bow windows and brick floors as clean as those in the manor house. Mahogany panels lined the walls and a dozen grooms laid fresh straw on the stable floors each morning. Now the place was dirty and decaying.

He paused at the threshold of the building and peered through the shadows, the musty smell of old hay creeping up his nostrils. A single light burned near the tack room. Miles walked toward it, focused on the distant drunken humming of his groom as the old man went about his business of mucking out the few occupied stalls.

"There's a girl. Good lass. Pretty pony. I'll just take a quick nip if ya don't mind . . . aye, it warms the cockles of me old heart, it does. Scoot. Scoot. Atta girl. Master Warwick'll be pleased that yer leg is healin'. Yes, he will."

Charles Fowles straightened, and finding Miles leaning against the stall post, brightened with a smile. "Well now. Look who's here, Perlagal. If it ain't the master himself come to share a bit of spirit with us, I wager."

Miles looked over at the gray mare who tossed her delicate dished head and whinnied softly. She was a beauty, no doubt about it, with her proud arched neck and flaring nostrils—her silver-white mane that shimmered in the lantern light like fine-spun silk. Her conformation was superb, and in her momentary excitement over seeing him, she pranced in place and cocked her snowy tail high over her back.

Miles offered his hand and she nudged it with her velvety muzzle. "Is she sound?" he asked the groom.

"Good as new, I reckon." Charles tossed some apples in a bucket and propped the rake against the wall. "I hear tell that congratulations are in order, sir."

Miles smiled. Few people in England referred to him as sir. Since the day Miles had arrived at Braithwaite thirty years ago, Charles Fowles had afforded him such respect.

"I'll be makin' the lady's acquaintance soon?"

"Of course."

Charles winked and reached a slightly trembling hand for a bridle on the wall. Slinging it across his shoulder, he hobbled toward the tack room, chuckling to himself. "Before ya know it we'll be hearin' the patter of little feet about the old place."

"Sooner than you think," Miles muttered to himself. "She has a son," he mentioned louder, and waited for the old man's response.

Charles stepped from the tack room and closed the door. "Well now, ain't that grand?" he said, and brushed dirt from his hands. "I'll be lookin' forward to meetin' him come tomorrow."

Miles watched the man limp to a chair, his whisky flask bobbing up and down in his oversized back pocket. It was just like Charles to accept the news of his sudden marriage to a woman with a child without so much as a raised eyebrow of surprise.

"I reckon we'll be seein' a few changes round the old place now." Charles dropped into the chair with a sigh.

"A few."

"Maybe you'll even drop a shillin' or two on these old nags, maybe spruce up the quarters a bit." He turned the flask up to his mouth and drank deeply, then wiped his lips with his shirtsleeve. "I 'spect ya might even wag down to that auction in a fortnight and buy back that black devil you were so fond of. What was his name?"

"As if you could forget. You were there when he was foaled."

"I was there when he put a hoof up agin me arse too. Damned brute. I ain't walked right since. But never mind. He were a magnificent stud. Made right pretty babies, did Gdansk. So, will ya be buyin' him back, sir?"

He didn't answer, just turned and walked to each of the stalls where the remaining four Arabians moved restlessly at the sight of him.

"I'll be turnin' in now, sir, if that's all right," came Charles's voice.

"Good night," Miles replied, listening as the man struggled up the steps to the second-level apartment that had been his home for the last fifty years.

Alone, Miles gazed about the worm-eaten planks, the floor with missing bricks, the broken stalls, and saw himself prostrating himself before his wife with his hand outstretched for money.

And he cursed under his breath.

Returning to the house, he went back to the kitchen and found Sally with her hands in a bowl of sticky dough, pounding, kneading, punching, flinging flour over the floor. She glanced up briefly, her hands pausing in their assault on the mixture as she saw his face. Any sarcasm she might have uttered in that moment was left unsaid as she recognized, and acknowledged, his dark mood.

"You can tell Her Highness that she'll have her bleedin' crumpets for breakfast," she said cautiously.

He made no reply, just continued to walk, choosing to take the servants' stairs to the second floor, where he moved through the shadows until rounding the corner where the family chambers lined the stately corridor. Walking directly to his own bedroom, he found it empty.

What had he expected, exactly?

Turning on his heels, he moved to the next room and knocked, then knocked again more forcefully. In that moment a door across the hall flew open and Bryan, dressed in a flowing white gown, burst forth from the chamber with a squeal. Olivia followed, dressed similarly, her hair spilling like a cloud over her shoulders and down her back to her waist. Neither child nor mother noticed Miles, but continued their dash down the hallway, Bryan in the lead, Olivia in hot pursuit.

"Oli—oli—oxen free," the boy cried. "Ya might run fast but ya can't catch me!"

"We'll see about that!" Olivia replied, then with the ruffled flounce of her gown tail bouncing about her shins, she swooped upon her son and swung him up into her arms, spinning him round and round while he filled the air with uproarious laughter.

Miles watched it all without breathing.

Then Olivia, turning back to Bryan's room, spotted him, standing with his back to her bedroom door. Her face flushed with her exertion, her eyes bright with the laughter that seemed to hang suspended in the air between them, she hugged the boy close to her bosom as if he were a shield to protect her from Miles's reaction— or perhaps it was simply to protect the boy.

"Sir," Olivia said, "we were told you were walking."

"I was."

Olivia gazed at him over the top of her son's disheveled hair, her breasts rising and falling with each breath.

Then, without a word, she hurried back to Bryan's room. Miles followed.

"Hush now," she whispered as she tucked the fidgeting boy into bed. "I fear we've disturbed Warwick. He's not accustomed to noisy little boys flying about his house."

"But he likes little boys, doesn't he?" Bryan asked, peering over his mother's shoulder at Miles.

"Of course he does. Yes, I'm sure of it."

"What shall I call him, Mummy? Shall I call him Papa?"

Olivia's busy hands fell still, yet she did not look back at Miles. "I'll speak to him on the matter," she finally replied, and continued tucking the bedclothes around his squirming little body. "Until then, why not call him sir?"

"All right." Rolling onto his side and drawing his knees up, he rested his chubby cheek into his pillow and peered up at Miles from the corner of his eye. "Good night, sir."

"Good night," Miles said.

Straightening, Olivia offered Miles a swift glance before dousing the light and hurrying from the room. Miles followed more slowly, hesitating as she dashed into the chamber—which was actually two small rooms, a bedroom and small sitting room—she had obviously chosen for herself. When she did not reappear, he moved to the door to find her sitting at a dressing table. Having hurriedly pulled a wrapper on over her nightgown, she stared fixedly at her reflection in the mirror and brushed her hair that looked the color of fine whisky in the candle-lit room.

"Olivia—"

"I'm sorry if we disturbed you," she interrupted, sounding a bit breathless. "Occasionally Bryan has difficulty settling down for the night. He's very excitable, as most children his age are, I suppose."

"You have beautiful hair," he said, loathing the almost aching quality of his own voice. He did not desire this woman, he told himself. By all rights he should scorn her and all she represented, this violation of his dignity. He did not desire her, yet here he stood with his feet rooted to the floor and the sight of her curves draped in soft flannel bringing a fine sweat to his brow, and a pressure to his loins.

She paused in her brushing, just briefly, then began again. "I wager he'll be up again before the night is over. He's very happy to be here. I earlier found him at the top of the stairs slaying imaginary dragons. He's blessed, or cursed, with a very vivid imagination."

Finally, her head turned and she met his study of her directly. He did not waver, but absorbed himself in the image of her sitting there on the tiny, crewel-cushioned stool, the nightgown buttoned high at the neck, and at her wrists. The gown shimmered pale gold in the candlelight.

"Do you mind that I took this room?" she asked softly.

"I thought . . ." He shook his head. "No, why should I?"

Gently, she put down the brush. "We'll begin on the books first thing in the morning."

"All right." He wanted no reminders of those damnable books in that moment.

"I fear . . ." Her shoulders rose and fell in a sigh. "I've made a bad impression on Miss Pinney."

"I know."

She didn't flinch, but raised her little chin and clasped her hands in her lap as if waiting for him to hurl judgment, like fire and brimstone, at her feet.

"You'll get your crumpets," he said. "But no orange marmalade."

She feigned a frown. "Oh dear. I wonder if I might expire for lack of it?"

They both laughed and fell quiet. The silence was palpable then, throbbing like a heartbeat in his ears. "May I come in?" he finally asked.

She raised her hand quickly to her cheek, then it came to rest at her throat. What emotion flashed across her features? Surprise? Distress? Nervousness? He wasn't accustomed to dealing with skittish women. And besides, she had no right to play the frightened virgin. Not with her past.

Frozen on the edge of her stool, she watched him approach her, her lips slightly parting and her hand grabbing the edge of the dressing table for support. Stopping before her, he said, "Are you frightened of me, Olivia?"

"I only wonder why you're here."

"I would think that that would be rather obvious, dear heart."

Suddenly, she moved from the stool to the far side of the room where she pretended to gaze out the window. "I thought . . . that we would at least come to know one another . . ."

"Is it him?"

She turned her head sharply and stared at him with hard eyes. "I beg your pardon?"

"You're thinking of your other lover, perhaps. Bryan's father. If you're worried that I should hold that against you tonight—"

"No. I . . ." She swallowed. "You must understand. All this"—she motioned toward the room—"has happened so swiftly. Forgive me, husband, but I'm not a woman who can so easily surrender herself intimately to a man who harbors no fondness for her at all, despite what you think of me."

"Is it not enough that I married you? That I've given you and your son a home of your own?"

She regarded him a long, unblinking moment, her countenance an odd mixture of fear and yearning. "If I thought you harbored one fiber of inclination for me, then . . ." She looked down at her hands that appeared very thin and white in the shadows. "Do you like me just a little?"

He stared at her while his blood rushed through his veins like a firestorm. How dare she demand affection from him before showing him what was his connubial right? He had every right to demand his husbandly privileges—after all, he'd paid dearly. His pride. His manhood. Yet, she stood there demanding some hypocritical vow of devotion so that she might feel better about her actions.

"Mummy!" cried her son, shattering the tense silence.

The lad flew across the room and grabbed Olivia's hand, tugging on it wildly. "Quickly. Come see! There's a crazy lady downstairs—"

Olivia frowned. "Hush! You've had a bad dream. You shouldn't be out of bed—"

"Please!" Turning to Miles, his eyes round, Bryan announced, "There's two men holding a crazy lady between them. They say they're from—"

"Amersham Private Hospital," came Sally's flustered voice behind them.

Miles turned. The maidservant gaped at him with flour on her face and her hands coated in crusting dough.

"And he's right," Sally added. "They got a crazy lady with them."

Miles briefly shut his eyes. "Oh my God," he whispered, and walked from the room and down the hall, his sight focused straight ahead, his heart beating like drums in his ears. It couldn't be. The bastards had given him until the fifteenth of the month to come up with the money.

Hesitating at the top of the stairs, gripping the balustrade with his left hand, he looked down the winding staircase to the trio of visitors waiting below. Then around them stepped a fourth, a tall man dressed in black with the demeanor of a corpse. Peering up through the shadows at Miles, the man said, "Mr. Warwick, I presume."

"What the hell are you doing here?"

"My name is Peabody, Dwight Peabody, and I am from Amersham Private Hospital."

Slowly, Miles descended the stairs, his eyes going from the gaunt, somber man called Peabody to the pair of white-coated attendants, and, last but not least, to the wild-haired, teary-eyed hag who trembled and wept between them.

"Miles!" the hag wept. "Oh my darling, darling Miles. Help me. Please!"

"Oh my God." Olivia gasped softly behind him. "Husband, who is that pitiful creature?"

"My mother," he snarled.

We saw it in each other's eye,
And wished, in every half-breathed sigh,
To speak, but did not.
　　　—THOMAS MOORE

CHAPTER TEN

OLIVIA AWOKE THE FOLLOWING MORNING TO DISCOV-
er Miles had left Braithwaite. According to Sally he
had departed at dawn, taking a few belongings with
him and leaving no word as to where he had gone,
or when he would return.

Their last words the evening before had been hard
ones

"She's suffering from a form of dementia. Occasionally
she's rational. But other times she lives in some imaginary
world where she talks to herself or stares blankly into
space," Miles explained as he ran his hands through his
hair. "Why are you staring at me like that?" he asked
Olivia.

"Because I understand now."

"Understand?"

"Why were you in such a hurry to marry me. You
thought to go to Amersham and pay your debt before
they released her. But they released her early and now
you're thinking you married me for nothing." Pulling her

173

wrapper more tightly around her, she gazed straight ahead and tried to stop the inner trembling that made her teeth chatter. Finally, when no further response came from her husband, Olivia quit the room and took the stairs slowly, pausing upon the first landing to steady her racing heart and shallow breathing as she again relived the moment she had looked into that wretch's face and recognized those shockingly familiar eyes.

And now he was gone.

Throughout the next days she did her best to keep her thoughts from straying to her errant husband by occupying herself with house matters—the hiring of staff, the planning of a new budget, the settlement of old debts. Word about Miles's marriage had obviously got out, for within the week she was called upon by numerous characters of questionable repute.

There were Messieurs Sydney and Lawrence. Olivia didn't like the looks of them. Sydney had pig eyes, beady, nearly colorless orbs set too closely together. Lawrence had the features of a bulldog, bulging eyes, flat nose, and sagging jowls. Both were nearly bald.

"We expected to speak with Kemball," Mr. Sydney stated with an air of pique that exaggerated his already pompous demeanor.

"Indeed," Mr. Lawrence blustered. "I didn't ride that blasted train all the way from London just to be received by a female who likely doesn't know the first thing about business, money, or the fine, upstanding nature of fair gambling. No offense intended, madam."

She stared at Lawrence without blinking until he began to squirm in his chair, crossing then uncrossing his legs that looked like tree stumps. They then declared that Warwick owed them a total of twenty-five hundred pounds. "Perhaps he does . . . and perhaps he doesn't," Olivia replied with a tolerant but less than believable smile. "But you show me no proof. You can't simply expect me to pay for vouchers that may or may not exist. It wouldn't be very good business, now would it?"

They settled for five hundred each.

Then there was Lieutenant the Honorable Brereton. He explained how he came to lose the exorbitant amount of money to Miles and his "underhanded cohorts." Then he produced the club vouchers, as well as written testimonies of witnesses who were present.

"I must have satisfaction, madam," he declared. "I hope you understand."

"I see," she replied in a gentler voice than she had used with Sydney and Lawrence. "A thousand pounds is a great deal of money to lose for a young man of your age. I'm certain that your annual salary comes to only a fraction of this amount."

He nodded and continued to stare straight ahead.

"And I suspect that, for you to meet your vouchers at the club, you would be forced to ask your father for help."

His Adam's apple slid up and down his throat, but he didn't so much as blink. "My father is dead. I would be forced to speak with my mother—"

"And of course, your mother would be heartbroken to learn that her son lost the money under those circumstances. It might even put her own financial stability into jeopardy."

He nodded.

"And it would not look good on your military record to have such a black mark against you."

"Indeed."

Olivia offered a smile to the young man, then took up her pen and wrote out the note. "May I suggest, Lieutenant, that you refrain from the tables until you learn how to better hold your spirits?"

A look of relief flashed over his features, momentarily alleviating his look of impassivity. He stared down at the extended note as if in disbelief. His hand slightly trembled as he took it. "Madam—"

"You're welcome, Lieutenant."

Certainly, she spent as much time as possible with Miles's mother and Bryan, assuring them both that Miles had only been called away on urgent business and was certain to return just any time. In the privacy of her thoughts, however, Olivia wondered.

What if he didn't return?

She told herself that it shouldn't matter. After all, she was his wife. She and her son lived in the finest house in Yorkshire. It wasn't as if they were dependent on Miles's money to survive. Yet, anxiety hovered about her shoulders like a cloud. She found her mind wandering back to that moment on her wedding night when he had stood before her with something akin to yearning.

Dear God, how many years had she fantasized about such a moment? She, who had grown up on an island of solitariness surrounded by the sea of indifference shown to her by her parents and sister; she had never ached so badly to experience a tender touch, a kind word, a genuine emotion of caring as she had in that moment of looking into her husband's eyes . . .

But she had turned him away.

When not entertaining her son or looking after Alyson's welfare, Olivia began frequenting the stables, finding delight in Charles Fowles's company, not to mention the horses.

She took an instant fondness to the white Arabian mare called Perlagal. Standing fifteen hands and with black points, the animal's wide dark eyes flashed with the fire of its desert ancestors. Olivia began sneaking out of Braithwaite before dawn, wearing little more than a woolen dress and her cloak. She mounted the mare bareback, and with her hair tumbling free, she drove Perlagal over the moor to Margrave Bluff, and once there, faced the sunrise and imagined that she would look around to find her husband there—come home at last.

He didn't, however. And Olivia redoubled her efforts on Braithwaite.

She began her restoration of the old house by posting announcements in Middleham for experienced servants. Her note to the French chef was successful. Within two days Jacques Dubois had shown up on Braithwaite's doorstep with baggage in tow.

Next Olivia tackled the chore of locating both carpenters and painters. Soon Braithwaite was buzzing with the sounds of hammering, scraping, footsteps, tittering servants, and whistling workmen. Occasionally, Olivia escaped to the privacy of Miles's office, sat in Miles's chair, behind Miles's desk, and peered at the hideous stuffed beasts with snarling snouts and glass eyes staring down at her from the walls. A

typical man's room, down to the gun cabinet that
held an impressive display of weapons, including a
long-bladed knife with a scrimshawed whale ivory
handle, a crossbow, and several rifles.

The desk was a massive but distinguished relic of
some ancestor who obviously preferred his furniture
overly big and overly ornate. Each side of the mammoth
fixture was intricately carved with scrolling leaves and
acorns, with an occasional squirrel peering out through
the branches. The walnut wood had turned pitch-black
from generations of oil having been rubbed into
it. She, of course, would have preferred something
more delicate, perhaps a dainty Queen Anne affair
with graceful curves. The one in her bedroom at
Devonswick would do very nicely. However . . .

Sitting back in the chair, her gaze scanning the
garish but strangely comforting room, Olivia reluctantly allowed herself to consider the fact that she
had taken on the challenge of renovating Braithwaite
without so much as a nod from her husband. She
shuddered to imagine what his reaction might be
when he returned home.

If he returned home.

Olivia propped her elbows on the desktop and
buried her face in her hands, knocking her glasses
askew. Where the blazes was her husband? Living
with his indifference was one thing. Dealing with
desertion was another. Then she reminded herself
that no matter what, her life now was infinitely
better than at Devonswick.

Freedom.

Dignity.

Usefulness.

If only . . .

Leaving her chair, Olivia moved to the window and gazed out on the rose garden. She recalled the look in Miles's eyes as he stooped beside her in the garden, and the sense of regret she'd felt over her appearance. Now, focusing on her reflection in the window, she tried to imagine how she would look with Emily's narrow, turned-up nose and Cupid's bow lips, without the sharp, angular contours that made her cheeks and jaw line too noticeably prominent. And her body . . . too tall by far. Standing five seven, she could look most men directly in the eye. Perhaps that's why she had always admired Miles. He towered over her by at least six inches.

Sighing, she rested her forehead against the pane and closed her eyes. She was being foolish. It was Bryan's future that counted most, after all.

Sally appeared at the door. "Yer sister is here," she announced.

Olivia stared at her, until the servant fidgeted. "Beg pardon . . . ma'am." She attempted a clumsy curtsy. "Miss Emily Devonshire of Devonswick Hall asks if yer in res'dence, ma'am. Are ya receivin' guests?"

Olivia nodded and awarded Sally with a pleased smile that lasted only as long as it took for the servant to disappear.

Emily swept into the room with a flourish of taffeta skirts, her pale hair braided into a silky rope that trailed over one shoulder. "There you are!" she cried. " 'Tis a wretched day when I'm forced to gallivant over the moor just to see you."

"Has something happened to Father?" she responded.

"Oh pooh. Of course not. Father may cry that he's feeble, but we both know he's strong as a mule. It's you who's the problem."

"I?"

"We never see you, Oli. At the most important time of my life, you're stuck out here in the middle of nowhere tinkering with this old house."

" 'Tinkering' is a slight understatement, I think. And besides, this is my home now, and my responsibility."

"But you're totally neglecting us."

"Hardly. And besides, it's time you and Father learned to look out for yourselves. I'm married now, Em."

"Married?" Emily laughed. "Olivia, you look perfectly miserable. No doubt you'll end up divorcing and once again you'll find yourself a source of Society's contempt."

"And when will you ever realize that I don't give a damn about Society?" Moving around the desk, Olivia watched her sister's face suffuse with color. "God forbid that I should ever imagine myself a member of your esteemed circle. As you've reminded me most of our lives, I'm not pretty enough, or mannered enough— of course, I was so busy raising you I was hardly given the opportunity. And there is the little matter of Bryan."

"Hush!" Emily implored her, and covered her ears. Then she sank into a chair, looking miserable. Olivia frowned, forgetting her pique.

"Oh, Oli, please. I didn't come here to fight." Emily was on the verge of tears.

Concerned, Olivia sank down beside her younger sister and took her hand. "What's happened, Emily?"

"It's Lord Willowby. We've argued, Oli."

"Everyone argues now and again, Em."

Sniffing, Emily glanced around for something to wipe her eyes. Spying a handkerchief tucked under a untidy stack of ledgers, she grabbed it and blew her nose. "I received a letter from Carolyn Cobb who knows Marcia Hutchinson who knows Belinda Delfries. Belinda declares that Lord Willowby has lost his heart to another, that he's even been seen with her at the theater."

"Rumors," she replied softly.

Her lower lip trembling and tears flowing down her cheeks, Emily wailed, "It's true! I asked him when he called on me this morning. Her name is Janelle Sheredon and he finds her fascinating but declares that they are friends and nothing more." Snorting again into the hankie, she added with emphasis, "She's a widow, and you know what that means."

"That she's older?"

"Older and more experienced, if you know what I mean. She's thirty-five. Practically dead of old age."

"How old is Willowby?"

"Forty-five."

"Has he spoken of crying off?"

Emily shook her head. "But I fear it's only a matter of time. We had set our date for eight months from now and when I mentioned our moving the date up, he refused."

"But there are so many plans to be made—"

"The old fizzle isn't getting any younger, Oli! He's been widowed twice and neither marriage has provided any living offspring. You'd think he'd be champing at the bit to get on with it. After all . . ." Her shoulders shook as she sobbed, "We all know that's the only reason he's marrying me—to bear him an heir."

"Nonsense. If that were the case Willowby could have chosen anyone. But he didn't because everyone knows you're the most beautiful young woman in the country. What man wouldn't lose his heart to you?"

Dabbing at her eyes, Emily managed to smile. "Well . . . I suppose you're right. Still." She frowned. "We both know there's no guarantee when it comes to men. There must be some way to convince him to move up the wedding."

There came a clatter from the hallway and a burst of laughter from the painters, snapping Emily from her reverie; she glanced around the room and wrinkled her nose. "Were I you, Oli, I would have those laborers muck out this room and start again. It's so typical Warwick."

"Agreed, Emily, but that's exactly what I like about it."

Leaving her chair, Emily shoved her used hankie into Olivia's hand and strode to the door where she peered up and down the corridor, where painters were slapping fresh color on the walls and servants were on their knees scrubbing the floor with brushes. "I don't like the shade of blue you've chosen for these walls." Tilting her head slightly toward Olivia, Emily rewarded her with a moue of displeasure then a sigh. "You were always cursed with terrible taste when it came to color, clothes, and men. And speaking of men, where is your husband, Oli?"

"Out."

"Out? According to the help you've sent traipsing to Devonswick to collect your personal belongings, not to mention staples, your husband has been 'out' for nearly two weeks. I hate to say I told you so, Oli—"

"Then don't," came the soft voice from the hallway.

Surprised, Emily turned to discover Alyson Kemball holding Bryan by his hand.

Olivia hurried to collect her son as Emily stared hard at the woman. Alyson, looking very thin and pale, offered Olivia a weak smile. "We were about to go sit in the morning room and have tea and biscuits. We hoped you'd join us."

"And who may I ask is this?" Emily demanded.

As Bryan wrapped his little arms around Olivia's neck, Olivia hugged him close. "This is Miles's mother."

Emily didn't move.

"And you must be Aunt Emily," Alyson said with one slightly raised eyebrow. "I've heard so much about you from Bryan."

"Oli, I'd like a word with you," Emily snapped, and reentered the office.

Allowing Bryan to slide to the floor, she said to Alyson, "I'll meet you in the morning room in ten minutes." She smiled as she watched the pair move leisurely down the corridor, noting how cautiously Bryan escorted his grandmama.

"How could you allow that horrible woman in this house?" Emily demanded. "It's no wonder Miles left. Have you any idea how he detests her?"

"She's very ill."

"If Earl Warwick were to learn of it, why, there's

simply no telling what he might do."

"Bryan is quite fond of her. He calls her Grandmama."

Emily paled.

Retrieving Emily's reticule from the chair, Olivia offered it to her and smiled. "Now if you'll excuse me I have a tea party to attend with my son . . . and his grandmama. Good morning, Emily. My best to Father."

Emily's eyes widened briefly. Without another word, she quit the room in a flurry of taffeta.

✻

You fear, sometimes, I do not love you so much as you
wish? My dear Girl, I love you ever and ever and
without reserve. The more I have known you the more
have I lov'd.
—JOHN KEATS

CHAPTER ELEVEN

"'AS I ROSE AND DRESSED, I THOUGHT OVER WHAT HAD
happened, and wondered if it were a dream. I could not be
certain of the reality till I had seen Mr. Rochester again,
and heard him renew his words of love and promise.'"

Alyson gently closed the ragged-edged copy of *Jane
Eyre,* and smiled a bit wearily at Bryan who lay asleep in
Bertrice's plump arms. "How like Miles he is," she said
thoughtfully as she turned her face to catch a momentary
shaft of sunlight that spilled through the clouds and into
the window. "I have often thought what it would be like to
look into a child's face and see my son's features. I imagined that I would spoil my grandchildren rotten, hoping to
make up for my failures with Miles. Now it seems I won't
have the opportunity."

Olivia dismissed Bertrice with a slight nod and continued to drink her tea, watching her husband's mother intensely. Since arriving at Braithwaite, Alyson's
mental health had improved considerably. Olivia suspected that the medications administered at Amersham

to help alleviate Alyson's pain had also affected her mind. These days she seemed remarkably lucid.

"Imagine, Olivia. After all these years I have finally come home to Braithwaite. You can't know how happy you and Miles have made me by bringing me here. It was my fondest dream that this should all belong to my son someday. Now it does and I can finally find peace within myself for sending him here when he was a child. Does he still hate me terribly for it?"

"I can hardly speak for my husband."

"You are a very tactful young woman. Of course he hates me. He hates me for bringing him into this world to suffer under the burden of illegitimacy. He hates me for so loving his father that I sacrificed my life, and his, on the ridiculous hope that Joseph would leave his family and marry me. He hates me for loving him enough to give him up. Tell me, Olivia, is he happy? Is he successful? What a stranger my son is to me. Is he a kind husband and loving father?"

Olivia regarded Alyson before responding. "Yes," she finally said. "He's a wonderful husband and father."

"And do you love him?"

"Oh, very much."

"And he loves you? Of course. Of course. Even the wildest creature can be tamed with a kind and tolerant hand."

Olivia would never have believed Emily could be so malicious as to ride directly to Earl Warwick's home—and on the pretense of visiting the Countess and offering congratulations on the birth of their third son—while slyly delivering the news of Alyson Kemball's arrival.

However, Olivia knew the very instant that Earl Warwick showed up at Braithwaite's front door the following morning that that was exactly what Emily had done.

Olivia received Warwick in the blue drawing room, glasses perched firmly on the bridge of her nose, prepared to do battle. He had no more than leveled her with one of those infamous Warwick glares when she blurted out:

"While I can appreciate your sentiments, my lord, you must respect mine. Surely you would not have me toss her out in the weather. She's homeless. She has no money. And she's desperately ill. She is a dying old woman who can hardly be faulted for loving a man who did not love her. And besides—" She took a breath. "Braithwaite is my husband's home. As Miles's wife I must stand by his decision to allow his mother to remain here."

Warwick didn't so much as blink, but, like his brother, stood with his broad shoulders erect and his dark eyes boring into hers.

"Very impressive," he said at last. "Most admirable. I wonder why you continue to defend him when, as I understand it, he left this house a fortnight ago and hasn't been seen since."

"He is my husband."

Warwick crossed his arms over his chest. His features looked sinister. "I'm not certain I have ever known a woman, or a man for that matter, who would so sacrifice for the sake of family."

"I hardly consider offering kindness to the sick and elderly a sacrifice."

"I wasn't speaking of the sick or elderly. I was speaking of your family in general."

Olivia frowned. "You talk in riddles, sir."

"You married my brother to satisfy your father's wishes. I wonder what lengths you would go to to protect your sister?"

"What has any of this got to do with Miles's mother?"

"Only that you are stubbornly determined to protect your loved ones at all cost, including your own good name and reputation." Relaxing, he glanced around the freshly painted room before continuing. "While the idea of Alyson Kemball residing in this house makes me ill, I confess that she is not my primary concern. Madam, I've only come to suggest to you that you might find your husband at Gunnerside."

"Gunnerside?"

"At the mines. There's been an accident—"

"Oh!" she cried almost soundlessly.

Earl Warwick stepped forward and took hold of her arm. "It's my understanding that Miles wasn't involved. But due to the rise of discontent with the workers, he was sent for immediately."

"Sent for?" Olivia frowned. "Do you know where Miles has been?"

He moved a little closer, as if to offer further support. "He keeps a cottage not far from Gunnerside. He's been known to go there on occasion . . . when he's troubled or needs time alone."

"You're familiar with this place? You know where it's located?"

"A few miles out of Gunnerside. It was the house my wife grew up in, until her father died. I should have informed you as to Miles's probable whereabouts as soon as I heard he was missing. But I was occupied by the birth of my new son, and besides, I couldn't be certain he was there . . . or who might be with him."

"You're meaning a mistress."

He shrugged and appeared somewhat chagrined. "As far as I know, Miles doesn't have a mistress. He can't afford one. However—"

"You thought it best not to take any unnecessary chances, my lord?"

"Something like that."

"You speak from experience, of course."

His eyes met hers. A slow smile curled his lips. "I think it would behoove us not to dredge up our pasts. Wouldn't you agree, Mrs. Warwick?"

Olivia turned away.

"I thought you should know about the mines," Earl Warwick said. "It seems there's enough trouble to warrant my riding over to investigate. Your husband is not well known for his ability to tactfully negotiate his way out of such annoyances."

Olivia nodded, but as Warwick turned to leave, she looked around. "I can be ready in five minutes, my lord. Please don't try to dissuade me. You'll find that I'm not easily discouraged. As you said yourself, I'm stubbornly determined to protect my loved ones . . . at all cost. Besides, if you refuse I'll simply go alone."

"No doubt."

Rewarding him with a faint smile, Olivia moved toward the door.

Miles strained his eyes to better see the walls of the old mines. Jake Delaney stood at his right, Herbert Wallace at his left. Both men were shorter than Miles by inches, but made two of him in girth. Their chests, arms, and shoulders resembled the rock surrounding them, and were, no doubt, just as solid. Both had worked the mines since they were children.

Deeper in the mines came the constant, jarring crack of picks on stone, and the painful sounds of men groaning as they hefted rock into the low-sided carts they used to remove the bouse from the mines. Jake removed a lantern from a hook jutting from a timber overhead, and held it up before him, casting elongated and grotesquely shaped shadows on the stone-strewed floor. Staring at Miles with furious eyes, he planted one hand in the middle of Miles's back and shoved. "After you, Mr. Warwick . . . sir."

Miles moved forward cautiously.

"What's wrong, Mr. Warwick?" Herbert asked in a surly voice that brought silt filtering down. "You ain't afraid of nothin', are ya? Just because two men was killed here yesterday in a cave-in don't mean it's gonna happen agin—it were no doubt a freak accident, right? Ain't that what the captain said last month when five workers escaped a collapse by the skin of their teeth?"

Staring at the barrier of fallen rock, Miles shook his head. "I've shoveled enough money into these pits the last year to insure its safety, Mr. Delaney." He glanced around at his manager, or captain as the supervisor was called by the miners, Bob McMillian, who stood like a stack of stone himself close by. "What happened, Bob?"

The hulk shrugged and rubbed his bearded face. "Can't rightly say until we've excavated, sir. Seems the stopes just give out," he explained, referring to the timber floors above the levels that held tons of partly wedged deads, rocks with no ore.

"I gave you explicit instructions three months ago to remedy that danger. So what the blazes happened to the new timbers?"

"They never come, sir."

"Never . . ." Miles walked over to his manager. "Explain, Mr. McMillian."

McMillian glanced about nervously and lowered his voice. "I was told, sir, that yer credit was no good."

"But they agreed in this case—"

"They reconsidered, sir."

"Well now, there ya have it," Jake said. "Seems all yer smooth talkin' and pretty promises ain't gettin' any of us anywhere, Mr. Warwick. Sir."

"Sure they are," Wallace joined in. "They are gettin' us dead."

Jake twisted his hand into Miles's coat sleeve and yanked him around. "Dead and starvin'," he sneered. "We've been listenin' to yer fancy pledges to turn our pitiful circumstances around for the last two years. And where has it got us? Soon we'll all be dead. Poor Billy— the best man in the mine. Ever'body liked him, we did, and him only married a year. We were forced to bring him up in a blanket."

"I'm very sorry for the loss, and of course I'll compensate the family. But rebuilding takes time, Mr. Delaney."

"And how many men is goin' to die in the meantime?"

"What would you have me do?" he shouted in frustration. "Shut her down?"

Dirt and stone rained from the ceiling, and the timbers groaned.

Jake smirked. "I'll tell ya what you can do, gov'nor. You can sell her off to Lubinsky."

"Lubinsky." Miles laughed sharply. "You idiot. If I sell these mines to Lubinsky, Gunnerside will die."

"Oh yeah? How do you figure that?"

"How long do you think you'll last working for a man who works his employees like animals? Who refuses to employ any man beyond his prime? Three quarters of these workers would lose their jobs before the ink dried on the contracts."

"My heart's bleedin'," Wallace said. "As if we're suppose to believe that the bloody Warwicks give a flyin' leap about us."

"Aye, yer right on that count," Jake agreed, then stepped closer to Miles. "Considerin' that our wives and children have been starvin' for years, I imagine they'd embrace a change of management."

Miles glanced at his manager, who remained oddly aloof, then he turned away from Delaney and Wallace and exited the mine. Immediately, he was surrounded by two dozen mine workers with soot grooved into their every feature. Too much work and too little food had left them looking like skeletons with muscles and barrel chests, brought on by overdeveloped lungs that had struggled to breathe what little oxygen existed deep in the earth's belly.

To make matters worse, there were women and children. "Murderer!" they shouted and shook their fists. "We're sick to our teeth with yer useless, high-stockin' way of doin' business!"

Someone flung sheep dung, another a stone, cutting the flesh over Miles's right eyebrow. Suddenly the world turned a red blur as the mob surged forward, engulfing him in a tide of driving fists and kicking feet that drove him to one knee as he attempted to shield his face.

"Stop it! Stop it!" the familiar voice shouted.

Then a gun blasted and the shouting crowd fell silent.

Slowly, a bit groggily, Miles stumbled to his feet and did his best to sleeve the blood from his eyes. At the back of the crowd stood two figures on a tumbrel: a man in a flowing cape carrying a rifle ... and a woman—oh Christ—wearing a fox-collared mantle with her hair pulled into a knot atop her head, and glasses on her nose. She pointed a riding crop at the crowd as if it were a cannon.

"People!" Olivia cried. "You resemble a pack of marauding hyenas."

"Who the blazes is she?" someone grumbled.

Miles groaned and briefly considered throwing himself at the mercy of the bloodthirsty crowd.

Damien jumped to the ground, then helped Olivia down. Chin up and eyes fixed straight ahead, she marched into the crowd, raising her eyebrows at any man or woman who thought to stand in her way. Finally reaching Miles, she stared at him. "Perhaps you would care to introduce me to your associates."

He gave her a cold smile in response.

"Very well then." Turning on her heel, she said, "I am Mr. Warwick's wife."

Silence, then someone guffawed. Someone else whispered, "I know her. That's Lord Devonshire's daughter. They call her old iron stays in Middleham."

The crowd moved back, giving them more room.

Damien swaggered up beside her, slapped his hand on Miles's shoulder and said, "I see you're exhibiting your usual tact and charm, Kemball."

Miles closed his eyes. "What the hell are you doing here?"

"I suppose it doesn't matter to you that your wife and I just saved your skin."

He tenuously touched his split lip, throbbing jaw, and swollen eyelid. "Seems you were a trifle bit late, Dame. Was that coincidence or intentional?"

"What do you think?"

"I think you probably encouraged them."

"You know better than that. I'm not an overseer; I tend more toward participation. I would've broken your jaw."

Olivia gave them a hard glance over her shoulder. "I think, gentlemen, that this is hardly the time and place for quipping." To Miles, she added, "I daresay, sir, that it would behoove you to remove yourself from this rather combustible situation lest they suddenly remember they are angrier at you than they are bemused by me."

Damien chuckled.

Miles glared at him.

"Good people," Olivia said loudly enough to be heard over the fresh rumblings of discontent. "Murdering your employer is most undignified, I'm sure. And what good would it do you?"

"Bring me a great deal of satisfaction," a man shouted.

"Indeed it might . . . until you suddenly discover yourself unemployed—or in the gallows. How sweet will your revenge taste when your children are starving?"

"Our children are already starvin'!" a woman cried.

A surge of approval reverberated through the crowd.

Turning to Damien, Olivia said, "I think we should find a neutral ground, my lord. I fear we're going nowhere until this situation is resolved."

The neutral ground turned out to be the White Horse Ale House and Inn. After much deliberation, the doors were closed to everyone except Delaney, Wallace, McMillian, Damien, Miles, and Olivia. Lining two sides of a trestle table, they all waited in silence as the proprietor of the tavern slammed steins of dark ale on the table, then stood with his hands on his hips and his mouth turned under as he regarded both Miles and Damien in displeasure. Damien returned his look with an intensity that warned him to keep his opinion to himself. Miles, however, regarded Olivia as she reached for her ale and turned it up to her mouth, her gaze sliding to his over the rim of her stein.

"This is a bloody waste of time," Jake grumbled. "I ain't in the habit of doin' business with women."

"Aye," Herbert agreed. "Since when did the Warwicks need a female to speak for them?"

"Understand that I'm speaking for no one," she replied. "But it's obvious you gentlemen are at loggerheads with my husband on the matter of the running of these mines."

"Damn right," Jake replied. " 'Cause we're sick to our teeth of empty promises."

"Understandably. Earl Warwick and I have discussed this matter at length, and I believe we all agree that the basic problem has been my husband's lack of monetary resources . . . and poor management."

Miles narrowed his eyes.

"Therefore," Olivia said a bit more cautiously, "I'm here to guarantee you that everything possible will be done to assure the men's, and their families', well-being."

Herbert looked at her strangely. "And how do you aim to do that, ma'am?"

"By drawing up contracts whereby my husband and myself will guarantee certain rights and privileges due to each man in our employment, including a guar-antee of company restructure, benefits, renovations, and—"

"I beg your pardon," Miles said, leaving his chair. Proffering Olivia an emotionless smile, he gently wrapped his scraped fingers around her arm and added, "I'd like to speak to you privately."

Olivia glanced at her companions' ambivalent faces, then joined Miles, offering little resistance as they moved to the back of the tavern. He did not pull her chair out for her, but straddled his own, back to front, and stared at her until she sat down, fingers folded around her reticule that lay in her lap. She met his look directly.

"First, I do thank you for helping me, but what the hell are you doing here in the midst of mine business?"

Olivia opened her reticule and extracted a handkerchief. She offered it to him. "Your head is bleeding."

He ignored the kerchief; his shoulders looked rigid. Olivia shrugged and returned the cloth to her lap.

"I would think that you had enough at Braithwaite to occupy you for the time being."

"Meaning your mother, I suppose."

He glanced toward Earl Warwick. "I suppose he knows about Alyson?"

She nodded.

Miles briefly closed his eyes. His features looked haggard, as if he had slept little the last weeks. "This business is no concern of yours," he said.

"Really?" Her gaze raked him. "Trouble is apparent here, and—"

"You and my brother determined that I'm incapable of dealing with it. Dammit!" He slammed his fist on the table and Olivia jumped. "I won't shut down these mines and I won't sell them to Lubinsky."

"Earl Warwick mentioned that the mines are virtually played out. It would seem a reasonable solution to your dilemma," she said.

Miles sat back in his chair and wearily gazed up at the old beams on the low ceiling. "I don't understand it. No matter how much money I sink into these damnable pits I get nothing accomplished. The men don't work any harder. And despite my efforts to assure their safety as much as possible, the mishaps continue."

"Then why go on? Why not sell?"

"Contrary to what you think of me, I care about these people. If Lubinsky moved in he'd bring his battery of gorillas in to work these mines and the good people of Gunnerside would be dismissed and forgotten. It's happened before."

"Yet they would risk that chance to be rid of you." Olivia looked over at the men. "Perhaps if I speak with them."

"No." Sitting upright, his soiled hands splayed on the tabletop, and his handsome mouth a sneer, he said, "I fear you've done enough already."

"Pride cometh before a fall," she replied with a setting of her chin. Then she left her chair and returned to the group.

"Gentlemen," she said, slapping her reticule onto the table. "Mr. Warwick and I have agreed that measures should be taken to remedy the dissatisfaction running rampant throughout the Warwick mines." Miles moved up behind her, and the air turned uncomfortably warm, yet she managed to take a steady breath and continue. "Mr. McMillian."

Warwick's manager shifted in his chair, but did not meet her eyes. "I would see your books and speak to you at length," Olivia told him.

McMillian looked at Miles, then at his men, who regarded Olivia as if she were an unusual bug that had settled on the end of their nose. "And," she added, "I'll wish to have a tour of the mines."

That brought them upright in their chairs. All except Earl Warwick, who remained relaxed, with that infamous Warwick curl to his lips.

"Yer bloody daft,"Jake Delaney cried. "Ain't no woman been down into the belly of them hills since Lord Ashley's commission legislated a bill prohibiting women from working underground."

"It's dangerous," Herbert Wallace added.

"Not to mention dumb." McMillian shook his head and crossed his big arms over his chest. "Besides, you'd get that pretty dress dirty."

The men snickered. Olivia adjusted her eyeglasses and stared at each man until he fell silent. "I will see the mines," she declared.

They glanced at one another dubiously.

"Mr. Delaney, I would advise you to talk with the others. Someone will be needed to speak on their behalf when it's time for negotiation. Until such time Mr. Warwick kindly requests that all mining be discontinued until further notice."

McMillian jumped up. "Now wait a bloody minute. Ya can't come in here and close us down. These men have wives and children to feed!"

"Agreed. Therefore it will behoove us all to make haste in emending this unacceptable situation."

*   *   *

After a great deal of consideration, Olivia agreed to leave the inspection of the mines until the morning. She did, however, spend the remainder of the afternoon shut up in the shop, a wooden hut that housed the blacksmith's smithy and the miners' shop, with Bob McMillian and the Warwicks, and came to the conclusion that she neither liked McMillian, nor did she trust him.

Just past dusk, she excused herself from the men's company, and hurriedly returned to the White Horse Inn and Ale House and, once learning that her husband had taken lodging at the shop, took a room, grateful for the little privacy the tiny chamber with paper-thin walls allowed her. The day seemed a blur now, as she lay on the bed and closed her eyes in the semidark and did her best to stop shivering. Her joints ached from the bone-jarring gallop all the way from Braithwaite to Gunnerside, and for the entirety of the afternoon her back and shoulders—indeed, her whole being—had been tense as a bow string in Miles's presence.

He was furious at her for being here.

He was furious that she'd helped him.

Well, what had she expected? That he would be skipping in glee because she and his brother had charged into this ugly fracas and saved his handsome neck? Were she and Earl Warwick simply to stand back while the irate miners killed Miles?

"Olivia."

Olivia opened her eyes and listened to the rattling of wind upon the windows. Her heart raced; the sounds of drunken laughter from below rolled over her in a thunderous wave.

"Olivia," came Miles's voice, then a tapping on the door.

How long had she slept?

She slid from the bed, gasping slightly as her bare feet touched the cold floor. She hurried to the door and opened it enough to reveal Warwick's dark face.

"Pardon me," he said, and moved into the room. "Did I wake you?"

Olivia glanced toward the door.

"Close it," he told her. Still, she hesitated and he looked at her with a trace of amusement on his lips. "Come, come, dear heart, it isn't as if we shouldn't be alone together." He waggled one finger at the door, and she eased it shut, leaned back against it and watched him slowly turn to face her.

Miles narrowed his eyes. Olivia had partially unbuttoned the bodice of her dress before lying abed. It fell open now, exposing a vee of white flesh and the pink bud of the tattoo on her breast. With her disheveled hair spilling from its combs, and her mouth and eyes appearing slightly swollen, it was obvious she'd been sleeping.

"Are you inebriated?" she asked in a faintly husky voice. "For if you are, sir, you may leave this moment. I have no desire to argue with a drunk."

"What makes you think I came here to argue?"

She frowned suspiciously and moistened her lips with the tip of her tongue.

"My brother has politely commanded me to join him for a tipple before supper—quite an occurrence, you understand. I suspect he intends to verbally whip me over my mother residing at Braithwaite. He'll no doubt remind me that Braithwaite is only mine by trial—being that if I don't show solvent by the end of next year, the properties revert back to him. And therefore he has every right to demand that Alyson Kemball be removed from the premises. Therefore, as a dutiful son and estimable human being, I'm supposed to relinquish my dreams of claiming Braithwaite and ride off to live happily ever after with the woman who tossed me out with a note when I was only eight years old. However, being the ever considerate husband that I am, I told him I should consult you before we had our tête-à-tête. Besides, we have so much to catch up on. Haven't we?"

"Indeed." She cleared her throat and slid her hand into a pocket in her skirt, withdrawing her eyeglasses. Her fingers fumbled with the stems, then lifted them to her nose.

Miles laughed and shook his head. He moved toward her, watching as her eyes grew large, then larger behind the thick-lensed spectacles. "You're not going to hide behind those atrocities tonight."

Before she could react, he grabbed the glasses from her face and dropped them to the floor. Then he ground his heel into them, pulverizing the lenses.

Olivia gasped. "Bloody idiot. What do you think you're doing?"

"This." Closing one hand around her throat, he eased her back against the door, watching as her blue-green eyes flashed with both fear and challenge, and her soft mouth fell open. She grabbed his wrist with both hands. For an instant, his anger over her and Damien's interference in his life and business matters were temporarily forgotten. An unexpected wash of desire for this infuriating woman overcame him.

"Sir, you don't frighten me. And," she added with emphasis, "I have another pair of eyeglasses at home."

His hard mouth curved faintly, and he lowered his face over hers. "Oh, I don't intend to harm you, dear heart. Walls are too thin. Might be witnesses. No, I only came here to look for something I lost this afternoon."

Olivia blinked slowly and appeared confused, then nervous, then startled as he nudged his knee between her thighs and pressed her back against the door. Her gaze locked on his face, she drew a sharp breath and made a desperate grab for his hand as it reached to tug up the hem of her skirt. "Wh-what are you doing?" she demanded in a tight voice.

She was naked under her dress. Her thigh felt warm and smooth and firm. "I told you. I fear I lost something today, or perhaps it was the moment I agreed to your father's conditions concerning your dowry. Have you guessed yet what I'm looking for, my darling wife? Hmm? Then let me tell you. I'm looking for my balls. You castrated me in front of those men today; just thought you might be hiding them here."

Her eyes locked on his, her lips parted; she only managed to whisper "Oh" as his hand cupped her moist, sensitive flesh.

He'd anticipated a fight, a lashing of her waspish tongue or a firm reprimand for treating her so coarsely. He'd meant to shock her. To make her feel the bite of humiliation he'd experienced. Yet, there she stood, like a doe frozen in the cross hairs of a rifle as her body warmed and turned liquid in the palm of his hand. Then again, why should he be surprised? This was her reputation, after all.

Frowning, he recalled the time he'd kissed her, experienced again that unnerving delight he'd discovered in the taste and touch of her mouth under his. If he stood here a moment longer, the recollection of her soft lips opening under his would stir the animal in him and he would forget the reasons for his present anger. He'd do something stupid, like toss her on the bed and bury his body inside her . . . take what was rightfully and lawfully his.

Damn, but she was tempting.

His fingers toyed with her, gently, until her face flushed with heat and her sex turned slick and hot and he heard her uneven breathing in the silence. Her eyes appeared glazed, her lips ripe and red, and her hips squirmed—just slightly—against his hand.

She liked this. Oh, yes. He wondered what else she liked—if she expected sex to be tender or full of rough passion—the way he liked it. Unrestrained. Wild.

Explosive.

If only he were a little drunker now . . . he could forget how she had manipulated—controlled—castrated him before the entire village of Gunnerside.

But he was too damned angry.

Removing his hand, he allowed the dress to fall down her legs, then he stepped away, flashing her a smile that kept her pinned against the door as forcefully as his body had seconds before, her entire being visibly trembling, her face suddenly pale. How young and vulnerable she appeared in that moment. Had she been any other woman—a virgin—he might have given her credit for appearing shaken and frightened by his sexual aggressiveness. No doubt it was simply her own wantonness that made her face flush with the blood-heat of passion. No doubt she was thinking of another time and place, possibly another man. Still, she faced him. Her eyes were unflinching, yet as the silent moments passed she regained her equilibrium and regarded him with her old defiance. And with challenge. As if saying, I dare you to take me. I dare you to want me, regardless of what I am, or what I was.

"Sweet dreams, dear heart," he said, and stepped around her for the door.

***

Love is a deep well from which you may drink often, but into
which you may fall but once.

—ELLYE HOWELL GLOVER

CHAPTER TWELVE

OLIVIA AWOKE TO THE DEEP, DISTANT MELODY OF
church bells. Wearily (for she had had little sleep) she left
her bed and peered out the window.

Along the village streets, and stretching off across the
downs, came a mass of black-clad folk, all with their
heads bowed and their weather-ruddy faces somber.
Silently, they moved in groups toward the church: the
youths neatly dressed, their parents walking in melancholy array, expressions of sorrow deeply creasing
their faces.

Olivia hurried down the stairs until she located the innkeeper, who was pulling on a black jacket over his dark
gray shirt and waistcoat. "Good sir," she said, "why are
these people descending on the church?"

"Why, there's to be a buryin', ma'am. A miner's
buryin' for poor Billy and Ian." He shook his head and
buttoned his jacket. "Poor, poor fellows was underground
in the 210 fathom level when a scale of ground come way
from the roof and crushed them both flat as pancakes.

Their comrades was wheelin' the bouse out to shaft;
and when they come back there was poor Billy and
Ian . . ." He wiped his eyes. "As dead as herrin's they
was. Sheeny Kilpatrick, he was their comrade come up
to surface, why he couldn't speak for five minutes, then
he calls for Kappen McMillian. Kappen goes barrelin' to
the 210 but there was naught to be done for the men. They
was dead, o'course, and all Kappen could do was tell their
widows and mothers. It were a pitiful and sad day, but no
sadder than this."

Olivia followed him to the door and stood on the stoop,
watching the hundreds of men, women, and children file
silently through the streets. "But where do they all come
from?" she asked softly.

"Other villages, ma'am. Other mines. When one of
their own is killed it strikes to the heart of them all,
because they all know that the next give could come
crashin' down on them or their loved ones." With his
jacket buttoned tightly, the innkeeper turned his collar
up against the cold and stepped out into the street, and in
seconds was swallowed up by the moving throng.

Olivia joined the procession from the church to the
cemetery. The knell, which had been tolling for some
time, ceased, and the Methodist minister stood before
the immense assembly of people and pronounced,
"Earth to earth, dust to dust. Please bow your heads in
prayer."

Shivering, Olivia set her gaze on her husband's broad
back and watched as he neither bowed his head nor
prayed, but looked out over the gathering of mourners
with his face blank of emotion, his gloved hands clasped
into fists.

The ceremony then concluded, Miles moved through the dispersing crowd toward the widows. As they saw him, they broke into fresh tears and huddled their children close to them.

From her place beside the cemetery entrance, Olivia watched her husband take the women's hands in his. He spoke. They wept. The children buried their cold-kissed faces in their mother's skirts as other children of other miners scampered from one hillocked grave to another, finding relief in their game.

"He'll be assuring the widows that they'll not want for bread for themselves or their children," came a soft voice behind Olivia. "Normally he would be joined by the good captain, but McMillian has hurried off to his dinner."

The woman moved around Olivia so they stood side by side. Olivia looked over at the striking brunette. "Certainly, how they'll continue to feed their children will be their main concern," she went on. "In years past, if there were no sons to take their father's place in the mines, the women would do so. Up until three years ago, McMillian allowed children, no older than those, to work their father's place in the pares. Your husband put a stop to it immediately. It was against the law to work the children, of course, but it's always been McMillian's theory that what the law doesn't know won't hurt them.

"Warwick will, of course, instruct these women to keep his generosity a secret." The woman lowered her voice slightly. "There are men killed occasionally for reasons other than mine accidents. Some, having grown weary of the drudgery, simply throw themselves down a hole."

"Suicide?" Olivia frowned.

"If the men were to learn that upon their deaths, Warwick would care for their families financially, I fear we would see a tremendous increase in suicide. As it is, these miners work themselves to death just to feed their families. Look into their faces, Mrs. Warwick. After years of ungodly toiling in the bowels of these hills, would death not seem a welcome respite?

"Then, of course, there are the accidents due strictly from carelessness. Men go in drunk. They get in fights. The mine owners simply cannot be expected to pay for a man's stupidity."

Olivia shook her head and clutched her cloak more tightly around her. "But they are all so angry with my husband."

"Not all. But there is a great deal of frustration, and it is commonly known that frustration breeds anger. I'll say this, Mrs. Warwick. There are those who would encourage disharmony among the men for their own purposes."

"Do you mean Lubinsky?"

"Others closer to Miles and the matter is growing worse."

"You speak in riddles, madam. Have you told my husband this?"

"You'll soon find, Mrs. Warwick, that despite Miles's appearance of cynicism, he will stubbornly, and often foolishly, choose to hang on to the trust he's invested in a man . . . or woman . . . until it's too late. Therefore, when a friend, or loved one, or business associate whom he's trusted turns on him, it makes their betrayal all the more bitter."

"You appear to know my husband very well, Mrs. . . . ?"

"Hooper. Janet Hooper."

* * *

In the past, Olivia had listened to her father's discourse on the Yorkshire mining industry with a modicum of interest. She knew that conditions in the mines left a great deal to be desired. She was also aware that mechanization, along with mine-owner reform, had done much to remedy the sorry conditions in which the miners had been forced to labor.

Flanked by Miles and Earl Warwick, Olivia managed to keep a brave upper lip as she, along with Delaney, Wallace, and McMillian, were trundled by rider into the very bowels of the earth.

"You'll be keepin' yer hands and arms tucked in close," Delaney explained to Olivia. "Or you'll find yerself limbless."

"And no whistlin'," Wallace added. "It's bad luck."

Olivia glanced over the rider's oaken side and watched water swirl around the wheels and rails. As the cart rocked into the darkness, Delaney leaned close and whispered, "If we're lucky we won't be seein' any pixies."

"Pixies?" she replied.

"Aye. The small people," Delaney explained. "They're somewhat like a kind of masculine fairy, but, unlike the softer sex of them diminutive folk, pixies like nothin' more than makin' mischief."

Leaning closer to Delaney's smirking face, so they were practically nose to nose in the semidarkness, she said, "Poppycock, Mr. Delaney. If you're thinking to scare me with such ridiculous superstitions you needn't bother. Such fables are given credit only by those of weak understanding and uneducated minds."

McMillian chuckled and poked Wallace with his elbow. "Got spunk, ain't she, Herbert?"

Herbert Wallace grimaced and looked at Miles, who sat with his elbows on his knees and his eyes on Olivia. So far, Miles hadn't spoken a word to her.

Listening to the sound of the rider creaking and groaning with the strain of its load, Olivia watched the daylight at the portal grow smaller and dimmer as they sank beyond the dressing floor, and the overwhelming sense of slowly being buried alive by the close stone walls made her feel slightly faint.

The dimension of the level they traversed was little more than six feet by four feet. Olivia was impressed by the stone arching that gave the mine a neat, orderly, and safe appearance.

"The upkeep on this masonry must cost a fortune," Olivia said, more to herself than to the men.

"Precisely six hundred pounds a quarter to secure the roofs and walls of each level," her husband replied, bringing her gaze back to his. Perhaps he was no longer angry over her presence here.

"It seems a phenomenal amount," she replied. "Is it necessary?"

"Absolutely, unless you wish to increase the risk to the men, not to mention impeding the roadway by which the bouse and deads are transported to the surface."

Olivia watched his face as he closely studied their surroundings. Occasionally they passed a tallow candle that had been affixed to the wall by bits of clay. The dim light reflected from his features, giving him the look of a young boy with his eye on a plate of confections as he spoke of the mine as if it were a living entity.

"The timber work is as costly as the masonry. More so because the timbers are constantly rotting or splintering, or generally in need of replacement. Larger companies, such as the London Lead Company, own their own woodyard, and in some cases, their own forests. To employ on-site millwrights or carpenters, however, would cost another fifteen hundred pounds a quarter."

As they reached the mouth of the nearest level, a sense of relief settled over Olivia as she did her best to take a deep breath in the thin air.

Delaney and Wallace stepped forward and grabbed a lantern that offered little more than a flicker of light in the oppressive darkness. Miles followed, glancing back at Olivia momentarily before offering her his hand.

Olivia stepped into the shaft, only to be brought up short as she sank to her ankles in mud. Startled, she looked at her feet, then up at Miles. He only offered her his hand again, and this time she took it.

She learned quickly that the dangers of the shafts were more numerous and varied than she had expected. With ceilings low enough that Miles and Earl Warwick were forced to stoop slightly to avoid hitting their heads, the mines were a catacomb of massive disasters waiting to snuff out the lives of the miners at any moment.

Olivia soon had enough. Still, she had asked—demanded—this tour. She needed to understand Miles's problems.

The stench was enough to force her into covering her nose with a perfumed hankie. While Miles offered her support by holding her left arm, and Earl Warwick her right, they moved down the bleak damp tunnels while McMillian explained how the ore was transported up steep inclines to the surface along wood rails. Occasionally they came to other pits that were little more than black holes with tiny orange lights flickering at the bottom.

"Down there is what we call hell. Man who volunteers

to work in hell signs his own death warrant. If disease or drownin' or cave-ins don't kill him, chokedamp will. Only way down there is by ladder."

The tour continued. The conditions worsened. The unbearable heat soon sapped Olivia's energy and parched her throat. A thermometer indicated the air at one hundred and eight degrees.

When Olivia could stand no more, she turned to Earl Warwick. "Sir, I've heard of your great philanthropy as well as your efforts to cooperate in the reformation of this country's industries. Yet you allowed your own employees to suffer under the indignities of these wretched conditions. You cannot let the workers point the blame at your brother. These problems have existed long before you ever passed them on to my husband, sir."

"Agreed, madam. However, I'll point out that it was my intention to close these hellholes down. As you can see, the cost of renovation would greatly outweigh any profit we might see from the remaining lead. If, indeed, there is any remaining lead."

"There's ore," Miles snapped. "I'd wager my life on it. And with ore we could improve safety and increase wages. But it'll take the excavation of new levels to get to it."

"And that takes money," Delaney reinforced. "How the blazes do ya expect to open new levels when ya ain't got the money to upkeep the ones you've already opened? I'm tellin' ya. You can do us all a favor and sell out to Lubinsky."

"Over my dead body, Delaney. I—"

At that moment a shout arose among the men as a section of earth and rock collapsed from the wall. As the miners scattered, Olivia suddenly found herself wrenched from her feet as Miles wrapped one arm around her waist and swung her away from the tumbling rocks and scrambling men. For an instant they seemed frozen in place, she pressed against his chest, his face above hers and his eyes reflecting the fire from the lantern on the wall.

As quickly, he passed her safely to Earl Warwick, who grabbed her up in his arms and spun away from the precariously tottering boulders that appeared to be crumbling stone by stone onto the shaft's mucky floor. Miles stumbled toward a young man no more than eighteen years of age who had tripped and sprawled heavily into the mud. Wrapping the lad's arm around his shoulder, Miles dragged him to his feet and hurried him from harm's way.

Fortunately, the wall collapsed no further, and as if the accident had not happened, Bob McMillian shouted for the men to get back to work—barking orders and sneering insults at those who dallied.

As the others retrieved their picks and ventured back into the tunnel, Olivia looked at Earl Warwick and said, "My lord, you may put me down. I'm perfectly capable of walking on my own."

He set her on her feet, her heart beating fast for numerous reasons. Anger toward the mine's deplorable condition, not to mention McMillian's heartlessness; the thrill and shock of Miles's rescuing her from possible harm. She offered Earl Warwick a glance and found him smiling. "I find little to smile about, my lord."

"I was only thinking that you remind me a great deal of someone very near and dear to my heart."

"Oh? Who?"

"My wife. I think you'll get on well together."

Miles reappeared, the beleaguered miners trailing after

him, McMillian bringing up the rear, his whiskered face red from heat and anger and his hands clasped into fists the size of ham hocks.

"Yer makin' a mistake," McMillian bellowed to Miles, who stopped and turned to face him. "Ya pull these men out of here and they won't ever come back."

"By the looks of these stopes they're lucky to still be alive, McMillian. Just what the hell have you been doing with the finances I've provided to take care of these problems?"

"Might as well be pitchin' yer money down them holes," he replied.

"It's like we said," Jake spoke up. "If yer smart, you'll sell out to Lubinsky. Otherwise you can barricade her closed and call it a day."

"You can both go to hell," he snapped, then turned on his heels, and grabbing Olivia by the arm, pulled her back toward the rider.

Olivia remained in her room for the next hours, gazing out the window at the rain-drenched countryside while her thoughts somersaulted. Her son was safe at Braithwaite, but she missed him and hoped she and Miles could return soon.

At least Miles was safe, and she was almost certain he would come home. She recalled Miles pulling her into his arms and kissing her those many nights ago . . . Miles climbing down into that dark, wet, and treacherous sinkhole at Margrave Bluff to rescue Bryan. For half of her life she had fantasized about Miles Warwick. Had experienced both envy and immense crushing grief when she'd learned Emily had become involved with him. Now . . . now Olivia was discovering that marriage without requited love could be far, far worse than no marriage at all.

A knock at the door brought her head up. "Yes?" she called.

"I'd like to speak with you," came Miles's voice.

Olivia grabbed for her glasses, feeling foolish as her fingers fumbled at the lensless wire frames. She checked her hair in the peeling silvered shaving mirror hanging above the washstand, gave a few wayward strands a pat into place, and smoothed her skirt with her hands.

She opened the door slightly. He stood there in the shadowed hallway, a whisky bottle in one hand, two cups in another. His eyes looked dark, his mouth partially curved in that familiar sardonic manner.

"Mrs. Warwick," he said. "You look as if you could use a drink."

"I, sir?"

He nudged the door open with his shoulder and stepped into the room. Olivia watched him walk to the tiny table where she had made copious notes about the mines throughout the last hours. He put down the bottle and cups and picked up the papers.

"Tell me." He looked at her and tossed the papers back onto the table. "Do you like children, Olivia?"

Surprised by the question, Olivia nodded. "Obviously—"

He waved away her response. "Just because you have a child doesn't necessarily mean you like children. There are a vast number of reasons why people procreate, the least of which is love for one another and/or love for children. You, of all people, should know that."

"Why do you ask?"

Miles poured a measure of whisky into the cups, then

took a long drink straight from the bottle. With ribbons of fading daylight making patterns on the floor at his feet, Miles stared hard at the bottle before looking up at her. "I've never given the idea much consideration, until recently."

"Oh?" He offered her the cup of whisky; she took it and gripped it with both hands.

"I've never spent a great deal of time with children. There are my nephews, of course, but seeing that I've not been invited over to Earl Warwick's home for any occasion other than a good dressing-down, I've not had the opportunity to get to know the lads. They seem like fine boys."

He drank again, this time from the cup. Then he took the chair where Olivia had earlier been sitting, and offered it to her. He, in turn, dropped onto the bed. With his back propped against the wall, and his legs stretched out before him and crossed at the ankles, he waited until Olivia sat down, nervously, on the edge of the chair. He looked at her bare feet, one eyebrow raised.

Curling her toes under the hem of her dress, Olivia asked, "Have you come here to discuss children, sir, or business?"

"In our case, I think the two go hand in hand. Don't you?"

Olivia put her cup on the table and retrieved the papers. She was feeling much too vulnerable—at odds with her emotions. The fact that he was staring at her with an intensity that would melt the lead he so worshiped didn't help. "I'm certain you are aware of the colossal amount of money it would take to save these mines," she said, changing the subject.

Miles looked into his cup.

"That's not to mention the increase in wages these men deserve. But all that is beside the point."

Leaving her chair, Olivia proceeded to pace and flip through the papers she carried. "You've seen zero profit from these mines in the last five years, regardless of the money you've invested. The reconstruction attempts and the safety measures have proven futile. Accidents have tripled in the last year alone. I wonder how you can justify spending another shilling on it?"

Miles tossed his empty cup onto the bed and watched Olivia move gracefully about the room, bare toes peeking from beneath the muddied hem of her dress. He wondered if he were drunk. Must be. Otherwise he wouldn't be enjoying this little scenario. The brazier of coals in the corner had warmed the tiny room capably. The lantern on the desk lit the stark walls in a hazy yellow glow, and the rain lightly tapped at the window and roof. The anger he'd earlier felt toward Olivia now seemed as murky as the weather. Perhaps he was just tired, or maybe defeated. Everything *Little Miss Know-it-all* was saying was absolutely true.

"You're right, of course," he said, bringing her to an abrupt stop in the center of the room. "Come, come, dear heart, you needn't look so surprised. I'm not totally illogical."

"I never implied that, sir. I only wished to point out—"

"You needn't bother. Damien has been telling me the same thing for the last years. His brother Randolf did likewise, and our father as well."

Olivia grabbed the little chair and pulled it next to the bed. She sat on it with her spine very straight and her hands clasped on the papers in her lap. Her eyes looked very large, her mouth moist. "Then why do you persist?" she asked.

"Because I believe in it. I can't tell you why, but in here"—he pointed to his heart—"I feel that we've only begun to tap the guts of those mines." Swinging his feet from the bed, he took hold of her hand, causing her to gasp softly in surprise. "Have you ever wanted something so badly, Olivia, that you would risk everything—your pride, your reputation, your money—to have it?" She blinked at him with her wide green-blue eyes, and he jumped from the bed, dragging her behind him as he moved to the window.

The panes were foggy with condensation. Miles rubbed a circle with his fingertips, spilling cold droplets of water on Olivia's toes. "Look out there," he told her. "Tell me what you see."

Standing on her tiptoes, she gazed out on the bleak village. "Dark buildings and no people," she finally replied.

"Once the population of this village was three times what it is now. Imagine what it could be again if we tapped a new vein of ore."

"But the dangers—"

"To hell with the dangers. With adequate renovations, the dangers diminish. There are five mines in the area that my father was forced to close completely due to a rash of explosions caused by lamp fire. There has been a successful lamp invented that will alleviate the danger of working those particular mines. They could be reopened, Olivia. We could employ another five hundred men to work those mines."

He rubbed another pane, and grabbing her shoulders, her back pressed to his chest, he said, "Do you see those two hills and the valley between them? If you travel directly east down that valley for twenty miles you'll run into rails. Train rails."

Rubbing a wider circle on the window, Olivia stared harder at the foggy horizon. "I see," she said thoughtfully. "Yes . . . I see. A train passing through Gunnerside would do wonders for the village."

"And there are innovations in steam pumps to drain the water and fans to expel methane. Then, of course, there is the Bessemer converter that could make the smelting hotching tubs and buddles in these mines obsolete."

Olivia turned to face him, her head fallen back slightly as she looked up into his eyes. Faint color touched her cheeks and the light from the nearby lantern made gold swatches among the mahogany coils of her hair. "These improvements would amount to a fortune. It would take every last shilling I own and then some. We couldn't do it alone. However . . ."

Pushing past him, Olivia moved tentatively around the small room, her head tipped forward as she studied the floor in deep concentration. Miles found himself smiling at her genuine interest.

"Investors," she cried, her eyes sparkling as she spun to face him. "We could sell shares in the mines—just enough to help finance the restorations and improvements. And certainly there are banks—"

"You can forget that. As you recall, dear heart, I'm a bad risk where they are concerned."

"But I'm not. And with my own money as collateral, and my father's influence, they wouldn't dare refuse us."

Miles frowned. "I don't want your father involved in this."

"But—"

"No," he said sharply. Moving toward her, he watched as she backed away.

Setting her bare heels to the floor, she lifted her chin and squared her shoulders. "First things first, sir. I haven't yet agreed to offer all, or any, financial aid in this matter. My comments to this point have been purely hypothetical. Besides, I haven't been convinced that there is any remaining lead in those hills to be mined. You have no proof, only a feeling."

"It's there," he said through his teeth. "I know it. Josiah Lubinsky knows it or he wouldn't be trying to buy me out."

"Then perhaps you should allow him to take the risk. He can afford failure. You cannot."

Miles glared down into Olivia's stubborn face.

"Think of it this way," she said a bit tauntingly. "With the money you could make off the sale of the mines, you wouldn't need to remain married to me. You would have sufficient funds to pay off your debts and live handsomely for the remainder of your days, as long as you stay away from the gambling halls, of course."

"Good God," he muttered. "I hadn't thought of that."

Olivia swallowed.

They stood in the center of the room, vaguely hearing the rain spatter against the window and the increasing sound of drunken revelers from the tavern below.

"Well," he finally stated, his mouth a sardonic curl. "Seems you've given me something to think about for the remainder of the evening."

Despite the surge of despair that shot through Olivia's heart, she did her best to focus on Miles's ruggedly handsome features and refused to allow him, even for an instant, to see that she'd been shaken to her naked toes by her own stupid comment.

At last, he moved around her, swept up the whisky bottle from the table, and walked to the door. Without turning to face him, she said, "Miles."

He stopped.

"I believe we are to meet Messieurs Delaney and Wallace at half past seven in the morning?"

"Right."

"That should give us both time to come to a decision."

"Both?"

"You must decide what is more important to you: your freedom and enough money to live comfortably for the rest of your life, should you decide to sell to Lubinsky. Or you risk the chance that I won't agree to finance the restoration of these mines."

"Either way, it looks like I lose," he said. Then he stepped from the room, closing the door behind him.

Olivia stood rooted to the floor, acknowledging the chill that was creeping into the room since the coals in the brazier had diminished mostly to ash. Then she fell onto the bed and drove a fist into her pillow.

※

Clare knew that she loved him—every curve of her form showed that—but he did not know at that time the full depth of her devotion, its single-mindedness, its meekness; what long-suffering it guaranteed, what honesty, what endurance, what good faith.

—THOMAS HARDY,
Tess of the d'Urbervilles

CHAPTER THIRTEEN

MILES STOOD AT THE WINDOW WITH HIS HANDS IN HIS pockets, watching the two dozen men and their families crowded near the entry to the White Horse Inn. It was almost time to join them. He didn't look forward to the task. Not after yesterday—and his wife's interference.

He took a deep breath and prepared to join them. Just as he was about to leave the room, there came a tap on the door. Before he could answer, the door opened and Olivia walked in, her step hesitant. Miles noted that she looked more than a little pale; there were circles beneath her eyes from lack of sleep. The dress she'd worn throughout the last two days was sorely in need of washing, but, as usual, she wore it as neatly as possible.

"Good morning, sir," she said in a matter-of-fact voice.

Miles relaxed against the windowsill and raised one eyebrow. "Olivia."

"I trust you spent a restful night?"

He shrugged. "And you?"

"Excellent, thank you."

223

Looking deeply into her eyes, he wondered if she were lying. He'd never known a woman who could so adeptly hide her thoughts and emotions. It was almost frightening—this lack of predictability.

"I suppose we each must now make a decision regarding our future," she said.

"I suppose."

"You sell out to Lubinsky, or you risk the possibility that I won't agree to finance the mines' restorations."

"Yes."

She continued to stare up at him, her shoulders back and her hands loosely clasped before her as she waited. Seconds ticked by while the voices outside the window grew louder and more impatient. Christ, he thought. She would make one hell of a card player. Most women would be a bundle of emotions at that moment—especially a woman in her position, whose possibly only chance to offer herself and her son a future hinged on whether or not he decided his freedom was more important to him than the mines . . . or marriage to her. She'd been absolutely right the night before—by marrying her, he'd sold his soul. By selling the mines, he sold his dreams. Which, he wondered, would be the lesser of two indignities?

"I'm not selling the mines," he said softly.

Olivia didn't blink.

"I said . . ." Miles turned away from Olivia. "I'm not selling the mines. I'll make a go of it with or without your help."

For a moment, Olivia did not respond, then she said quietly, "Agreed, sir. The mines will continue to operate . . ." Miles frowned as she moved to join him, her big green eyes locked on his. "The mines will continue to operate," she continued, "and you can be guaranteed that no money

will be spared in the renovation and updating of the mines.
I'll do everything possible to help you."

"As long as you can control—"

"No. Perhaps we'll simply consider my financial help
as . . . a loan. When you hit that new vein, I'll expect to be
paid back with interest."

"You could lose everything, Olivia."

She shrugged. "Or gain a great deal. Life's choices are
a constant gamble, are they not, husband? The trick is to
hold on to your faith that all will turn out for the best.
Without hope, and the belief in our dreams, what dreary
existences we would all lead."

Olivia, somewhat hesitantly, placed her hand on his
arm, and smiled up into his intense, watchful eyes. What
emotions did she see reflected there? "Your employees
are waiting, sir."

"You'll be joining me, of course."

"I think not. I'm quite certain you can adequately deal
with the situation. Simply inform them that no money will
be spared in the mines' renovations and improvements.
Perhaps you should also tell them that a wage increase will
begin at once. Hurry, sir. I'll wait here for their response."

By late afternoon they were finally in sight of
Braithwaite Hall. The ride from Gunnerside had been
wet and cold. Miles's horse had come up lame and they'd
been slowed to a walk the last five miles home.

Just outside Middleham they bid Damien goodbye and
rode the last few miles to Braithwaite in silence. So far,
she hadn't managed to work up the courage to tell him
about the renovations she'd made to his house during
his absence. Since their awkward meeting that morning,
conversation had been strained.

They stopped at the front door. Miles caught Perlagal's bridle and looked up at Olivia. The heavy humidity had caused his dark hair to curl riotously. His cheeks were kissed by cold. His jaw flexing with suppressed irritation, he moved up beside her, wrapped his hands about her waist and swung her from the saddle, plopping her hard on her feet.

The door was flung open in that moment, spilling light over the front steps; warmth washed over them in a welcome wave. A tall, thin stranger filled up the entranceway, dressed in a black suit and crisp white shirt. His thinning gray hair was swept back from his forehead, and he looked at Miles down a sizable beaked nose.

"Good God," Miles muttered under his breath, then mounted the stairs until he stood toe to toe with the man. "Who the blazes are you?" Miles demanded.

"The butler, of course. And who, may I ask, are you?"

Miles slowly pivoted on his heel to stare down at Olivia, who peered at him with wide eyes over the withers of her horse. He crooked his finger at her. She shook her head.

"Come here," he ordered her.

"Madame Warwick!" cried a voice from within the house. Miles moved aside as Jacques Dubois rushed through the doorway, chef's hat bobbing up and down and his clothes smelling like fresh baked bread. "Madame Warwick, what a great pleasure to welcome you home."

Olivia chewed her lip and watched Miles's face go from dumbstruck to incredulous. Jacques kissed her hand, then gently escorted her up the steps. "You are just in time for supper. I have prepared my specialties: almond soup, pomflet, quenelles of partridge, and for dessert, lemon pudding. It is *magnifique, oui?* Ahh!" Tugging her toward the rigid majordomo, he offered her a hopeful if not apologetic smile. "Madame will be pleased to meet my cousin Armand. Hopefully you will consider him to remain butler—he is very experienced, you know. He worked for ten years in the Tuileries."

"Oh." She focused on the butler's face and refused to so much as glance toward Warwick.

Armand tapped his heels together and slightly bowed at the waist, then he turned his attention back to Miles, adequately barring his way into the house. "And who, sir, might you be?"

"Warwick," Miles said in a hoarse whisper.

Armand's eyebrows went up and his expressionless eyes swept Miles in a glance, from the top of his wet head to the bottom of his muddied Hessians. He addressed Olivia without turning. "Shall I call for the footman, madame?"

"I don't have a footman," Miles said smoothly.

"Yes you do," Armand replied.

"No I don't."

"Yes you do," Jacques joined in, nodding so vigorously that his hat flopped over his forehead, then stepping into the well-lit foyer, he clapped his hands and cried, "Gustavea!" Shrugging, he laughed and added, "He is Armand's son, oui?"

A skinny young man scrambled up the corridor, smoothing his overly large livery coat and stumbling slightly in boots that were too big for his feet. He spoke not a word of English, but babbled excitedly at Armand, who babbled back and pointed to Miles's muddy boots with an air of distaste.

Miles narrowed his eyes and stepped around the butler, into the foyer where scaffolds and ladders adorned the walls and tins of paint, brushes, hammers, and saws littered the floor. Workmen moved about the house like ants. His hands clenched. His shoulders grew tense, his face thunderously dark.

"That will be all," Olivia said to the curious servants, then held her breath as they dispersed without a word.

"What the hell is going on here?" Miles demanded.

"You aren't pleased?"

"I s'pose you thought you'd just take over the old place while I was gone."

"I—"

"Just who the hell gave you the right to come into my house and drive one goddamn nail into my goddamn walls without my goddamn permission?"

"I—"

"You're so accustomed to lording it over Devonswick, including your father and sister, that you thought you'd do the same here."

He moved toward her. She backed away.

"Well?" he shouted.

"You needn't raise your voice—"

"Just who the hell do you think is going to pay for all this?"

Raising her chin, she replied calmly, "Why me, of course."

One eyebrow shot up. "You," he finally replied in a sneering, slightly caustic monotone. "Of course. How could I forget? You're the one with the money. The power. The influence. I'm simply the beggar with his hand out."

They glared at one another, Olivia thinking he looked red-faced enough with anger that the top of his head might go shooting toward the ceiling just any minute, and Miles thinking she looked as if she'd just taken an overzealous bite of a green persimmon.

"It's quite obvious," Olivia began in a more controlled tone, "that if this lack of appreciation is any indication of what marriage to you will be like, I don't think I'll care for it."

He stared at her.

She proffered Warwick a thin smile and moved toward the stairs. "What the blazes are you doing?" he demanded.

"I'm retiring to my room, of course."

"Now wait just a bloody minute," Warwick said behind her. "You can't simply waltz out of here. I have a few things I intend to say to you."

"Oh?" Tipping her chin, she glanced at Miles over her shoulder. He stood in the center of the foyer, legs slightly spread and his cloak dripping rain and mud on the spotlessly clean floor. His mouth was pressed thin and his eyes looked troubled.

"Perhaps," he said with more control, "you would care to join me in my office so we can discuss this in privacy."

His face drained of color, he walked less than gracefully down the corridor, stepping over a ladder and knocking a can of paint with his boot. Taking a deep breath, Olivia followed at a safe distance, entering the office behind him.

He fell into the chair behind the desk, appearing to relax as he took a visual inventory of his surroundings and found nothing amiss. He barely glanced at the stack of ledgers placed neatly to one side.

"I admit to having overstepped the boundaries of good judgment, sir. I apologize. My only excuse is my extreme love for . . . this house, and my desire to please you. If I've caused you any ill feelings, I'm truly sorry."

Miles wearily closed his eyes. "Ah, God. What am I to do with you? I've never known a woman who, one minute makes me want to strangle her, and the next . . ."

"And the next, sir?"

He regarded her with heavy-lidded eyes, then left the chair and strode to the decanters of liquor on a table against the wall. He splashed a portion into a snifter and tossed it back before slamming the fragile glass onto the table and refilling it. "So tell me. How is my mother? No doubt the two of you have become great friends in my absence. She was always very good at making . . . friends."

"I thought by now that you would have grown more accustomed to the idea of her remaining here."

"Then you don't know me nearly as well as you think you do, dear heart." He drank again, more slowly. "Ironic, isn't it? That the woman who cared so little for me when I was only eight is now dependent on me."

"I'm certain she must have had her reasons—"

"Certainly. She could hardly carry on her affairs with a child underfoot. As you well know, my love, bastards have a way of disrupting a woman's love life."

The caustic comment speared Olivia senseless for an instant. "That's very unkind," she remarked softly.

"But true."

Her hands clasped together, she joined Miles at the decanters. "Do you hate her for what she did?"

"Do you mean for deserting me for most of my life, or for giving birth to me in the first place?"

"For having you."

He tipped his head and his stormy eyes met hers. "What's wrong? Has the idea just occurred to you that your handsome, strapping son might one day grow up to resent you for his parentage, or lack thereof? I think you needn't worry, dear heart." He cupped her cheek in his big palm. "There is a difference between you and my mother. You love your son."

The fleeting pain reflected in Miles's eyes and in the tone of his voice made Olivia's heart skip a beat. The fact that he was cradling her face so tenderly—almost like a lover—made her breathless.

Sally appeared at the door, wearing a freshly laundered uniform. Her hair had been brushed and knotted at her nape and secured with a black net and satin bow. She curtsied and politely said, "Good evenin', sir and madam. Armand says Mr. Warwick is in need of a bath."

Olivia rewarded the obedient servant with a smile and a smug lift of her eyebrow as she caught Warwick's disbelieving expression. "Armand is correct, Sally. Please have Mr. Warwick's bath drawn."

"Will ya be needin' me to help with his bath?" Sally asked, bringing Olivia's gaze to hers, then to Warwick's.

"Do you normally attend Mr. Warwick with his toilette?" she asked, taking note of the color creeping up the girl's throat.

"Well, mum, it ain't as if he has a valet . . ."

"I see." Olivia pursed her lips in disapproval. The images of the two of them gamboling about in some sort of sordid disport brought a burning to her cheeks. "I feel Mr. Warwick is capable of bathing himself," she replied as indifferently as she was capable. "Just see to the hot water, please."

Olivia took dinner with Bryan, Bertrice, and Alyson. Miles was conspicuously absent. Olivia, of course, did her best to make excuses for her husband: important business to attend to. Simply exhausted and must have fallen straight into bed.

By the time Jacques carted out the lemon pudding, Olivia had lost what little appetite she had. Alyson had obviously taken great pains in preparing herself for the meal. Bertrice had plaited her hair and fixed it into a coronet about her head. She'd dressed in one of Olivia's gowns, which was loose on her frail body.

At last, unable to tolerate the hurt in the woman's eyes another minute, Olivia excused herself and went in search of her husband, her anger mounting.

According to Sally, Olivia could find her husband in the pool room, a vast marble chamber reached through a brick and mortar tunnel off the east wing of the house. Olivia had visited the rooms only once, during her initial investigation of Braithwaite. Consisting of two immense rooms with pillars and skylights, they each held a large pool, one cold, the other hot, filled with steaming water from an underground hot spring. Upon her initial visit, the rooms and pools had been empty and frigid, reminding her of a mausoleum. Tonight, however, as she marched through the tunnel and into the cold pool room, lights from the sconces on the walls reflected in gold puddles from the surface of the water.

Miles wasn't in the cold room, so she took a deep breath and entered the steam room, only to be brought up short by the sudden blast of humidity that fogged up her second pair of glasses and made her gasp. Carefully, she walked to the edge of the pool and did her best to see through the steam.

"Miles," she called. "A word with you, please."

Nothing.

"Sir, I know you're here. I wish a word with you and I have no intention of leaving until we've spoken."

There came a splash of water near the far end of the pool. Removing her glasses, Olivia stared hard through the condensation, finally locating her husband where he partially reclined upon the pool's marble steps, buried to his waist in water. "Oh," she said, and straightened at the sight of his naked, glistening torso.

"What did you expect?" he asked softly, a bit drunkenly. "Isn't a man allowed the opportunity to bathe nude in the privacy of his bath?"

"Perhaps we'll speak later." She began to retreat.

"We'll speak now," he replied, stopping her in her tracks as the water splashed again and it became obvious that he was leaving the pool. Staring straight ahead, her heart beating against her ribs, Olivia listened to the drip of water splashing on the marble tiles at Miles's feet. Then came the slight clink of glass against glass as he poured himself another drink from some decanter buried amid the mist.

"You'll join me, of course," he said, and she heard the glass clink again. "A man may have no say in the running of his house, but he should have a say in whether his wife joins him in a drink. You, of course, being the wife, will no doubt argue the issue."

"I've no wish to argue with you at all, sir."

"No? Then what are you doing here? Surely it wasn't to join me in a bath, though I admit I find the idea appealing. Tell me, Olivia, have you ever bathed with a man? Come, come, sweetheart. You can tell me. I'm your husband, after all."

Olivia stared straight ahead and said nothing.

"Really, dear heart. Any woman who would dance with Gypsies and brand her breast with a tattoo has surely bathed naked with a man. Did you enjoy it?"

"I came here to ask for your consideration," she said.

"For whom?"

"Your mother."

"Ah. Of course. No doubt she wept pitifully over her quenelles of partridge."

"No."

He was silent.

"She has her pride," Olivia added.

"Don't we all, dear heart?"

Her frustration mounting, Olivia turned to discover Miles lounging on a bed of tapestry pillows with bright-colored tassels. He lay completely naked but for a red cloth towel wrapped across his loins.

Placing her drink on the floor beside him, he smiled up at her.

Speechless, Olivia could do nothing for a moment but stare, all too aware, suddenly, of the oppressive heat and the discomfort of her heavy woolen clothes that clung damply to her flushed skin. "Why are you so damned angry?" she demanded.

"I'm not angry. I'm drunk. I'll warn you now because I'm very unpredictable when I'm drunk."

"Has it occurred to you that your mother simply wishes to make peace with you?"

"My mother wants to soothe her own conscience before she dies. No doubt she's terrified of writhing in hell for eternity with the memory of her sins eating away at her. Besides, I don't believe for a minute that's why you came here."

"I beg your pardon?"

"You didn't come here to discuss Alyson. Oh, you may be using her as an excuse. No doubt you're angry because I haven't fallen to my knees in gratitude over the mines."

"I hadn't thought about it."

He laughed softly. Disbelievingly.

"If the reason why you've buried yourself in this . . . tomb is because you're brooding over my involvement with the mines, then, sir, the problem can be easily resolved. I can wash my hands of it completely."

Miles drank his sherry without taking his gaze from hers. "Blackmail suits you, my love. The concept puts fire in your green eyes and color in your cheeks. You're quite beautiful when you're angry."

"It isn't my intention to blackmail you, sir."

"What a shame. I do so enjoy sparring with my adversaries. I used to be quite good at it, before I ensconced myself in this house and attempted to turn my life around—to put my hedonistic ways behind me and start anew. I was once very, very good at being very naughty. Would you care to see how naughty I can be, love?"

Frowning and feeling unbalanced by his mercurial mood, Olivia forced her eyes away from his, finding the effort to ignore his exposed, heat-flushed body impossible as he sat up. His shoulders glistened with sweat and candlelight. His chest was lean and hard, tapering to a stomach that was rippled by muscle and flat as the floor on which he sat.

"I have agreed to help you any way that I can with the mines and I shall do so," she managed. "You'll find that I'm not a woman who goes back on her word. I'm also not a woman who can turn a blind eye to the needy."

"Obviously. No doubt in a hundred years the religions of the world will vie to make you a saint. The question is . . . the saint of what? Saint Olivia of the sick and dying? Of the ruined and destitute? Or of the bastards of the world?"

"Why do you hate me so when all I want is to help you?"

" 'Hate' is such a harsh word, and inappropriate. I don't hate you, dear heart."

"But you don't love me."

"You mustn't take it personally. I've never vowed such an emotion to anyone."

"Are you incapable of love, sir, or just afraid of it?"

"Afraid?"

"Of not being loved in return. Perhaps you're still that little boy who loved his mother desperately, but felt unloved in return. You're terrified of experiencing that pain again."

He reached for her drink and turned it up to his mouth, pausing only long enough to say, "You talk too much, love. Besides, you give me far too much credit. You should know by now that I'm not a very nice man."

"I disagree. According to Janet Hooper you're a very concerned, kind man."

"Ah." He flashed her a smile. "Now we get to the crux of this visit. You want to know about Janet."

"I—"

"Jealous, pet?"

She suddenly wanted to run. She felt foolish. Chagrined that he could see through her motives even better than she—and he had the audacity to acknowledge it when she wouldn't.

"Well?" he said. "Are you jealous?"

"Should I be?"

"You're wanting to know if she's my mistress. Don't deny it. I've sensed there's been something bothering you since you showed up at Gunnerside. At first I attributed your mood to irritation over my sudden disappearance. Just now I considered your apparent pique to be over my not showing at dinner. Then I suspected differently. Janet," he said, then laughed lightly.

"Well?" she said.

"Well what? Are we lovers?" He smiled. "Tell you what, dear heart. If you confess your peccadilloes, I'll confess mine." He stood and the red cloth spilled to the floor. Olivia stared, transfixed, vaguely aware that her body had turned as incapable of moving as the statues of nymphs gazing out at her from the shadowed and misty corners of the room.

Warmly I felt her bosom thrill,
I pressed it closer, closer still,
Though gently bid not;
Till—oh! the world hath seldom heard
Of lovers, who so nearly erred,
And yet, who did not.
—Thomas Moore

CHAPTER FOURTEEN

Miles moved toward her like some deity of Greek mythology, perfect in form—far more perfect than she had ever imagined—his body slick and wet and aroused.

"So tell me, wife . . ." His hand slid around the back of her neck. "What name or names will you cry out when I make love to you? Hmm? Don't look so shocked. The consummation was inevitable. We both want it and, of course, it's necessary. If you wish, you can close your eyes and pretend that I'm someone else." Tipping back her chin, he smiled down into her upturned face. "That's why you really came here, isn't it? You thought to play coy on our wedding night, then, when you realized that I may or may not be satisfying my basic urges with another woman, you realized that you had better take what you can get before it's too late. I simply haven't met a woman yet who, once having tasted the nectar of forbidden fruit, didn't ache to sample the sweetness again. It's nothing to be ashamed of, love. Whether you like to admit it or not, you're human. Your son is proof of that."

Her knees trembling, Olivia did her best to make sense of this sudden turn of events. What, exactly, was he doing?

His fingers moved to the buttons on her blouse, and he plucked at them playfully, his eyes never once straying from hers as she felt the steamy air grow hotter and too unbearably thick to breathe. She suddenly felt as if she were drowning.

"Take it off," he commanded softly, meaning her blouse as he peeled back the damp drab fabric to reveal the transparent chemise beneath. "I want to see what I've purchased with my desperation. I've been curious ever since our wedding night, when I saw you running like a child down the hallway in your flannel nightgown. You're a study in contradictions, Mrs. Warwick. One moment you're some iron maiden, the next a wanton with passion aflame in her face. Yet, the wanton trembles in consternation when she's touched by a man. Are you afraid, pet? You speak to me of the fear of loving when it isn't I who begs shallow vows of devotion."

She tried to turn her face away. He would not allow it, but, with a firm grip on her jaw, forced her to look up into his dark features and falconlike eyes. He watched her with an intensity that frightened her. Her every instinct cried out in alarm, yet she forced herself to remain steady and call his bluff, for surely he only meant to frighten her as he had at the inn.

He forced the blouse down over her shoulders and tossed it away, then he pointed to her skirt. "Remove it," he ordered.

"And if I don't?"

"Then I'll rip it off you."

Olivia removed the skirt and stood before him in her underthings, stockings, and shoes. Miles smiled and caught her arm, ushering her to the pillows where he ordered her to lie down. Then he poured her another drink and offered it to her.

Unable to think coherently, Olivia settled into the pillows and continued to numbly watch her husband move around the steamy room, his body flexing and rippling with each lithe, graceful movement. Remotely, she wondered if she were lost in some erotic dream. In truth, the sudden disquieting turmoil in her own body shocked her. Left her breathless and light-headed.

The smell of burning oil from the sconces on the walls stirred in her nostrils, and the yellow light reflected from the marble floors like fire. The bed of pillows around her cast a hazy glow of colors: gold, purple, red— slick silk and nubby weaves that both embraced her and repelled her—heaps of cushions and enameled and filigreed screens depicting Orientals in explicit acts of copulation lined the walls. She wasn't shocked. She'd seen similar likenesses before.

Still, she hadn't come here to seduce, or be seduced. A tiny voice in the back of her mind cried out to flee—she wasn't prepared for this no matter what her heart—and body—felt.

Miles waded into the pool, little by little sinking to his hard thighs in the crystal-clear water while condensation dripped from the ceiling and made tiny circles upon the surface. "Olivia," he said, and the sound echoed in the cavernous room. "Join me."

"I . . . think not."

"But I insist."

"You cannot force me."

"Think again." He splashed the water with his fingertips.

The realization swept her then, just what this domination meant to him. Carefully, she put down her drink and unlaced her shoes, refusing to look at Miles again, but concentrating on calming the unreasonable anxiety that made her hands shake. Her husband had been right. The moment was inevitable. She had put it from her mind by convincing herself that Miles Kemball Warwick wanted nothing more from her than financial security. Emily had known. Emily had warned her. Deep in the night she had awakened with anticipation and fear and Emily's admonitions making her heart pound and her body burn.

Tossing her stockings and shoes aside, Olivia stood and moved toward the pool, vaguely aware that the cotton of her chemise and drawers had become transparent as it clung to her moist skin. She eased into the hot water, gradually sinking into its steaming midst, softly gasping at the heat as it climbed her ankles, calves, and thighs, and crept like liquid fire between her legs.

Standing in the center of the pool, steam swirling around him, Miles regarded her with glittering eyes. His black hair was swept back, curling behind his ears. Olivia stared at the black curly hair between his legs, and the organ curving up out of the dense thatch and thought it more beautiful and frightening than she had imagined.

He pointed to her hair and said, "Let it down."

She raised her arms and her fingers fumbled with the combs. At last, her hair tumbled, heavy and damp over her shoulders, and clung to her rapidly rising and falling breasts.

Miles lowered his head and regarded her with an intensity that made her quiver.

"Beautiful," he said softly, yet the very faintness of it made her jump and look about for some easy way of escape. "Come here," he commanded her.

She moved, feeling the water lap at her buttocks until she stood before him not unlike some slave before her master—despising this sense of control, and loving it too. She felt weakened, yet exhilarated. Unmistakably alive but sensing that at any moment she would find herself hurtling into some abyss from which she could never return.

He reached out and placed his hand upon her breast, brushing her nipple with one knuckle, causing her to inwardly groan and close her eyes as a lightning-hot spear of desire sluiced to every throbbing nerve in her body. She thought she might swoon. She wouldn't, she told herself. She couldn't. To lose control now . . .

Then his fingertips lightly touched the colorful flower on her skin. "Are there others?" he asked.

With great effort, she slowly shook her head. "No."

"Turn around and let me see."

Slowly, as the water swirled about her hips, she circled, allowing him an unobstructed view of all sides of her. Dear God, but the heat of the water, the humidity, the flushed surface of her skin made her feel as if she were engulfed in wet fire. If he touched her again . . .

When she faced him, he smiled and said softly, a bit drunkenly, "No dragons."

"Sir?"

"They say you have dragons on your backside."

"I'm certain they say a great many things about me. Do you believe them all?"

"They appear to know you better than I."

"They think they do."

"Do you like this?" he asked, gently squeezing her breast.

She swallowed. Or attempted to. Lowering her gaze, she watched his big hand gently massage her. How dark his hand was against her white flesh. The image made her breathless. She felt dangerously careless. "Would you stop if I say no?" she murmured.

"Do you like this?" he said more firmly.

Olivia nodded and gasped and, placing her hand over his, pressed it harder against her, until her nipple drew up tight and hard and tingled with feeling. "Yes," she finally replied.

"Then why are you shaking? Do you want me to make love to you so badly?"

She did not respond, but watched a drop of water bead upon his neck and drop into the soft, fine hair on his chest. He looked as if his hazel eyes actually held some form of affection. Or was it simply—as he had earlier termed it— the base urges that made men so often indiscriminate in their choice of lovers.

Oh, how she ached to touch him—but dare she? To feel, even for an instant, her hand upon his hard, smooth flesh. He was her husband, after all. Yet . . .

Catching her hand, he put it on his sex. His eyes narrowed. His breathing quickened. The powerful organ stirred in her fingers and a low growl emanated from his chest. "Nice," he whispered and moved her hand gently forward and back, until the rhythm turned her warm inside and as liquid as the water softly lapping at her hips.

Someone groaned. Perhaps herself. She couldn't be certain. The heat, the steam, the dim sconce light flickering erratically in the mist made the responses of her body and mind too confusing. Control was slipping through her resolve as easily as the water through her fingers. If she didn't stop now she would surely regret it. Her past would be laid before him as shockingly conspicuous as his body's hunger.

Still, she couldn't move, and when he suddenly slid his arms around her and lifted her onto the hard marble edge of the pool she could do little but close her eyes and futilely shake her head in resistance. "Please." She groaned.

"Please," he repeated softly. "Please what, love? Make you feel like a woman for a change?" He laid her back on the tile and she stared up through the ghostly condensation at the dim skylight overhead, feeling the warm water drip like rain onto her face, hearing the water stir with his every movement, her heart pound with his every touch.

His touch—oh God—his touch was everywhere at once. His hands on her breasts, her thighs, and in between, making her gasp and jump and quiver—her mind whirling, her senses reeling with unrecognizable feelings.

"Look at me," he commanded her, and she forced open her eyes to find him over her, half in, half out of the water like a sea god seducing some earthbound mortal, black hair coiling around his temples, ears, and neck, sconce-light reflecting like fire from his wet face and shoulders. With his knees, he eased open her thighs, and his fingers slid through the slit in her drawers, causing her to cry aloud from the sudden, startling awakening there.

"Tell me what you like," came his voice through her mental fog. "This?" His fingers tugged at the ribbons on her chemise, and nudged aside the wet, filmy material until her breasts were exposed completely to his eyes. Lowering his dark head, he closed his lips around one nipple, then the other, drawing the high, hard, and rosy points into his mouth, between his teeth until she arched her back and breathed sharply, haltingly, and prayed that this was no fantasy—like the fantasies that had so often plagued her since their wedding night.

But it was real. So real. The reality came in the delicious wash of his tongue over her sensitive nipples, the scattering of tender love bites along her stomach, the hot breath he breathed against the transparent cotton covering her womanhood.

Then—dear Lord.

She wanted to scream. To cry. To laugh. How sinfully, deliciously wicked, this intimate kiss.

She rolled her head from side to side. She buried her fingers in his wet, black hair and felt her hips tip up, inviting him nearer, deeper—yes, oh yes—this was much better than fantasy. Never in her wildest imaginings had she ever fantasized this—

He raised up and his eyes regarded her with something like flames dancing in them. He must be the devil, she thought, for making her feel so wicked and wanton. She wanted to cover herself. She wanted to spread her legs wider and beg him to continue.

The water stirred as he moved his hips up between hers. Then came the pressure, the shocking nudging, searching, exploration of his being against her wet, aching threshold, and, for an instant, the idea of succumbing to the moment made her eyes meet his in blatant need, and invitation.

Suspended, locked in mutual desire, they watched each other for what seemed like an eternity—but couldn't have been more than mere seconds—before Olivia shook her head and cried softly, "I can't."

She rolled away and clutched her chemise closed over her breasts. "I can't," she repeated, hearing her words reverberate back to her from the marble walls. "Please don't ask me. Not yet. Not until . . ."

"Until what?" he shouted behind her.

Clawing her way up the pool steps, she glanced back to see his face a mixture of startlement and fury.

"Until what?" he demanded again, grabbing her up against his wet, aroused body so her breasts were flattened against his chest and her face was just below his. "What the hell is wrong with you? You're my wife, Olivia. I have every right to expect—to demand a consummation. You come down here and undress and tease me with your body and then tell me I can't have it." He shook her. "Are you simply attempting to make a fool out of me? Is that it? Is it me that you hate, or men in general?"

She turned her face away or surely she would forget her idiotic fears and allow him the liberties he was so desperate to take. "Let me go," she managed to say.

He did, suddenly, allowing her to fall back to the hard floor so she was forced to scramble upright, to back away cautiously while her mind and heart waged a battle that neither could win. "I'm . . . sorry," she offered. "Perhaps later—"

"Later. Of course. Fine, dear heart. You will let me know when you're ready, won't you? Because I vow here and now . . . I won't touch you again until you beg me."

Olivia fled and didn't stop running until she stood in her bedroom, her back against the locked door, and water running in runnels to the floor at her feet. She could not rid her mind of the image of her husband's outraged face as she ran from the room, and of the oath he'd made not to touch her again—until she begged him.

Closing her eyes, experiencing again the unabashed thrill of his hands—and mouth—on her, Olivia longed for that day. Almost as much as she dreaded it.

*   *   *

Winter descended, and with it the cold, wind, and rain barreled down from Scotland and turned the moor into a dim and ice-burdened landscape. Travel to anywhere beyond the nearest hamlet was virtually impossible. Night after night Olivia lay in her bed, staring at the ceiling, listening to the low moan of wind and the slash of rain against the windows. One day blurred into another, and yet another, as she buried herself in the routine of business . . . as she had at Devonswick, occasionally rousing herself enough to spend time with her son and Alyson, whose health varied by the hour.

Since her childish flight from her husband's company Olivia had found herself married to a recluse. She rarely saw or spoke to Miles. He spent his days asleep and his nights prowling the house, scribbling messages to the mine, or galloping the frost-bitten countryside on horseback. Even Charles Fowles had begun worrying about him.

Olivia blamed herself for Miles's erratic behavior. She had taken over his house. Much of his business. His mother. She had foisted her odd behavior and unwelcome company on a man who wanted nothing more than normalcy in his life.

How very ironic that she, who ached for that same normalcy, was spoiling her chances for happiness—and his—because of her own fears and dreads. Then again, what did she expect? By marrying Miles Warwick, she'd backed herself to a wall, and the only way to remedy the situation was to own up to her doings.

Christmas and the New Year passed quietly and January arrived with a slight break in the weather. Frost thawed from the trees, and the roads were no longer slick with black ice. Olivia took to riding Perlagal every day at noon, driving the mare across the moor until reaching Margrave where she sat atop the bluff and turned her face to the sun and tried to make some sense of her life. She could not continue this way, living like strangers with a man who was her husband. Avoidance had never been a part of her nature, yet that's what she was doing. Avoiding the inevitable.

Returning to Braithwaite after one such ride to Margrave, Olivia had convinced herself that the time had come to confront.

Much to Olivia's surprise, she found Emily waiting for her in the blue drawing room.

"For heaven's sake, Olivia, do you make a habit of disappearing from this house at such ungodly hours?" Emily demanded from her chair by the hearth.

"Good day to you too, sister," Olivia replied.

"There is absolutely nothing good about it. How could it be? The air is bitterly cold and by the looks of the horizon I suspect rain again by nightfall." Dabbing a hankie at her nose, Emily frowned. "Oli, you look like hell."

"Thank you." Olivia tossed her crop aside. "You're not looking at all well yourself, Em."

"You've lost weight."

"You haven't."

"Your eyes look as if you haven't slept in weeks."

"You are becoming observant. Will you have tea? Sally!" The servant appeared in a blink and bobbed a curtsy. "We'll have tea and biscuits—"

"I'd prefer toast. And marmalade. I didn't take the time for breakfast." Emily added, "And plenty of milk and sugar for my tea."

Olivia frowned as she took the chair across from her sister. "You don't normally take sugar in your tea, Em."

Emily lowered her eyes and wrung her hankie. "I've missed you, Oli. Truly I have. Papa's extremely hurt because he never hears from you."

"I write Father regularly. However, I find that ironic since the two of you couldn't wait to get rid of us."

"How is dear little Bryan?"

Olivia blinked in surprise. "Why, Em, what's got in to you? You've never asked about Bryan's welfare before."

"You needn't be so nasty or vindictive, Olivia."

"I wasn't aware that I was being either. Only truthful."

Emily pouted and continued twisting her hankie. "You've changed, Oli. Dreadfully."

"Oh? How, pray tell?"

"You're bitter. Don't deny it. It virtually shouts from your face. You're miserably unhappy. Why, even your appearance has changed. Look at the way you're wearing your hair. It looks like a wild woman."

"I've just returned from riding."

"And look at that dreadful habit you're wearing. Where on earth did you get it?"

"It was once yours. I believe this was a costume you had whipped up in Venice, only you never wore it. It cost Papa a small fortune, if I remember correctly. Someone might as well get some use out of it."

Emily left her chair, and, for a moment, leaned against the arm of it while she blotted the hankie to her cheek. In a more weary voice, she said, "I didn't come here to trade insults with you, sister."

"No? Then why are you here, Emily?"

She sighed deeply. "I miss the days when we were friends."

"Friends?" Olivia laughed to herself and said more softly, "Were we ever friends, Emily?"

Emily looked somewhat frantically toward the door. "Where is that bloody servant with the tea and toast? I declare, but good help is dreadfully hard to find anymore. All the decent servants are moving to London where the pay is higher, they say."

"I take it you're having trouble with the help."

"Idiots. They're constantly taking advantage of me. You spoiled them horribly, Olivia."

"I only treated them reasonably. You might try it."

Waving the comment away, Emily moved around the room, her skirts making soft swooshing sounds in the quiet. "You're not at all happy, are you, Oli?" she asked.

"Why do you ask?"

Emily turned back to face her. Her cheeks were colorless, her eyes glassy blue pools. "Do you ever regret your decisions?"

"That would depend on the decision, I suppose."

"Come, come, Oli, we both know that you and I have made choices in our lives that will affect us for the rest of our living days."

"Very well, Em. Yes. I think as long as we live and breathe we'll make choices that we will, at some time, come to regret. Why do you ask? Is something wrong? Has something happened?"

Offering a watery smile, Emily hurried to Olivia, and dropping to one knee, took Olivia's hand and pressed it to her cold cheek.

"Emily." Olivia touched her sister's smooth face. "Something's dreadfully wrong. What is it?"

"Remember the days and nights the two of us used to talk for hours? You were always there for me, Oli.

Always! No matter how big a fool I made of myself, you were always there to look on the bright side, to make me feel better about myself, to protect me. I miss those days when we confided in one another. Don't you?"

"Certainly." Olivia smiled and cupped her sister's small chin in the palm of her hand. "I was only thinking this morning how grand it would be to have someone to talk to again . . . someone with whom to share my secrets."

"Are you as lonely as I, Oli?"

She nodded.

"And wouldn't you do anything—anything at all—to end the dreadful loneliness if you could?"

"Withinreason.Emily . . . What'shappened?Whathave you done?"

Sally entered the room in that moment carrying a tray laden with a china tea service and a plate of toast. A tiny pot of lemon curd stood to one side. Taking her chair again, Emily glared at the pot and frowned. "I wanted marmalade. You've brought me curd, you imbecile. I won't have it. Take it back."

Sally's eyebrows shot up.

"And you haven't trimmed the crust from my toast."

Dismissing the servant with a nod of her head, Olivia reached for Emily's toast. "You'll like the curd and I'll trim your toast. You needn't take your anger out on the help."

"Oh, pooh. You treat the lot of them as if they were your equal. It's so unseemly, Oli." Snatching the toast from Olivia's hand, Emily proceeded to pile the lemon curd on the bread. Then she heaped sugar into her tea as Olivia poured it, then splashed in a good portion of milk. She gulped it down, burning her mouth. Closing her eyes, she appeared to relax, and sank back into her chair, pressing her hankie to her lips.

"Don't be angry," Emily finally said. "I can't seem to control my emotions these days. I'll apologize if you wish."

"I've never known you to apologize to anyone," Olivia replied, stirring sugar into her own tea.

Taking a deep breath, Emily briefly closed her eyes, allowing Olivia the opportunity to sip her tea and cut her wedge of toast into a triangle. When she looked up again, she found her sister regarding her with an odd expression, her lids heavy, her lips slightly parted.

"How is Miles?" Emily asked.

"Well, I think."

"You think? Don't you know?"

"Why do you ask? I was under the impression you would be quite thankful if he suddenly dropped dead."

"I've heard the servants talk at Devonswick. Rumor is he's hardly home, and that the two of you rarely speak, and never share a bed. Is that why you're so unhappy?"

Olivia smiled thinly. "Obviously I should use better discretion when hiring the help. I fear they gossip too much."

"Is it true?"

"Would it please you if it were?"

Nibbling her toast, Emily shrugged. "I'm not surprised. I told you he would make you unhappy."

"Would it surprise you to know that Miles is not at fault?"

"Then who?"

"Me."

"Why?"

"For all the reasons you pointed out before I married."

Emily put down her toast. "So you're truly married in name only." She laughed dryly. "My God, Oli, I've never known a woman with more fortitude, especially in light of your feelings for the bastard."

Olivia winced at the term, but chose not to scold her sister. What good would it do? "I have little choice, Emily. I agreed to marry Warwick because he vowed that the partnership would be strictly business. I was naïve enough—imagine my being naïve enough—to believe it would, or could, remain that way forever."

"Then he desires you."

Olivia reached for her cup of tea, refusing to meet her sister's inquisitive gaze.

"I'm not surprised," Emily said more softly.

"Why? Because he's an indiscriminate rutting heathen?"

"Because you're a very pretty woman."

Stunned, Olivia sat back.

Emily laughed almost sadly. "Don't look so surprised. It's not as if I said you were a raving beauty—like me . . ." She rolled her eyes, mocking herself. "But you're passably attractive. The arrogant idiot could do much worse."

"Well . . ." Olivia put her tea and toast aside. "It doesn't matter. I've turned him away twice. He's hardly liable to forgive and forget that."

"Seduce him."

"I can't. Not under the circumstances. To do so could risk everything, Emily. I won't take that chance. Not where my loved ones are concerned."

"There are solutions to the circumstances, Oli. I know someone who is most trustworthy, and very discreet. He could help you with your 'problem,' and your husband needn't ever know the truth."

Olivia left her chair. Emily followed, catching Olivia's hand. Angrily Olivia said, "Are you suggesting I have an affair? What sort of game are you playing now, Em?"

"I admit to motives—"

"I thought so."

"I also admit that I've been a sorry sister. I truly had no idea how much I depended on your strength and support until after you'd gone. Now there's no one, Oli, and for the first time I realized just how alone you must have been all those years. I was never there for you, and I'm sorry. Can you forgive me just once more?"

"Emily . . ." Olivia closed her fingers around her sister's hand. "I want desperately to believe all that you're saying, but I cannot help but question this sudden turn of disposition."

Emily appeared to falter, and her cheeks blanched gray as ash.

"For the love of God." Olivia gasped, and as her sister swayed into her arms, she eased her back down into her chair. Grabbing the hankie from Emily's palm, Olivia gently pressed it to her sister's forehead.

Her eyes glazed, her lips colorless, Emily did her best to smile. "Dear Olivia. I knew you wouldn't forsake me. Regardless of my sins, you do love me."

"What's wrong, Em? What's happened? Are you ill? Shall I call for Dr. Whitman?"

"I'm in trouble, Oli. Dreadful trouble. You'll see me through it, won't you? You'll help me tell Papa?"

Sitting back on her heels, Olivia stared into her sister's pinched face and frightened eyes, the cold chill of awareness snaking up her spine. "Emily—"

"I'm pregnant," Emily whispered.

'Cautious, very cautious,' thought Emma; 'he advances inch by inch, and will hazard nothing till he believes himself secure.'

— JANE AUSTEN,
Emma

CHAPTER FIFTEEN

THE VAGUE SOUND OF RAIN SLASHING AGAINST THE windows needled its way into Miles's consciousness, rousing him from sleep. The previous day he had traveled to Gunnerside, returning last evening near midnight, bone-weary and half frozen. He'd discovered his wife asleep on a settee in the blue drawing room. The image of her mahogany-colored hair spilling from the cushions to the floor still burned behind his eyelids . . . as did the memory of her gossamerly draped body standing before him in the pool.

He opened his eyes, and caught his breath.

Bryan lay beside him, his little head on the pillow near his.

"Mummy's cryin'," the boy said.

Blearily, Miles blinked and raised his head. "What?"

"Mummy's cryin'. She's been cryin' since yesterday after Aunt Emily came to visit."

"Well then. That explains it." Rolling onto his back, Miles rubbed his eyes and stretched. Bryan did the same.

"Will you play with me when Grandpapa leaves?"

"Grandpapa? Lord Devonshire is here?"

Bryan nodded and mounted Miles like a horse, bouncing up and down on his stomach. "You never showed me them secret passageways, sir."

He winced and caught the lad in mid-bounce. "What's your grandfather doing here?"

"Don't know. He told me to bugger off just before he slammed the door and began yellin' at Mummy. Will you take me for a ride on your horses?"

"It's raining. What the blazes are you doing in my bedroom anyway?"

"Helpin' Bertrice to find her cat. Can I call you Papa now?"

Frowning, Miles slid Bryan onto the bed and tossed back the bedcovers.

"Can I?" Bryan asked.

"Can you what?" Reaching for a green silk wrapper emblazoned with dragons, Miles slid from the bed.

"Call you Papa?"

"No."

"Why not?"

Miles yanked the wrapper closed and secured it with a tie.

"Why not?" the lad insisted.

"You ask too many questions."

"Grandmama says that you don't spend enough time with me and Mummy."

"Grandmama," he said in a sarcastic tone, "should learn to mind her own business. Besides, she hardly has room to criticize."

*   *   *

"Pregnant. For the love of God how could she do this to me?" Lord Devonshire fell into a chair before the hearth and buried his face in his hands. His brow was flushed and sweating when he again looked up at Olivia. "One scandal in this family was enough. What did you do to influence her? Tell me, girl. No doubt this was all some plot you contrived—"

"I can hardly be blamed for this," Olivia replied hotly.

"Do you expect me to believe that Emily fell without encouragement from you? I don't know who to strap first. You or that bastard Clanricarde." Sinking in his chair and gripping the coat over his heart, Devonshire shook his head. "I should call him out—after he's married her, of course."

"Someone was taken advantage of, Papa, but it wasn't Emily."

"Are you insinuating that Emily—"

"Papa." Olivia hurried to her father and dropped to one knee beside him. "Emily was desperate. Clanricarde had become evasive about setting a wedding date and she was afraid of losing him. We all knew that the reason for this marriage was to give Clanricarde an heir, and that's exactly what Emily's doing."

"Are you saying that Emily intentionally got herself with child . . . to trap the scoundrel?"

"That's exactly what I'm saying, Papa."

He glared at her in fury. Then he slapped her face hard enough to send her sprawling against the floor. Rising out of his chair, his fists clenched and trembling, Devonshire said, "You would sully your sister's reputation so that you might feel better about your own. Admit it. No doubt the bastard raped her—"

"He didn't!"

"I'll make certain he regrets the day he was born. I'll bring charges—"

"He intends to marry her as soon as possible."

"Wicked girl. You've been jealous of your sister since she was a child. You would say or do anything to spoil her in my eyes. Admit it!"

"That's not true, Papa."

"No doubt this is some plot you've contrived to make me suffer for foisting you on Warwick. Everyone in this bloody county knows how miserable you've made him. Where is he now, gal? Off with his mistress?"

"He's standing right behind you," came Miles's dispassionate voice from the doorway.

Devonshire turned as Olivia struggled to sit up, her hand pressed to her throbbing cheek.

Miles filled up the threshold, shirt only partially buttoned, the tail of it hanging to his hips. His hair looked a glorious curling mess that framed his lean face and coiled against his shoulders. His dark eyes shifted to Olivia, then slowly back to her father.

Without speaking, Miles moved gracefully across the floor and offered his hand to Olivia. She stared at it, as taken off guard by his sudden appearance as she was by her father's unreasonable behavior. At last, she put her hand in his and he helped her to stand, though she kept her face averted.

Taking her chin in his fingers, he tipped her jaw and acknowledged the mark on her cheek. "Did you strike her?" he asked her father softly.

"Keep out of this, Warwick. It's no concern of yours."

"Ah, but I beg to differ, my lord. When you invade my house and abuse my wife, it most definitely is my concern.

I should call *you* out for what you've done here."

"He's upset," Olivia tried to explain, but he cut her off abruptly by raising his hand. He moved in a slow, catlike manner toward her father, who backed away until coming up against a chair.

Towering over the smaller man, Miles fixed Devonshire with eyes that glittered with a wild and threatening expression—yet contained. "Upset," he said in a deeper voice. "About his dear, sweet, innocent Emily. My lord, I will tell you about your dear, sweet, innocent Emily—"

"No!" Olivia grabbed his arm.

He turned his dark head and stared down at her. "Very well, pet. Then you tell him."

She shook her head.

"Tell him or I shall."

"Tell me what?" Devonshire demanded.

"That Emily is a whore," Miles snapped.

Devonshire gasped. He groaned. He drew back his hand and tried to drive it across Miles's cheek, but Miles quickly dodged the blow. Crying out, Olivia flung herself at her father, only to be brought up short as her husband shoved her aside.

Twisting his hands into Devonshire's lapels, Miles raised the short man onto his toes. "I should kill you, Devonshire. But I won't. Your punishment will come in knowing that I fucked your darling daughter Emily some years ago. And if that's not enough to turn your stomach, maybe the fact that I wasn't the first will."

"Liar!" he blustered. "Emily would never allow the likes of you to take such privileges!"

Miles laughed and gripped him tighter. "Really? Then how could I possibly know that she has that dainty little mole on the inside of her thigh—"

With a howl of rage, Devonshire twisted from Miles's grip and stumbled toward the door. With his eyes bulging, he turned on Olivia. "How can you stand there and allow him to disparage your sister in such a manner? Slut! After all I've done for you—you'll stay away from me from now on. Do you hear? And you'll stay away from Emily or I'll—"

Spinning on his heels, Devonshire stormed from the room. Olivia ran after him. "Papa, please! You're being irrational. Please—"

Suddenly she was yanked off her feet as Miles hefted her up against him, dragging her back into the parlor.

"He's my father, damn you. I can't allow him to leave this way."

"And I am your husband!" he roared in her face. "You will do as I say and I say you won't allow him to degrade you and hurt you any longer."

But he released her, allowing her to run to the door before he stopped her by saying, "If you follow him, Olivia, you might as well take your son and his crazy old nanny with you."

"What do you mean?"

"Simply put, dear heart, it's your father or me."

Laughing almost hysterically, Olivia shook her head. "What a tragic ultimatum you offer me, sir. A choice between two men who couldn't care less if I live or die—whose lives I've obviously made miserable with my idiotic attempts to help them."

"Don't you mean control them, pet?"

"Oh. Is that your problem, husband? Is that why you disappear from Braithwaite for days? Why you prowl this house in a brood? Why you stumble through life ignoring the fact that you're married—"

"Married?" He barked a laugh and moved toward her. "You speak to me of marriage and its obligations when it is you who avoid the marriage bed as if I were some leper whose touch disgusts you."

Olivia covered her ears with her hands. He grabbed them down and pinned them to her sides as she raised her chin and met his fierce and furious eyes with her own.

"Do you ache for him so badly?" Miles said through his teeth.

"Wh—"

"Don't play daft, sweetheart. It seems to me there's only one reason a woman like you would turn her husband away and that's because you're still in love with Bryan's father."

Olivia shook her head.

"Can you deny it? It's strange you never speak of this man you've sacrificed your life for. Well, I'm tired of the evasions. If you're still so goddamn in love with him, then go the hell back to him, Olivia. If you can."

Outside, the snow swirled in blinding clouds, and somewhere in the distance the clouds thundered. It seemed the entire world thrashed in an undertow as Olivia watched her sister weep.

"Fiend!" Emily cried at Miles. "Detestable fiend! That you should tell my father of our affair—oh! I would kill you if I could. I shall! I swear that I'll kill you as you sleep. I'll cut out your heart as you have my father's." Turning her wild eyes to Olivia, Emily ran to her sister, and fell to her knees beside Olivia's chair. Emily gripped Olivia's hand. "I beg you, Oli, come home. You mustn't stay here another hour with this horrible brute. Come back to Devonswick where you belong. I need you, Oli. Papa needs you. He's a madman. I'm frightened, Oli. Horribly frightened. I've never seen him so angry. Not with me."

Numbly, Olivia looked away. "I cannot," she said. "I do love you, Emily. But I cannot help you. Not this time. Were I to leave Braithwaite and my husband for you and Papa, where would I be then? Soon you'll marry and where would I be? Where would Bryan be?"

Furious, Emily stumbled to her feet. She looked at Miles, who stood with his back to her and his gaze fixed on the fire in the hearth. With the speed of lightning, Emily flew to the desk and snatched up a brass-blade letter opener, and wielded it threateningly.

Miles turned and deftly wrestled it from her hand.

"Emily!" Olivia cried, jumping from her chair. "Armand! Gustavea! Quickly!"

The servants materialized from the near shadows. Turning her eyes toward her sister, Olivia said, "Get her out of here. See that she gets home as safely as possible."

Wrenching herself from Warwick's grasp, breathing hard, Emily sneered. "I'll never forgive you for this, Oli. Never!"

Armand firmly caught Emily's right arm, Gustavea her left. They ushered her toward the door gently.

"If you turn your back on me now, Oli, I'll make certain everyone knows . . . everyone! There won't be a soul in England who won't know the tricks you've played, including your husband—and *your* son."

"Then you and I shall sink together, won't we, darling?" Olivia replied calmly, if not sadly.

After several eternal minutes, all became quiet, but for

the constant drone of the wind. Stiffly, Olivia walked to the window and looked out, watched the dense flurries whip back and forth across the frozen rose garden. "It isn't safe to be traveling," she said quietly. "I wonder if I should have her stay."

"She's gone," her husband said.

"Yes. She's gone. I suppose I should be thankful, yet . . . why am I so saddened? And afraid. I feel as if I've been cast adrift on a sea. Alone."

"You are not alone," he said so softly that Olivia wasn't sure she'd heard him correctly.

"No, you're not alone."

Olivia turned. Miles's mother, looking exceptionally frail, leaned on the cane she had recently obtained. Her face appeared bloodless. "You have your friends," Alyson said. "As the saying goes: Fate gives us family; choice gives us friends."

Olivia hurried to help Alyson into the nearest chair. Once seated, Alyson looked at her son. "Is it not ironic that we are continually forced to acknowledge our past mistakes?"

"Note how she looks at me when she mentions mistakes," he said in a droll voice to Olivia.

"Fool," Alyson said. "You would rather dwell on your past than exalt in your present. You would rather weep over your burned bridges than rally and rebuild them."

"Haven't we become wise in our old age?" he replied.

"Age does that to you," she quipped, offering Olivia a smile. "In our youth we're arrogant enough to believe we already know everything there is to know, and that the wisdom of age is nothing more than the cynicism of old minds—or senility."

Alyson gripped Olivia's hand and squeezed it reassuringly. "You're upset."

"Yes," she replied.

"You mustn't feel bad for your sister, dear. At least the scoundrel intends to marry her."

"I feel as if I've abandoned her."

"She'll have her husband. It's obvious that she's in desperate need of some strong influence in her life. Perhaps Clanricarde will succeed where your father has failed her. Husbands are supposed to be good at that," she added pointedly while looking at Miles.

Miles gave her a thin smile. "You, of course, are the expert on husbands."

"Certainly. Your father taught me a great deal on the subject of marriage."

"Like how to cheat?"

"Quite the contrary," Alyson said. "He taught me about responsibility, and of accepting our decisions with grace and dignity. He taught me to make the most of our future instead of dwelling on what cannot be undone. Sadly, it's a lesson I ignored. But I needn't educate Olivia on that fact. I have a feeling she could teach the two of us about commitment and the responsibility that goes with it."

Olivia turned and smiled wearily at her mother-in-law. Alyson relaxed in her chair. Her thin white fingers toyed with the crook of her cane. "I've asked Jacques to prepare us tea and shortbread," Alyson said. "Bryan and Bertrice will be joining us." To Miles, she added, "I hope you'll join us as well."

Miles regarded his mother with a look as fierce as the frozen hurricane that howled outside the house, and just as cold. And yet . . .

"I think not," he finally replied, but his tone was gentle.

As he moved toward the door, Alyson said, "I do so enjoy spending time with your son, Miles. We're becoming great friends. I would love nothing more than to be your friend as well."

Hesitating at the doorway, he stopped.

"I fear you're thirty-nine years too late," he replied.

" 'Tis never too late, son," she said. "Never . . . if you can find it in your heart to forgive."

Olivia stood in the dark, watching Bryan sleep. Somewhere in the house, a clock struck three.

A movement in the shadows caught her eye. Bertrice materialized from the deepest corner of the room and held out her arms to Olivia. Without a word, Olivia sank into them.

"I'm so frightened," she whispered.

"I know ya are, lass."

"I've only seen Emily like that one other time, Bertrice. Why does she hate me so? I fear she'll destroy everything. Me. Bryan. My happiness here with Miles."

"Have faith that it'll all work out for the best."

"I used to have nightmares that I would come to Bryan's room and discover him gone. Now those dreams seem far too real."

"Hush," Bertrice soothed her.

"I don't know what I would do if she took him."

"It's Clanricarde she wants, love. She'll give him his own son and leave yours alone. Besides, she won't want no one to know the truth about her—that she gave birth to Bryan. Especially not Clanricarde."

"But what if something happens—"

"Ain't nothing goin' to happen, dearie."

Closing her eyes, Olivia did her best to relax. "Oh God," she whispered. "I hope you're right."

*

I wish I could remember the first day,
First hour, first moment of your meeting me . . .
—CHRISTINA ROSSETTI

CHAPTER SIXTEEN

OLIVIA OPENED THE LETTER FROM JANET HOOPER AND read it silently to herself.

"I have arranged for the widows to each supply the Warwick Mining Company one hundred tallow candles a month. The cost to the company will be approximately 30s every four weeks per miner, a savings of some 225 pounds a year—compared to the cost of supplying candles by contract from York. The ladies are greatly pleased and muchly appreciative for this endeavor to allow them to earn this extra bit of pay."

Removing her glasses, Olivia sat back in her chair and closed her eyes. How ironic that, over the last weeks, she and her husband's . . . friend had become allies in an attempt to rally the people of Gunnerside.

Bryan dashed by the door, wielding an imaginary weapon, leaping, dodging, thrusting, and pirouetting. "En garde!" he whooped, and let out a bloodcurdling cry that made Olivia grab her ears and laugh. Hurrying to the door, she looked out just as Miles leapt from around a corner, his head covered in an armor helmet of steel that was badly in need of polishing.

"Good Lord." Olivia gasped, unable to believe her eyes.

"Yer days are numbered, Black Knight!" Bryan discoursed as he waved his invisible sword through the air and added a "Whoosh! Whoosh!" for effect. "I'll be slayin' the dragons round this castle from now on. And I'll be wooin' the wenches."

" 'Wooin' wenches'?" Olivia repeated. "Oh, dear."

Miles replied, though the helmet muffled the words into a garble as he, too, brandished his imaginary sword in the air.

With a shriek, Bryan gave his phantom charger a kick and raced down the corridor, his trusty sword now a lance aimed at destroying his foe. "Take that!" Bryan cried, thrusting the spear at the helmeted knight.

Miles bent double, and holding his stomach, backed down the corridor with a wounded cry of pain, stumbled, spun on his heels, then collapsed, arms and legs splaying in an exaggerated manner as he hit the floor.

Beaming Olivia a smile, Bryan bowed before her. "Behold, my queen, I have slain the Black Knight."

"So you have," she replied, moving toward her husband's twitching form.

"So what are ya gonna give me for it?" Bryan asked, scratching his little nose.

Stopping at the Black Knight's side, Olivia peered down into his helmeted face. "Are you certain he's dead, Sir Bryan?"

Bryan frowned, and bending, caught the visor with his fingertip and slid it up, over Miles's forehead. Miles's face was red and sweating. His eyes were closed. "I could kill him again," Bryan said. "Just to make sure."

"I think dying once a day is enough. Besides, you're late for your reading with Grandmama. I believe Jacques has prepared you a plum pudding as well."

"Puddin'?" His eyes sparkling, his mind suddenly on something besides slaying rogue knights, Bryan dashed down the corridor toward the morning room.

Miles opened one eye, then the other. "Is he gone?"

"Like a flash." Olivia smiled. "Would you like me to help you out of that?" She pointed to the helmet.

Miles sat up. Olivia caught the heavy metal contraption and tugged it off. His hair lay in loose wet curls, and it was all Olivia could do not to touch it. "You die very impressively," she told him.

"Thank you. Comes from practice."

"Oh? Do you die often?"

"Every day for the past three weeks. Sometimes two or three times a day." He ran his hands through his hair and took the helmet from her, flashing her a smile.

"Odd that I hadn't noticed," she said thoughtfully.

"If you would ever come up for air you might notice a great many things, Mrs. Warwick."

"I happen to be getting a great deal accomplished."

He stood and tucked the helmet under his arm. "Such as?"

"I've arranged to have a number of the village women make candles for the miners. It'll be much cheaper than purchasing them from your previous sources, and it'll keep the money in Gunnerside."

They moved down the corridor, side by side.

"We received a letter from Bob McMillian. The timber we ordered has been held up until the weather clears. Fortunately, there's been no more accidents, and since the pay has been coming in regularly and on time, the men's attitudes have improved drastically."

They walked on in silence before Olivia said, "I understand that Emily and Clanricarde were married last week."

"What? And we weren't invited?"

Olivia could find little humor in his remark.

"May they live happily ever after," Miles said cryptically.

"I understand that Father was with her. I suppose he forgave her after all."

"Did you doubt it?"

Stopping outside the door of the morning room, Olivia replaced the glasses on her nose and gazed up at her husband. Many days had passed since she had last shared company with Miles, and as she stood there looking up at his profile she realized that he had changed.

His olive face seemed less intense. His jetty eyebrows, deep eyes, and strong features were not so grim. He surveyed her in a way that made hope stir in her heart.

She had hoped before, had yearned before, had ached with her every fiber that he should come to care for her. And she had had her expectations dashed by disappointment.

She dared not hope now. Olivia left him.

Miles watched her enter the morning room where Alyson and Bryan sat in a chair before the wide windows. Alyson's weight had dropped severely the last weeks. She had lost the use of her right arm. Therefore, Bryan held the book for her and turned the pages. Standing in the hall, his back to the wall, Miles closed his eyes and listened,

his memory tumbling back to his childhood, when he had
dreamt of sharing such a moment with his mother.

That time of year thou mayst in me behold
When yellow leaves, or none, or few, do hang
Upon those boughs which shake against the cold,
Bare ruin'd choirs, where late the sweet birds sang.
In me thou see'st the twilight of such day
As after sunset fadeth in the West,
Which by-and-by black night doth take away,
Death's second self, that seals up all in rest.
In me thou see'st the glowing of such fire
That on the ashes of his youth doth lie,
As the deathbed whereon it must expire,
Consum'd with that which it was nourish'd by.
This thou perceiv'st, which makes thy love more strong,
To love that well which thou must leave ere long.

"Miles, darling, will you get Mama her cup of tea? I fear
my throat grows too dry."

Bryan glanced at his mother before shimmying off
Alyson's lap and retrieving the china cup and saucer.
Alyson smiled and cupped his rosy cheek. "Such a good
lad," she said in the weary, dreamy voice that had become
the norm of late. "If I didn't have you to live for, I don't
know what I would do. Now come; sit again in Mama's
lap while I read you more Shakespeare."

Settling in her chair and wrapping her chilled fingers around her cup of hot tea, Olivia listened to
Alyson read to the child she, for a moment, anyway, believed to be her own son, and she focused
on the dim reflected image in the gray windowpanes.

Believing himself hidden, her husband stood in the hallway with his back to the wall and his eyes closed, absorbing every word.

Perhaps today she would confront him and invite him to join them in the enjoyment of Alyson's sweet renderings. But dare she?

Carefully, she put aside her cup and left her chair, moving as quietly as possible toward the door so as not to disturb the reading or frighten away the secreted audience.

How serene he appeared as the words flowed like music in the stillness.

She touched his hand. His eyes opened slowly.

"Husband," she whispered. "You've hidden here during your mother's readings every day for the last two weeks. Will you not join us?"

"Tell me why I should."

"For your pleasure. And hers. Did you not tell me the first day you brought me to Braithwaite that your greatest desire was to have sat with your mother as she read to you? Well, listen now, sir. Her illness is allowing her the opportunity to recapture those lost hours with you. Will your heart allow you the same opportunity?"

She waited, forgetting to breathe.

At last he straightened, and with his hand still holding hers, they entered the morning room.

CHAPTER SEVENTEEN

THE THREAD OF PEACE WHICH BEGAN SO TENUOUSLY between Miles and his mother grew stronger. And every day, it seemed to Olivia that her own relationship with Miles also became more and more solid. For long hours they closeted themselves in the office and discussed business. They'd come to a comfortable understanding on how each of them was involved in their various business undertakings. Renovations on the mines were going smoothly. Excavation on the new levels were started, and the morale among the miners was high. Braithwaite itself glistened like a newly polished gem. However . . .

When evening approached and the discussion of the mines dwindled to an occasional afterthought, and there was little that remained to say about the house, a new sort of tension settled in.

A dozen times Olivia had caught her husband watching her from afar—his gaze extreme in its intensity, almost desperate . . . or perhaps she only imagined it. Night after night she heard him prowl his room until the wee hours, occasionally moving to their adjoining bedroom door where he tried the handle, only to find it locked.

Often, as she lay in her bed in the dark, recalling the strange and wonderful incident in the pool room those many weeks before, she considered unlocking the door.

That, of course, wasn't possible. She still hadn't decided how to overcome her biggest problem. As Miles was a man who valued honesty, she was afraid that Bryan's story would separate them forever. This quandary kept her up at night.

She awakened early after one such sleepless night. Dawn had barely crept through her draperies and transformed the dark into ghostly gray when she dressed and wearily made her way to the office. There would be correspondence to answer. The week's menu should be discussed with Jacques, and she would attempt one last time to communicate with Emily, though she wasn't certain why. Her last three notes had been returned unopened.

Olivia stopped short at the door upon finding her husband propped against the desk, sipping a cup of steaming coffee.

"Good morning," he greeted her somberly.

"This is a surprise," she replied.

"Really? Tell me why."

"I wasn't aware you turned out so early."

"I turn out early every morning. You simply fail to notice. Would you like coffee?"

She nodded and entered the room.

Miles poured her beverage and handed it to her as she took her chair behind the desk. Withdrawing her glasses from her skirt pocket, she eased them onto her nose and glanced about the cleared desk, concerned. "The books seem to be missing," she said.

"So they are."

Despite her resolve, her eyes were drawn to his face. These last sun-kissed days had darkened his complexion. He looked like a Gypsy, with his black hair curling wildly to his shoulders. "Do you know where they are?" she asked.

"I put them away." Digging into his pocket, he withdrew a key. "I've locked them in a safe place for the time being."

"But why?"

"So that you might be forced to spend time with your family."

Frowning, Olivia did her best to ignore the precious pleasure of finding herself the center of her husband's attention.

"Are you insinuating, sir, that I don't spend a great deal of time with my family?"

"Yes. I am."

"That's ridiculous."

"Oh? When is the last time you joined Bryan, Charles, and I for my mother's reading? Most evenings you take your dinner in here."

"You exaggerate. I took dinner with you only—" She chewed her lip.

"Last Sunday," he supplied. "Five days ago. Could it be that you are avoiding me?"

"Don't be ridiculous. There's no reason why I should avoid you."

"Oh? I can think of several reasons. The same reasons why our conversations are limited strictly to business. You're attempting to evade any possibility of our becoming . . . closer."

"Absurd. Now give me the key, please."

"Your glasses are fogging, sweetheart." As she reached for her coffee, he covered her hand with his. She gasped and jerked her hand away, burying it in her lap. "What the hell are you afraid of, Olivia? I've given you time. And Lord knows I've met all your father's conditions. What is it?"

She jumped from the chair and made her way around the desk. He moved before her, blocking her way. "You're not running this time, my love. You're not locking yourself in this room and burying yourself in those damned books. I've learned to enjoy playing the Black Knight. I've made peace with my mother. I've even grown accustomed to Bertrice's endless cat hunts. But I haven't won you over. I'd like to try."

"That's very kind of you, but I'm afraid I'm very busy today," she replied, and made a quick move around him.

"Oh no you don't." The next moment she let out a squeal as she found herself tossed over his shoulder.

"What do you think you're doing?" she cried.

"Passing the time with my wife, wife. It just so happens Jacques has prepared us a picnic breakfast. John has saddled the horses, and you and I are going for a ride."

"Perhaps I don't care to—"

"I don't give a leaping lizard what you want. I've lived in this frigging house with you for five months and have yet to spend one relaxing hour alone with you. That, my love, is about to change."

"But—"

"Shut up," he said, and slapped her on the butt.

They rode in no particular direction, but ambled down Dodsley's Road at a leisurely pace, then cantered up and over the ramparts of grass and rock, allowing their horses enough rein to stretch their legs. Around them, the dales were greening, and beyond them, they could see the spires and chimneys of Braithwaite Hall.

When they reached the head of the dale Miles dismounted and removed the horse's bit, allowing the animal to graze. Upon helping Olivia to the ground, he repeated the procedure with Perlagal, and watched as, with head up and tail curled up over her back, she pranced down the moor in gleaming white splendor.

Sitting upon the moss-blackened granite crag overlooking the moorside, Olivia and Miles shared Jacques' croissants, tiny meat pies, Cheshire cheese, and wine.

Except, Olivia had a difficult time swallowing.

How often had she daydreamed of a day such as this, but now she felt unbearably nervous.

Stretching his long legs out before him, Miles fixed his gaze upon her and sipped his wine from a wooden cup. "Relax," he said. "I don't intend to maul you, though the thought has, occasionally, crossed my mind."

Olivia said nothing.

"I've been remiss in voicing my appreciation over your helping me with Braithwaite and the mining company. If your melancholy stems from feelings of inappreciation—"

"It doesn't."

"Then why are you so damned unhappy, Olivia?"

"I'm not unhappy, sir. Braithwaite has truly become home to me."

"And what about me?"

"You, sir?"

"What have I become to you?"

She thought hard for a moment—her mind searching desperately for an appropriate answer. "A friend, I think," she finally replied.

"A friend. Describe to me your definition of a friend."

"A confidant. A companion. A conspirator in dreams."

"A confidant? You've never confided in me, girl, about anything."

"Surely you're wrong—"

"You've never once told me how you really felt about your family's desertion—or more, my behavior toward them during our last meeting. Are you angry with me? Do you want to rail in fury? And what about your travels. I know little of your past. I don't even know the story behind that tattoo."

She felt her face flush, and cast him a chagrined glance.

He grinned. "Don't tell me your lover was an Oriental tattooist."

"Hardly. But the gentleman was most persuasive. He assured me that I had the exotic beauty that such a work of art would enhance to unimaginable proportions." Raising one eyebrow, she looked away, over the moor, and allowed the gentle breeze to cool the heat of embarrassment from her cheeks. "It is my body," she replied almost defensively. "What right does anyone have to condemn me for what I chose to do with it, as long as I've not broken laws or hurt another human being? Some women paint their faces with kohl and powders and rouges. I chose to place a very small painting of a rose on my breast because it makes me feel . . . special. Unique. And . . . sensual."

Olivia looked at Miles again. His eyes had suddenly grown very intense. "Does my admitting such an emotion shock you, sir?" she asked him pointedly.

He slowly shook his head. "Would it shock you to know that I, myself, find the tattoo extremely sensual?" His lips curled provocatively, and Olivia felt her heartbeat skip.

Miles laughed softly, as if he were toying with her. She wouldn't have been surprised if he reached out to touch her in that moment. He didn't, however. He relaxed against the ground and said, "What is your favorite color, Mrs. Warwick?" He regarded her drab dress. "I assume it's brown."

"Blue."

"Ah. Yet you don't even own a blue dress."

"What good would a blue dress do me?"

"Bring you pleasure, I would think."

"Perhaps." Olivia gazed up at the cloudless sky. "There was a dress, once, in a tiny shop in Paris. A very pretty gown of pale blue organdy with ivory lace trim. I imagined how I would look in it every time we came in for one of Emily's fittings. Then one day I put it on, it fit me perfectly; for the one and only time in my life, I actually felt beautiful."

"Why didn't you buy it?" he asked softly.

"There was Emily to buy for. And my father needed new boots. Besides." She shrugged offhandedly, finding she felt both thrilled and anxious at this new closeness she was sharing with Miles. She was actually revealing a very small part of her soul, and he was listening—what's more, the compassion she saw in his eyes meant he cared. "Would a blue dress keep me warmer in the winter? Or cooler in the summer? Would blue, as opposed to brown, feel better against my skin? I think not."

"Perhaps not. Silk, as opposed to cotton, does feel immensely better against the skin, however."

Olivia looked directly at her husband at last, one eyebrow raised. "You're referring, of course, to the fact that recently I instructed your tailor to seam your shirts in cotton instead of silk. Cotton is much less costly, and better falls within the limits of your budget."

"I assume the same goes for my boots?"

"There is an excellent cobbler in Middleham who can make your boots for a third of the cost of your London maker."

"Do tell."

Her enthusiasm for the subject grew. "Not only that, but by our investing money in the local businesses, I'm certain the townspeople will regard us in a more favorable light."

"What gives you the idea that I give a damn about the townspeople's attitude toward us? Personally, I like my boots made in London. Milo Jones has been making my boots since I was twelve."

"Obviously, you're opposed to change. Very well. If you insist—"

"Good God." Sitting up, Miles tossed out his wine and pitched his cup to the ground. "You must be more miserable than I thought."

"I beg your pardon?"

"I can't even get a rousing argument out of you any longer. But never mind. Back to this friend business. I've pointed out that I'm hardly a confidant. I think you mentioned a companion, yet you avoid me at every opportunity."

"We're together now."

"And you look as if you're about to scramble to safety like a frightened rabbit if I make a single untoward advance—as if any advance toward my wife could be considered untoward by anyone except you. Explain to me, Mrs. Warwick, how you can find a man acceptable to marry, yet unacceptable to bed."

She shifted uncomfortably on the granite crag and watched the horses. "I vow Charles Fowles has grown more than a little fond of your mother. He's taken to writing poetry for her."

"Answer my question," he snapped.

Somehow, Olivia managed to take a deep breath. "Simply put, our marriage was to be strictly for convenience— or so I thought."

"Otherwise you would not have married me?"

"I'm not one to dwell on what ifs. It serves no purpose. What's done is done."

"Just what the blazes are you afraid of?"

Olivia put down her uneaten croissant and swiped crumbs from her lap. Afraid. Yes, she had many unspoken fears. Her face felt warm, growing warmer by the second, and her body became tense. Yet . . . her heart raced with the realization that Miles Kemball Warwick wanted her in that moment as desperately as he had that night in the bath. It showed in his rigid posture, in his burning gaze.

Leaving her perch, Olivia walked a short distance and turned her face into the warmish breeze. Miles moved up behind her; she could feel the heat of his body—the fierceness of his stare. She thought: If he touches me I'll crumble. I'll confess my every sin, uncover all the lies. I'll melt in his hands like warm wax—as I did that night in the bath.

"Olivia . . ."

She moved away, farther up the incline where the wind gusted more briskly.

"Look at me," came his voice from below her.

Gradually, she turned. He stood amid the bracken, the wind fluttering the sleeves of his white shirt and scattering his hair over his brow. "I'd like to make love to you," he said.

Briefly, she closed her eyes, overwhelmed by the thrill of hearing him speak the words . . . but just as shaken by the blow of desire.

"No," she replied softly.

His face turned dark and almost savage. "As your husband I demand to know why."

"It was agreed that this marriage—"

"To hell with old agreements! God, but I grow weary of this wheel, Olivia. Two strangers in the depths of desperation. We're hardly strangers any longer." He moved up the incline, sending stones bouncing down the hillside.

Olivia backed away.

"On our wedding night," he began with strained patience, "you asked me if I cared for you a little. Another man might have lied to you. He might have replied with a lot of pretty lies in order to enjoy the use of your body. I didn't. Now if you asked me if I care, I would happily say . . . yes. I've grown quite fond of you, Olivia. I care for that crazy old nanny, and I care very much for your son. You said once that you thought I was worth saving. I thought you an idiot—I was beyond saving. But lately . . . God, Olivia, I feel saved.

"I'm actually enjoying my life. Looking forward to the time spent with your son—and with you. For the first time in a very long time I feel hope." He laughed shortly, almost angrily. "Listen to me. I'm baring my soul to you and you stand there like wood. For the love of God, talk to me. At least assure me that we have a future."

She longed to cover her ears with her hands. She did not want to hear his vulnerability, his honesty. She would rather that he declared his loathing. It would make living this shameful lie easier.

Suddenly, he moved up beside her; his hand firmly gripped her arm as she attempted to turn away. He turned her to face him, his head lowered over hers. "Tell me the truth, damn you. Are you still so in love with Bryan's father?"

"Why must our conversations always come back to my past?" she demanded heatedly, and struggled to escape.

He only gripped her more tightly. "Because part of your past makes you what you are now. Because somehow your ties to your past bind you so tightly that you can't allow your own husband inside your heart."

She stared at him hopelessly, unable to reply.

"Do you feel *anything*, Olivia, or has he so slain the woman who once loved with such an intensity that she sacrificed her life to have—and keep—his son that you're simply no longer capable of loving?"

She didn't say a word, as she watched his gaze turn from pleading, to frustration, and then fury.

Grabbing her with both hands, his fingers dug painfully into her arms. He shook her until she cried aloud, "Stop. I beg you to stop!"

"Beg? The Olivia Devonshire I first met would never have begged me for anything. She would have clawed my face. For the love of God, I would rather be married to the wanton who danced with Gypsies than the icicle you've become."

"But you don't understand—oh, God, it's so hopeless . . ."

Finally, he loosened his hold, and Olivia turned away, refusing to look at him while she stood with her back to the wind and hugged herself as tightly as she could, praying the emotions churning at her insides would not spill forth. What was the solution? They couldn't pass the rest of their years in this state of limbo.

At last, she looked around and found that he had walked down the hill toward the horses, the bridles swinging from his hand. She thought of going after him—considered confessing.

If she weren't so certain the truth would destroy her.

✳

The rest is silence.
—William Shakespeare

CHAPTER EIGHTEEN

Bryan leapt from behind the door and flung himself on Miles's back. "I have you now, Black Knight!" Bryan crowed then giggled with the pleasure of having surprised Miles and Olivia as they entered the house. Jacques dashed from the kitchen, the mouth-watering aroma of freshly baked bread wafting around him.

"Madame! Monsieur! You are just in time for my *déjeuner à la fourchette*. I—"

"I'm not hungry," Miles grumbled to the stunned cook, and swung Bryan to the floor.

"I'm sorry, Jacques. Maybe later," Olivia said.

She took Bryan's hand and they walked without speaking down the gallery to the morning room. Coming to the doorway, Olivia paused and gripped her son's hand tightly, a sense of despondency sweeping her.

Alyson sat in her usual chair—the one Charles had made for her—a blanket tucked snugly over her lap. The morning sun spilled through the sparkling windowpanes, warm and as yellow as pale butter. It flowed over

Alyson's face and closed eyes, and onto the hands lying limply in her lap.

Olivia's gaze shifted to her husband.

He stood at Alyson's side and gazed out at the moor, a book in his hand.

"Is Grandmama sleepin'?" Bryan whispered.

Olivia closed her eyes against the sudden burning of tears. "Go find Bertrice and Charles," she ordered him firmly, but gently.

"But—"

"Quickly, Bryan!"

The boy dashed away; his hurried footsteps faded in the quiet.

Olivia moved silently into the room, and to Miles, who continued to stare out the window.

"It seems she went peacefully," he said.

Olivia, very tentatively, put her hand on him.

He tensed.

"I'm desperately sorry," she said.

He took a long, shuddering breath, but his face showed no emotion. "Just as we were becoming close . . . she's left me."

"She's free of pain—"

"She's free," he repeated. "What about my pain? No one has ever given a damn about me or my pain." His fingers gripped the book tightly—so tightly his finger-tips turned white, then he made a clumsy attempt to flip through the pages to the poem Alyson had marked with a satin ribbon. "What the hell am I supposed to do now?" Miles whispered.

The decision to see Earl Warwick, and ask—plead, if need be—for his permission to allow Alyson to be buried in the Warwick crypt had been precipitous. Her only thought had been to ease her husband's emotional suffering. She hadn't considered how foolhardy the request would appear to a man who'd previously voiced his disapproval of Miles's mother in no uncertain terms. Yet, as he had so often done of late, Damien Warwick had complied, though with extreme reluctance.

Olivia returned to Braithwaite with a sense of relief that quickly turned into shock the moment she stepped into Braithwaite's front door.

"He were like a madman," Sally declared as she swept up bits of shattered glass from the foyer floor. "I've seen Warwick in some moods, but nothin' like this. He were drunker than the proverbial skunk—breakin' vases and kickin' over the furniture. It were right frightenin'."

Olivia surveyed the ravaged room, her heart sinking. Armand stood calmly amid the confusion and directed the cleanup. To have caused such destruction, her husband must surely have been in tremendous emotional pain. What could she have been thinking to have left him, even for a moment, when he was so obviously unable to deal with his fresh loss?

"Where are Bryan and Bertrice?" Olivia asked.

"They took to their rooms and locked the door. They ain't been out since," Sally explained. "I don't blame them either. He were like a mad—"

"Where is my husband now?"

"Took off to the stables 'bout ten minutes ago."

Stepping carefully around the glass fragments, Olivia hurried down corridor after corridor until, exiting the house, her pace grew faster and more frantic as she ran down the bricked pathways to the stables. Charles stood at the door, preparing to mount Perlagal.

"Wait!" Olivia called, and the old man looked around. Breathing hard, Olivia joined him. "Where has my husband gone?"

"Out there." Charles motioned toward the moor. "I'm goin' after him. He shouldn't be alone in his frame of mind, lass."

Olivia snatched the reins from his hand.

Charles caught her arm. "I ain't seen him like this since his father died. Even then he weren't so desperately grieved. I ain't certain ya should be alone with him, darlin'. Ya know how his bloody temper can get the best of him."

"He's my husband," she told him. "He wouldn't hurt me. Now give me a leg up, Charles Fowles, or must I be forced to search out a step?"

Reluctantly, Charles caught Olivia's bent leg and heaved her up into the saddle. The horse pranced nervously. A moment later the mare surged forward and stretched her arched neck out toward the moor.

Olivia flew across the countryside, the wind roaring in her face and ears.

Instinct led her to Margrave Bluff.

There Alhabac grazed peacefully in the deep heath. Olivia dismounted, and not bothering to tether her mare, made her way up the steep incline toward the bluff. She found Miles standing at the ledge, his face to the wind and setting sun.

"Miles," she said softly and urgently. "I fear you're standing too close. Come away from there. Please!"

"How did you know where to find me?" His voice sounded slurred.

Calmly, she moved up beside him, and held out her hand. "There are safer places in which to grieve," she said.

"Grieve? What do I have to grieve for? Because Alyson is dead? I've wished her dead a thousand times in my life. When her health deteriorated and I interned her in Amersham, I fantasized her dying there as alone and as unhappy as she made me."

"But you loved her or you never would have experienced the intensity of those emotions."

His dark brows drew together.

"And in the end," Olivia added, "you forgave her."

Miles focused on some distant object, and for long minutes he was silent. How incredibly approachable he seemed in that moment: a child suddenly orphaned and desperately lost. She ached to press him to her breast, to soothe the confusion and pain from his features. But dare she? To do so would risk everything—all the secrets she had tried so desperately to conceal these last long months.

"It wasn't time for her to die," he murmured thoughtfully. "We had only grown to know one another. There were so many lost years . . . My God, all the years I damned her with my anger." He closed his eyes. "I want to take it all back, and I can't."

"You have! All the kindness and concern you've shown her the last months was your way of making amends. She understood. Her peace came with knowing that you forgave her."

He shook his head, and in his inebriated state, lost his balance and stumbled. Olivia's heart leapt to her throat as he appeared to totter for an instant on the craggy precipice. Cautiously, she caught his arm and attempted to pull him away from the ledge.

He jerked his arm away. "Go away," he said, drunkenness slurring his voice.

"I think not. Not, at least, until you come away from this bluff."

His eyes flashing, his lips curling under, Miles turned on her suddenly, sending stones scattering over the edge of the cliff and causing Olivia to stagger backward before catching herself. "Don't you understand?" he shouted, and the sound echoed across the desolate dale. "I have no one. No family. Not a solitary soul to call my own. I'm alone, goddammit, and I'm scared!"

"Alone? Sir, I am your wife. You're hardly alone."

"Wife? Do you want to know what *my* wife is to me? She's a signature on a worthless piece of paper. She's an object behind a desk who spouts budgets and figures and percentages, and no doubt croons debits and credits in her sleep. She's a martyr who would devote her life to a father and sister who couldn't give a damn if she lives or dies—yet she hasn't got the time of day for me." He grabbed her arm with one hand, the other he buried along her scalp, destroying the tightly coiled chignon so her hair spilled through his fingers and down her back. Dragging her near—so near she could easily detect the strong scent of liquor on his breath, he said, "She rejects me."

Olivia touched his face with her fingers. His need gave her strength to confide what was in her heart. "I dream of no other man," she replied firmly. "Only you."

He laughed sharply and his fingers twisted more fiercely in her hair. "Liar," he snarled.

"You. Only you. I swear. Are you so blind you can't see it? My every action these last five months has been for you, to help you, to rally you, to champion you. I love Miles Warwick. No other man has ever owned my heart."

He shoved her away; his face looked frighteningly savage. "You mock me."

Olivia shook her head. "I would not mock you for the world."

"You profess to have loved only me, yet there's Bryan. You refuse to speak of your lover, or the pain of his abandonment. What sort of life can we share—what sort of love can we share—when you keep such secrets? Why the hell can't you understand that your past doesn't matter to me any longer, Olivia. All I care about is honesty. Without that we can *have* no future."

Allowing him a shaky smile, her heart racing in her breast, Olivia stepped up against her husband and tentatively touched his rigid cheek. Pleasure surged through her in a warm wave. She trembled.

"Love and affection matter more than parentage. I am Bryan's mother because I chose to be. And you have become a true father to Bryan as well. Bryan's father is a man capable of great tenderness, passionate love, and intense anger. Every atom of his being is as dear to me as my own son's." Rising up on her toes, she lightly pressed her lips to his, and became breathless. "I . . . understood the language of his mind and body, for we were of a kind, both desperately yearning for a future, and a family in which we could belong."

Lightly, she kissed him again, lingering, breathing softly against his mouth until she felt him shudder in response to her touches. In his hazel eyes she saw anguish, outrage, disbelief, and desire.

"In my heart, there has never been another. As long as I am living, there never will be. I love you."

"Oh, sweet Jesus." He groaned as if in pain.

She kissed him fully, cutting off his words, burying her hands in his thick hair as she had often imagined doing as she lay in her empty bed at night and wept tears of longing for him. She kissed him until the world careened, and the sky and clouds and dale became a kaleidoscope of colors that swirled around her and dragged her down.

And she pulled her husband with her, until his face and shoulders blocked out the sky and his hands on her naked flesh—impatiently shoving aside her clothes—made her body explode in a thousand directions, until she was little more than an aching, straining sensation of long denied desire—of the desperate need to forget the idiotic fears that had kept her from knowing her husband completely these last months. How foolish those fears seemed in that moment, as his fingers slid inside her and he kissed her with his whisky-sweet mouth. She would have thrown caution to the wind even had he not been drunk and swept away by his passion for her, and his grief for his mother; she wanted him that badly.

"Make love to me," she cried, unable to stand the waiting a moment longer—ignoring the nagging forebodings that screamed out their warnings. "Make love to me," she pleaded, gazing up into his face. His features looked pained, yet there was a smile on his lips, and in his eyes, and there was an urgent gentleness to his hands as they moved on her, and in her, doing wonderful things that made her want to scream.

And her body responded. A deep stirring of passion turned that aching place between her legs soft and hot and fluid, and her fear of the unknown vanished with the onslaught of desire. She barely noticed the brief pierce of pain as he drove his body into hers, but instead, cried aloud at the glory of consummation.

Oh God, at long last . . .

He stretched her out in the flowing grass atop the bluff, the sky a blue bowl above his head and his hair slightly mussed by the wind and the easy, flowing motion of his body moving into and out of hers. How splendid he was. How handsome! She loved every tiny crevice in his dark face. She worshiped the feel of his naked skin upon hers—slippery flesh and coarse black hair, the muscles of his buttocks flexing with each penetration. Suddenly, she was lost as she had never been lost before, helpless to the fall, the overwhelming flood of wet fire that sluiced through her lower body and drove the breath from her lungs.

She returned his kisses feverishly, her mouth opening to receive his hot tongue even as his hips rocked almost violently back and forth upon hers, bringing with each deep thrust a frantic new feeling of delectation and pain, of uncontrollability. Twisting her fingers into his hair, she rose up to meet each movement of his swollen sex, loving him back with all the pent-up fervor she could no longer contain.

Her world became a pinpoint of immense, unfettered pleasure, and joy. His kiss laid open her soul, and she succumbed in body and spirit until she felt overcome with the heat of each little spasm, the apogee rendering her helpless, and free at last.

"Jane, you look blooming, and smiling, and pretty, truly
pretty this morning. Is this my pale little elf? Is this my
mustard-seed? This little sunny-faced girl with the dimpled
cheek and rosy lips; the satin-smooth hazel hair, and the
radiant hazel eyes?" (I had green eyes, reader; but you must
excuse the mistake; for him they were new-dyed, I suppose.)
"It is Jane Eyre, sir."

— CHARLOTTE BRONTË
Jane Eyre

CHAPTER NINETEEN

MILES AWAKENED SLOWLY, THE MORNING SUN THROUGH
his window a white pulse behind his eyelids. His head
pounded, and the previous day's memories tapped at his
throbbing skull in misty images.

Christ. How long had he been drunk?

Raising up in bed, he looked at the twisted covers
beside him, and burying his fingers in the pillow, he pulled
it to his face, detecting the faint hint of violets.

He rolled from the bed, pausing long enough to allow
his spinning head to settle. Naked, he assessed the
discarded clothes strewn about the floor—boots there,
breeches here, shirt (cotton) lying in a heap by the chair.
Stooping, he lifted a feminine stocking with one fingertip
and grinned.

"Bryan, get down from that wall this minute," came
Olivia's distant voice.

Miles moved to the window and looked down in the
rose garden just as Olivia swung her son away from the
garden wall. For a moment, they spun round and round

in a circle, mother and son laughing aloud in the brilliant morning sun.

He dressed quickly, even though his head and body felt disassociated, and hurried down the stairs. The servants tiptoed about, casting him cautious looks as he strolled through the corridors. Seeing Sally peeping at him from behind a door, he stopped and frowned. "Come here," he ordered her.

"Only if ya promise ya won't be hurlin' nothin' at me again."

Raising one eyebrow, he repeated, "Come here . . . please."

Reluctantly, she moved down the hall, stopping a safe measure from him.

"I would like some very strong black coffee. I'll have it in the morning room."

She looked at him funny. "Sir . . . yer mother is laid out in the mornin' room."

"My . . . ah, God. Never mind then."

Miles continued down the corridor to his office, exited through the door into the garden where Olivia was gathering up her trowel and gloves, while Bryan collected several stones he had discovered during his exploration of the dirt. Moving up behind his wife, Miles wrapped his arm around her waist, making her jump in surprise and spill her gloves.

"Good morning," he whispered in her ear.

"Who's that?" she demanded in a teasingly stern voice.

"Your husband, of course."

"Oh, is that all? I thought, perhaps, it was the groom from the next estate. We meet here every morning at ten."

He laughed and swept her unbound hair aside, exposing the pale curvature of her neck. "I never realized that you wore violet water behind your ears."

"There are a great many things you haven't noticed about me, sir."

He turned her to face him. His eyes searched her features, his fuzzy mind slowly registering the startling changes in the woman before him. Olivia's complexion bloomed with color; her eyes sparkled like gems. Her flowing hair reflected the morning sun like polished copper, and he wanted like hell to bury his hands in it. But she smiled somewhat tentatively, and pulled away.

"How are you?" she asked a little too formally as she bent to retrieve her gloves.

"Hazy and pounding."

"I don't doubt it." She glanced around at Bryan, who continued stacking his stones in a pile.

"What the blazes went on here yesterday? Everyone looks at me as if I'm a two-headed warthog."

"I would say that sums up your behavior nicely. Don't you recall?" Olivia moved toward the house.

"Some of it," he replied, falling in beside her.

"How much?"

Stopping suddenly, he took her arm and spun her around to face him. Her eyes widened and her pink lips parted just before he kissed her, at first briefly, then fiercely, drawing the breath from her and making her quiver as he touched his tongue to hers. With his mouth against hers, he said softly, "I remember everything important."

"What, exactly, do you remember, sir?" she replied as softly.

"Not much. But it'll all come back to me eventually. I'd much prefer to make new memories, however."

Olivia wiggled free and returned his smile, though less than enthusiastically. "Your mother . . ."

"I'll make arrangements in Middleham—"

"I've taken care of that for you," she interrupted. "I spoke with Earl Warwick. He's given his permission to intern Alyson in the family crypt. With your father." Taking his hand, she added, "The clergyman is to arrive here at two."

Alyson Kemball was laid to rest alongside Joseph Warwick in the Warwick tomb. Earl Warwick and his wife attended, though kept at a distance—their appearance strictly for Miles's sake, not to pay respects to the woman who, once, had nearly destroyed the Warwick family. Olivia stood at Miles's side, her presence lending him strength. Bryan stood on the other, holding Miles's hand.

When at last the funeral was over, and they were leaving the tomb, Miles glanced at his brother, who stood some distance away. Their eyes locked briefly, then Earl Warwick, with his wife, turned and left the estate.

His hands in his pockets, Miles watched them go. "I never thought he would come," he said to Olivia. "He's done me a very great service. I cannot imagine what he must have sacrificed to do me this favor."

"Isn't it odd how death can bring friends closer?"

"Are you speaking of me and my brother, or you and I?"

"Both, perhaps." She flashed him a smile, then moved away, down the path. Bryan remained, gripping Miles's hand.

He awoke with a start, heart racing, body sweating. But for the stream of pale white moonlight pouring through the window, the room was dark. A movement near the window caught his eye.

Olivia moved into moonlight. "Husband," she whispered. "Are you awake?"

Miles focused hard, blinked twice, and focused again. Olivia stood at the bedside, her hair flowing over her naked shoulders. Her breasts shimmered like alabaster in the dim illumination.

She eased onto the bed, stretching her slender body out beside his, running her hand over his naked chest and down, under the sheet covering his loins. Gasping, he caught her wrist.

"Shh," she said, and drew her knee across his thigh. "Do you have any idea how long I've waited for this?" she whispered in his ear, and nipped playfully at his lobe with her small teeth.

He didn't speak. He couldn't. But his body spoke for him, turning rigid, growing hard. His flesh felt on fire. His earlier numbness flooded with exquisite sensations. He reached for her, but she shook her head and slid her hips over his, straddling his sex with her hot, moist cleft, sliding it against him, forward and back until he groaned and grabbed her, making her laugh in a deep, husky way that sent a fissure of wild hunger surging through his loins. "My turn," she said simply.

Rising slightly, she impaled herself on him, softly crying aloud.

He caught her tiny waist in his hands as she poised there upon the tip of him, her head thrown back so her hair spilled in a glorious silken pool upon his thighs, her heat and closeness making him crazy with the need to drive himself into her. Yet, her whimper confused him.

"Is there pain?" he asked, concerned.

Her glorious breasts rising and falling with each labored breath, she replied breathlessly, " 'Tis the scrapes on my thighs." Catching his hands, she moved them to the scratches on her legs. "From the heath yesterday." She eased his fingers to the small discolorations on her hips.

"I'm sorry."

"I'm not." She sank onto the full length of him, slowly, like one feeling her way into unknown depths, her face uncertain, yet eager, in pain, and in ecstasy. "Christ," he murmured. "Was I that rough on you?"

"Don't you remember?"

She rocked him slightly, and he caught his breath, squeezed closed his eyes and wondered if he were still dreaming—but the dreams that had awakened him with a slamming heart weren't this splendorous—they were confusing . . . He wished he could recall.

"Oh God," he moaned as she began the rhythm, sweeping away all other thoughts.

Her father's letter arrived at just after ten the next morning. Upon reading her father's hurriedly penned scrawl, Olivia felt as if the ground had opened beneath her feet. Emily had returned to Devonswick. She had lost her baby, and Clanricarde had sent her packing home to their father.

She found Miles and her son at the stables, Bryan perched bareback on Alhabac as Miles lunged the horse in a cantering circle. The image stopped Olivia in her tracks.

How beautiful they were together, with the sun reflecting from their dark hair, the thrill of the ride flushing Bryan's face with vibrant color. How well he sat! Heels down, legs relaxed, his slender body rocking with the seesaw motion of the horse. Soon Miles would have him riding with the hounds.

Spying his mother, Bryan waved a hand in the air. "Hello! See what Papa's taught me!" he called.

Papa?

Olivia watched Miles for his reaction. Her husband only laughed and waved, then turned his attention back to Bryan. "Heads up!" he ordered. "Pretty ladies are not supposed to interrupt a true horseman's concentration!"

Papa.

Feeling light-headed, Olivia sank onto a stone bench. It seemed only a minute passed before she looked up to find Miles standing before her, the lunge line wrapped around one hand, his hazel eyes intense.

"You look as if you've just seen a ghost," he said.

She looked beyond him. Bryan continued cantering in a circle on the Arabian bay. "Is it safe?" she asked. "He's so very small. What if he falls?"

"He will . . . eventually. One doesn't learn to properly ride until he can boast of a few broken bones." Miles eased onto the bench beside her. "You seem upset. If his riding Alhabac—"

"That's not it," she replied more abruptly than she intended. At last, she managed to pull her attention from her son to find her husband with his elbows on his knees, his gaze on the ground between his feet.

"You don't like his calling me papa, perhaps," he stated quietly.

"I simply thought you were opposed."

"It seemed to mean a great deal to him. That's all." Sitting straighter, his mouth tight with irritation, he said, "That's not true. Suddenly, for whatever reason, his calling me papa means a great deal to me. Occasionally I look at him and . . ." He watched the boy bring the horse to an easy trot.

"And what?"

"I imagine that he's mine. I don't think I could love him any more if he was mine." His eyes came back to hers. "You wouldn't ever attempt to take him away from me, would you?"

There was a fierceness, an urgency in Miles's features that gave Olivia pause. Her response was cut off, however, as Gustavea came plodding down the path in his overly big shoes. He carried a letter in one hand, which he delivered with practiced ceremony to Miles. Despite the earlier bad news about Emily, Olivia couldn't help but smile at the boy's clumsiness, taking little notice as Miles tore open the envelope and read the missive silently to himself.

"My God," Miles said, his voice deep and breathless. "Oh my God."

"What's happened?" Olivia demanded in a voice verging on panic. "Husband, what—"

A smile stretched over Miles's mouth, and his cheeks flushed with bright color. Suddenly, Olivia found herself picked up and swirled around, while behind them Bryan brought the cantering Alhabac to a stop and slid to the ground, his little legs carrying him up the path at breakneck speed so he, too, could join in the impromptu celebration.

Sweeping the lad into his arms, Miles spun Bryan and Olivia round and round, laughing at the top of his voice until Olivia found herself joining in.

"Will you tell me what is so wonderful, sir, so I know exactly why I'm laughing like an idiot?"

"Tell us, Papa," Bryan joined in, hugging Miles's neck as hard as he was capable.

"We're rich," Miles shouted.

"Wh—"

"Rich! Ah, God, Olivia, I'll buy you a thousand blue dresses and two thousand bottles of the most expensive perfume in Paris. No more violet-scented water for my wife. And Bryan—we'll have the money to send you to the most prestigious university in the world. Dear hearts, I was right!" He swung Olivia and Bryan again, kissed Olivia on the mouth until she felt breathless and dizzy.

"I was right," he repeated again and again.

"Right about what?"

"The mine. They've hit a new vein, dear heart, the biggest vein found in this county in a hundred years."

Some are born great, some achieve greatness, and some have greatness thrust upon them.
—WILLIAM SHAKESPEARE

CHAPTER TWENTY

UPON ARRIVING AT GUNNERSIDE, MILES AND OLIVIA had expected to find jubilation. What they discovered were the stunned, shock-stricken faces of miners and village folk, of weeping women and children, and a dozen corpses lined up on the ground outside the church.

"Explosion." Miles stood in the shop door and watched the frightened and confused miners mill about the mine entrance, some with fire-blistered faces, others with bandaged heads, arms, and legs. Olivia and Janet Hooper moved among them, administering aid to any man who needed it.

"Aye," Jake Delaney replied. "One minute we were all congratulatin' each other for a job well done and lookin' forward to an evenin's celebration at the White Horse, the next . . . it were like hell opened up under our feet. Those of us who were in back managed to run for it. Them others weren't so lucky."

"Was it methane?"

Jake left his chair and joined Miles at the door. "Sir, we been down that level every day for the last four months, includin' this very mornin'. And, sir . . . the canaries was singin'."

The canaries were singing. Miles frowned.

"Where is McMillian?"

"Away, sir."

Miles looked at Delaney. "Why the blazes wasn't he on the job?"

"Said he had business in Newbiggin. He intended to hire more men for the new level."

"I didn't give approval to hire new men."

"I'm only tellin' ya what he told me, sir."

Turning away from the door, Miles asked, "Are all the men accounted for?"

"There are five missin'."

"Why hasn't a rescue attempt begun?"

"The men feared diggin' any deeper. Not much chance of survival anyway. If they hit more gas—"

"It wasn't gas that caused that explosion, Delaney. I think you know that. You said yourself that the canaries were singing."

"They're afraid, sir. Pure and simple. Many of those men lost fathers and brothers—we were all friends." Jake's face fell as he added, "Herbert Wallace is one of the missin'."

"What if those men are alive?"

Jake shook his head. "The men refuse to go in, sir. They've all said for some time that the damned shafts are cursed by the pixies."

"That's ridiculous. They're grown men, for God's sake."

"Most of 'em are sayin' now that they don't want no more of the Warwick Mining Company. That it don't matter about the new vein—the new vein won't do much for dead men."

"Damn." Miles left the building and walked directly to the mouth of the mine where he picked up a tin bucket and a stick, and beat the bucket as hard as he could, until the addled miners roused from their stupor and turned their attention on him.

"I need volunteers to go in!" he shouted. "There are five men—"

"I ain't goin' back," someone replied.

"Nor me!" came another voice.

"Ain't enough men died in yer bloody pits?" cried a voice. "Would ya make ever wife a widow before yer satisfied that these shafts ain't safe?"

Miles flung the pail to the ground. "That was a new level. Every measure had been taken to guarantee its safety."

"The damn levels are cursed!"

Swearing, Miles spun on his heels and moved toward the portal, rolling up his sleeves as he stepped along the discarded tips.

"Miles!" came Olivia's voice. She grabbed his arm from behind. "You're not going in there," she said.

"Someone has to."

"You can't do it alone."

"There could be men alive in there."

"Then I'll go with you."

He stopped and looked around. Her face was smudged with dirt and sweat, her dress stained with blood. "The hell you say."

Jake Delaney stepped from the shop, a pickax gripped in one abraded, massive hand. "I'll be goin' in with ya, sir," he announced, then glanced among the miners' tense, watchful faces as he moved toward the portal. "That'll be our fathers and brothers and friends buried in there," he shouted.

A big man with a bandaged forehead stood up. "Y've certainly changed yer tune, Jake Delaney. It weren't so long ago that you were espousin' the closin' down of these deathtraps."

Delaney took a stance beside Miles and Olivia. "It weren't twenty-four hours ago that ya were slappin' each other on the back and makin' toasts to Warwick, regrettin' the mischief ya caused him those months back, and praisin' his determination to open these new levels." Lowering his voice somewhat, he added, "I admit I was one of the loudest protestors, but the fact of the matter is, we're lookin' at a vein that could guarantee us all, and our children, employment for the rest of our days. Think of what it will do for Gunnerside."

Janet Hooper stood and looked from man to man, and the wives who huddled near their injured husbands. "My own husband and son were killed in these mines. They knew the risks. You all do."

The men grumbled among themselves, and shifted restlessly.

"Bill Foster!" Janet called, pointing to the man who had earlier stood. "Your cousin died working for the London Lead Company. Riley Davis, your brother and father-in-law died in Boltsburn Mine in Rookhope when the damn stopes gave way."

"So what's that prove?" Davis responded angrily.

"That all mines are dangerous." Janet faced Miles and Olivia. "I'll be going in with you."

A woman slowly stood up by her husband. "If that were my Quinton down there, I'd surely be frantic to know for certain if he were dead or alive."

Little by little, the men who were not incapacitated stood and moved toward the mouth of the mine, leaving their weeping wives. Olivia turned her eyes on her husband, her heart climbing her throat with fear. "Please," she said as quietly and as calmly as possible. "Don't go."

Miles gave her a twisted grin, and touched her cheek. "Dear heart, if you keep looking at me like that I just might begin to believe that you really love me."

He bent his head and kissed her mouth lightly, then pressed his lips to her forehead.

And then he was gone.

The hours passed. Olivia paced the grounds, doing her best to offer aid to the wounded miners, or to the grieving families of the men who had died. All the while, her fear mounted, and her eyes continued to return to the mouth of the mine, hoping against hope that she would soon see her husband emerge from the damnable, dangerous pits.

Why had no one heard from the men who ventured into the level in hopes of finding survivors?

Rumors ran rife concerning the cause for the explosion. But no one knew for certain. It wasn't until Bob McMillian returned from Newbiggin that the shocking and ugly suspicion began to formulate in Olivia's mind. McMillian did not return to Gunnerside alone.

Josiah Lubinsky was with him, and he wasted little time in rousing the battered, frustrated, and angry workers from their state of lethargy and shock. He stood before the two hundred miners and their families, the shopkeepers, farmers, and the scattering of clergy who had been feverishly praying over the dead, dying, and injured. "I can promise you that this sort of thing won't happen if you work for me," he announced to the tension-charged crowd. "I can happily say that my company hasn't recorded a solitary accident attributed to explosions or cave-ins in three years, due, I might add, to the utilization of the most modern safety devices available today."

Olivia watched the miners' intent faces as they listened to Lubinsky's blatant propaganda against her husband's company, then made her decision.

Olivia worked her way down the level by following the iron cart rails. For six hours those up top had heard nothing from the excavating group. Some had predicted that gas had killed them. Others argued more cave-ins. Since Lubinsky's arrival all hell had broken loose.

Breathing hard from exertion and the lack of oxygen, Olivia paused long enough to catch her breath. There didn't seem to be a dry thread on her body; her feet ached from stumbling over stones. The dripping tallow from the candle she carried had raised burn blisters on her fingers. Where was her husband?

Had she, possibly, taken a wrong turn in the dark? Were there offshoots in the level?

Was she, as many up top maintained, already too late?

Briefly closing her eyes, she refused to believe her husband had perished.

She looked back the way she had come. Darkness; silence loomed back at her, as deep and seemingly impenetrable as the darkness and silence stretching ahead. Closing her eyes briefly, she did her best to force back the panic threatening to overwhelm her and rob her of logic.

A sound.

Olivia caught her breath. Her senses surged to a pinpoint, and for an instant her pounding heart crashed like
cymbals in her ears, drowning out all else.

Candle held before her, she ran along the rail, eyes
searching, ears straining, her mind struggling to remain
rational—to think clearly. Again! a noise.

"Oh God oh God," she whispered aloud, running faster
as the noise grew louder and she recognized it as men's
shouting voices and the clink and clatter of picks on stone.
At last, up ahead, a dim light began to show, growing
brighter the nearer she came, until the shadows on the
walls took shape, and finally became men.

"Miles!" she cried. "Are you there?"

Suddenly Miles materialized before her, his dirt- and
sweat-covered face incredulous as he watched her stumble toward him out of the dark.

"What the bloody . . . Olivia?"

Laughing in relief, she flung herself against him, dropping her candle to the floor. He held her fiercely against
his wet body.

"They all said you were dead," she said.

"Tired, but not dead." He pushed her to arms'
length. His face looked haggard, but relieved. "They're
alive. We should be breaking through any minute." Frowning, he looked beyond her. "Are there
others?"

She shook her head.

"You came down here alone?" he demanded angrily.

"I had to. There's trouble." Olivia swallowed and did
her best to catch her breath. "McMillian's returned from
Newbiggin, and he's not alone . . . he's brought Lubinsky
with him."

*   *   *

By the time Olivia and Miles reached the surface, her lungs were burning from exertion—her ears ringing with Miles's silence. She was well aware of the thoughts running through his head. Their future hinged on the outcome of this confrontation.

The crowd, apparently divided by loyalty, applauded and hissed, then fell silent as Miles moved from the mouth of the adit, and directly toward Lubinsky. A woman leapt to her feet and screamed, "My husband, sir? Have you found my husband?"

A man grabbed her and dragged her away while she wept, frantic for some word on the trapped miners. Lubinsky slowly turned, his eyes widening as Miles, dirty, sweaty, and bloody, advanced on him in a slow, confident, and threatening swagger. For an instant Lubinsky appeared stunned, then confused, then frightened.

Then Bob McMillian stepped from the night shadows and placed himself protectively between Miles and Lubinsky, stopping Miles short. Standing face to face with his manager of seven years, Miles glared into Bob's eyes and said through his teeth, "Why, damn you? You've worked for my family for eight years. We took you from the mines and put you in control."

"It ain't nothin' personal, sir. You've been more than fair to me. But a man's got to think of his future, and Mr. Lubinsky is offerin' me a share of this operation."

"A share of nothing is nothing, McMillian. I don't intend to sell. Why should I when we've just hit a new vein? Lubinsky doesn't have enough money to pay me what this company is worth now."

"Unless ya got the men to bring up the bouse, sir, yer company is worthless."

Olivia moved up beside Miles, and took his arm. Miles looked at her briefly before shifting his gaze to Lubinsky. "So that's the way of it. You turn my men against me and force me to take a pittance of what the mine is worth."

Lubinsky shrugged and smirked with an exaggerated air of importance. The gray mutton-chop whiskers growing low on his jaw made his beefy face appear all the wider. He hooked his thumbs in the vents of his waistcoat, and smiled. "It's not as if you'll be left penniless," he said. "After all, you have your wife's money."

Miles lunged at him, only to be grabbed from behind by McMillian, who hauled him off his feet and slammed him to the ground hard enough to knock him breathless. He heard Olivia cry out, then a pressure buried into his back, and he gritted his teeth and tasted dirt.

With his knee in Miles's back, McMillian said, "I think we should let the men decide who they want to work for. Don't you, sir?"

"Bastard," Miles said through his teeth. "If they walk I'll simply hire new men."

"I don't think so. Not with these mines' reputation for cave-ins and explosions—at least, not until Mr. Lubinsky can take over and guarantee their safety."

Closing his eyes and doing his best to breathe, Miles tried to focus on something besides the pain and sense of hopelessness and frustration pounding at his temples. He'd come so close—so goddamn close, not only for himself—proving to himself that he was capable of succeeding—but for Olivia and Bryan. For a few short hours he had experienced the exhilaration of looking forward to a future of *giving* to his loved ones . . . as opposed to taking.

"Now, Kappen, sir," came a voice from the dark. "Is that any way to be treatin' a fine gentleman like Mr. Warwick? And after he risked his life to save our friends here?"

The crowd fell silent as Jake Delaney stepped from the portal of the mine, his pickax gripped like a weapon in one hand. Behind him came the battered and bruised survivors of the cave-in.

A woman screamed in joy and burst from the pressing crowd, tripping and stumbling her way to her smiling husband, who grabbed her in his weakened arms and did his best to spin her around. For a moment, disbelief maintained an electrified silence that shattered into a great roar of fervor as realization set in. The miners were safe! Men, women, and children poured forth, sweeping around the survivors like a tide.

Lubinsky frowned and slowly dropped his hands to his sides. McMillian eased off Miles and moved away, watching Lubinsky, then the men, uneasily. Olivia elbowed her way through the crowd and fell to her knees beside Miles, taking his face in her hands.

He sat up as Delaney leapt upon a stack of timbers and waited until the last hurrah had fallen silent, and all eyes were locked on him.

"I ask ya, what other owner would have risked his life to go in there and save these men? Lubinsky? I don't think so. He'd have forced the lot of ya down there before him, I wager. Need I remind ya that the rest of ya were willin' to write these men off? If it weren't for Warwick they'd have died there."

"But the accidents," someone shouted.

Herbert Wallace limped his way over to Delaney. Delaney offered his hand and helped his obviously weak and injured friend up beside him. "Maybe you'd like to talk to Wallace here about *accidents,*" Jake said.

Herbert held up a blackened, ragged fragment of some object. "This weren't no accident," he announced. "We come across this as we were diggin' our way out."

The men pressed closer.

"Dynamite," Wallace explained.

"What is it?" someone called. "And what's it got to do with the explosion?"

"Everything," Jake replied. "It's an explosive."

"I ain't never heard of no . . . dynamite," a man yelled.

"It was just patented last year by a Swedish chemist, Alfred Nobel. It's just bulgin' with nitroglycerin—and we all know what nitro can do. This dynamite was set off in that level to sabotage our minin' of the new vein. There's only one man I know who uses dynamite in the excavation of his mines. And that's Josiah Lubinsky."

Lubinsky backed away, and turned on McMillian, who stood rooted to the ground, apparently uncertain if he could, or should, turn tail and run. "You idiot!" Lubinsky roared. "I never instructed you to go to these extremes. I only meant for you to scare them."

Miles slowly stood, and shrugged Olivia away. Janet Hooper materialized through the crowd and wrapped her arms around Olivia's shoulders and refused to allow her to follow.

"You sonofabitch." Miles moved toward Lubinsky, who backed away, only to come up against a wall of shoulder-to-shoulder miners. "It's been you all along— all the mishaps. The convenient 'accidents.' So what the hell if a man had to die every now and again. I wager it was you who had my credit cut off at the lumbermills as well. You and McMillian made damn certain that any measures

I took to maintain safety were less than adequate, and no doubt McMillian made certain that rumors of your authority and management abilities reached the men."

His brow sweating, Lubinsky shook his head. "I never ordered McMillian to endanger anyone. Tell him, McMillian!"

All heads turned toward McMillian. He backed away as the miners moved toward him, picks and shovels in their hands.

"Someone get the sheriff," Miles said.

"My life is a burden without you," he exclaimed, in a low voice. "I want you—I want you to let me say I love you again and again!"

—THOMAS HARDY

CHAPTER TWENTY-ONE

IT WAS NOON OF THE NEXT DAY BEFORE OLIVIA AND Miles arrived home at Braithwaite. Olivia's mind felt fuzzy from lack of sleep, her body drained from the previous day's and night's fear for her husband's safety—not to mention the grief she'd experienced over the death of the miners. She looked forward to a leisurely hour spent in a bath of hot, steaming water, as did Miles. With his hands bandaged and his clothes in tatters, he wearily mounted the steps with Olivia, just as the front door was flung open, and Bertrice stumbled toward them, her lined face rigid with distress.

Olivia and Miles stopped short as Bertrice burst into tears.

"I didn't know what to do, lass," the nanny cried. "She come here with no warnin' and said you had given her permission to take him."

Olivia took the old dear's trembling shoulders in her hands. "Bertrice, what are you talking about?"

"Bryan."

A coldness crept up Olivia's spine.

Miles grabbed Bertrice fiercely. "What are you saying? Speak up, blast you, and quit blubbering. Where is Bryan?"

Her face white, her eyes round, Bertrice replied, "With Emily. She come here yesterday afternoon and said you had given her permission to take him for a ride. She swore she'd have him back to Braithwaite in an hour."

"Oh my God." Olivia sank toward Miles. He caught her and held her tightly.

"When she didn't bring him home, I sent Mr. Fowles to Devonswick. She told Mr. Fowles Bryan wished to stay the night with her, and that she would have him home first thing this mornin'. When she didn't bring him home I sent Mr. Fowles back . . ."

Bertrice burst into tears again, and Olivia roused enough to shake her. "Oh Lud," the nanny wept.

Robbed of breath, unable to reason coherently, Olivia turned away and stared down the long, curving drive. After a night fraught with fear and pain, how pleasant the morning had been. In the space of a moment, however, Olivia's world turned gray, her eyes unable to acknowledge the gardens of bold purple auriculas and golden-eyed pansies, of pink thrift and brilliant crimson double daisies that bobbed their majestic heads with the slightest movement of the wind.

Gradually, voices wormed their way into her consciousness.

" . . . Bring the coach up . . . Ride to Devonswick . . . Regret the day she was ever born . . . Bring charges of kidnapping . . ." Miles's arms came around her. He pressed her head to his chest and stroked her hair. Only then did she realize she had begun to silently weep.

"Hush," he said in her ear. "Everything will be fine. We'll find our son and bring him home. I swear to you, Olivia. I won't let anything happen to him."

She tried to breathe, tried to focus on the accelerated beating of her husband's heart, hoping it would calm the increasingly irrational fear centering in her chest. Of course Emily would not harm Bryan. Emily might be a great many things, but a murderess of children she wasn't.

She allowed Miles to lead her into the house, and into the closest drawing room, where he sat her on the settee and ordered a hovering servant to fetch Olivia hot tea.

Olivia shook her head. "I don't want anything."

Miles watched her for a minute, his heart breaking. He watched her small body draw in on itself. Her fear for his safety had been immense the previous day, but this emotion she was experiencing now was beyond simple fear. They had returned to Braithwaite with only one thought: to share their newfound happiness with her—their—son.

Now this.

Armand stepped into the room. "Sir, your coach is waiting." Frowning, he added, "Perhaps you'd care to change your clothes before leaving?"

"There isn't time."

As Miles moved toward the door, Olivia looked up. "Where are you going?" she asked.

"To see your father."

She ran after him. "I'm going with you."

"Absolutely not."

Her face white as alabaster, her eyes turquoise pools of unshed tears, Olivia shook her head. "How can you think I could remain here ignorant of what's happening with Bryan? If my father is in any way involved in this,

I would rather know. If we find Emily, I should be the one
to confront her. She would never listen to you."

Taking her face in his hands, Miles asked, "Why the
blazes would she do something like this? She's never
given a damn about Bryan before."

"She's . . . confused and upset." Olivia did her best
to steady her breathing. "Emily lost her baby and
Clanricarde intends to divorce her. He sent her home to
Devonswick."

"But what's that got to do with Bryan?"

Olivia averted her eyes. A moment passed before she
could speak. "I fear she's . . . desperate. No doubt she's
suffered a great shock and disappointment over losing the
child, and the failing of her marriage. Women in the throes
of such upset occasionally feel powerful emotions . . ."

"Is she capable of hurting him?" he asked. As her face
blanched whiter, he shook her and demanded, "Answer
me, Olivia? Would Emily harm Bryan in any way?"

"No," she said. "I think she wants to keep him."

After half an hour's wait in Devonswick's foyer, Lord
Devonshire received Olivia and Miles in the formal drawing room reserved for greeting guests. Miles was livid,
and it was all Olivia could do to keep her husband from
thrashing her distraught father.

Standing toe to toe with her father, Olivia said as
calmly as possible, "Tell me where Emily has taken
Bryan."

"How the blazes am I supposed to know?" he replied,
sweating profusely. His round eyes looked sunken, and
darted nervously, furiously, toward Miles every few
seconds.

"You're lying, Father," she said.

"Why should I lie, for God's sake? The gal has been insensible since Clanricarde sent her packing, muttering about husbands and children and babies—even in her sleep. For the love of Christ, I don't know the gal any longer." Lowering his eyes, he added wearily, "I suspect that I never did. Emily has turned into . . ."

"Into what, Father?"

"A stranger. A . . . monster. Blaming me for expecting too much of her—claiming the only reason I loved her so dearly was because she reminded me of your mother. She had the audacity to tell me that I 'suffocated' her with attention, demanding that she live up to her mother's reputation."

Devonshire dropped onto the settee. Olivia sat down beside him, and took his hand. "Please, Father. If you have any idea at all where she might have gone, tell me."

He turned his gaze to hers. His brow showed lines of confusion, his eyes a tumbling of questions, and regret.

"The things she told me about herself . . ." he said softly.

"Father," Olivia whispered, squeezing his hand. "Please."

"Are they true? Blast it all, tell me the truth, Olivia. Was Emily capable of those things? The lies? The deceits? How many times have you covered up for her? Protected her?" He covered his gray face with his hands and began to weep. "How I must have hurt you—all those times I accused you, ridiculed you, shamed you. All the while you were only protecting your sister, and me, knowing how the truth about her would have destroyed me, and ruined her."

Gently, Olivia removed her father's hands from his

face. She tried to smile. "All is forgiven, Father, if you will only help me find Bryan."

His eyes came back to hers. "If I had been half the parent to you and Emily as you are to Bryan, all this grief might have been avoided." He blinked, and fresh tears spilled down his face. "Right, then," he said hoarsely. "She mentioned something about a picnic at the bluff . . . then she intended to return the boy to his rightful father . . ."

Miles stared out the coach window at the passing countryside and did his best to focus his thoughts on the undulating hills and dales, and not on the stomach-turning events unfolding around him. For the last hour his wife had sat like a cold stranger on the opposite seat, in the far corner, her gaze fixed straight ahead, her hands clasped like vises in her dirty skirt, refusing to acknowledge his existence. It was as if Olivia had gone into shock the moment her father had confessed that Emily intended to search out Bryan's father.

Closing his eyes, resting his head back against the seat, Miles did his best to breathe calmly while he flexed his bandaged hands into fists, and winced from the pain. It was all too goddamn confusing. Why had Olivia refused to direct the driver to Margrave, where Emily purportedly had taken Bryan for a picnic? That wasn't the burning question in his mind, however.

He looked at his wife. His every bone and muscle ached with the fatigue of last night's digging, not to mention the many hours he had gone without sleep. He felt sick, and bone weary.

"I want the truth," he said softly.

Olivia offered him a shadow of a smile. She lightly touched his cheek with her fingertips. "Forgive me. But my mind and heart are confused. I don't know how or where to begin. I keep thinking about how happy we've been recently—how truly fond you've become of Bryan—not to mention the tremendous success you've found with the mines . . .

"This has all been caused by my own stupidity. I should have known it would come to this. It was unavoidable. I knew that, yet I prayed that, somehow, it could be delayed a lifetime, or until our love was strong enough to weather the storm of truth."

Miles sank back into the cushions. "Olivia. Dear heart, do you know where Emily has gone? If you do, for the love of God, will you please tell me?"

"As Papa said, to see Bryan's father," she replied, looking at him in a calm, unblinking manner.

"So . . . I'm finally going to learn his identity."

"I fear I can hardly keep it from you any longer. I do hope you won't hate me too severely. After we find Bryan, everything will be clearer."

They rode in silence, with Olivia gazing out the window watching the sun set beyond the west horizon, while Miles studied his wife's perfect profile until the deepening shadows made his eyelids grow heavier and heavier, and finally close.

He dreamt that Olivia, thinking he was sound asleep, wept openly at last, allowing her quiet sobs to flow freely into her hands while she whispered repeatedly, "I don't want to lose either of you. I simply couldn't bear it. The two of you are all I've got in the world."

And he dreamt that he sleepily responded, "I'll kill anyone who tries to take either of you away from me."

"Sir?"

He awoke with a start. Olivia was gone. The coach was still.

The driver, dressed in his finest livery, stood at the coach door looking up at him, concerned. A blaze of light poured through the house windows behind him and lit up the twilight. Stiffly, Miles sat up, rubbed the back of his tense neck, and asked, "Where is my wife?"

"Already inside, sir."

Forcing the fog from his mind, Miles focused on the familiar front door and exited the coach.

On her knees in the foyer, Olivia held Bryan tightly against her as Miles entered the house behind her. She listened to his footsteps approach, and gradually, she lifted her eyes to his as he stopped beside her, his visage confused yet relieved upon finding her with Bryan.

"Where is Emily?" he asked.

"In the morning room," came Bertrice's voice from a doorway. The nanny then hurried to Olivia's side and protectively put her arms around her charges. Her features appeared completely lucid, and stubbornly determined.

Without speaking again, Miles moved slowly toward the morning room, his footsteps ringing like bells in the quiet. Olivia could not bring herself to watch him, yet she knew the moment he reached the room, knew by his silence that he had at last confronted her sister.

"Close the door," came Emily's voice in the distance.

"What the hell is going on?" Miles demanded. "I should have you arrested for kidnapping."

"I said to close the door, damn you."

After a long hesitation, the door clicked shut.

Slowly, Olivia stood, her hand still resting on the top of Bryan's head as he continued to grip her tightly, his tear-streaked face buried in the folds of her skirt. Olivia looked to Bertrice.

Bertrice reached for him. He shrugged her aside and almost frantically grabbed for Olivia as Bertrice attempted again to escort him from the room.

"Go now," Olivia whispered, and smiled comfortingly. "We'll read later. I promise."

At last, Bryan allowed the nanny to lead him out of the foyer, and Olivia, taking a shallow, shaky breath, moved down the gallery to the closed morning room door, the muffled voices within becoming more distinct until Olivia could, at last, hear each dreaded word as Emily spoke.

"I lost Clanricarde's child and the physician informed me that to have more children would be suicide. My husband then sent me packing, declaring our marriage was over. At first I panicked. I honestly believed that if I produced a child—any child—that he would accept the child as his own. I was still arrogant enough to believe that he loved me enough to accept another man's son as his own.

"He didn't, but by that time, the truth was out."

"What the blazes are you trying to tell me?" Miles demanded.

"*I* am Bryan's mother, of course."

Olivia closed her eyes. Her knees turned to water, her face to fire. Fear squeezed off her air so she could hardly breathe.

"You're insane," came Miles's eventual reply. "Olivia is—"

"His aunt. Nothing more."

Silence.

Oh God, the silence. Why didn't he say something?

At last, he said in a deep, tight voice, "You're a liar."

"You know Olivia. Always sacrificing herself for others. It became quite nauseating at times. She'll never know how jealous of her I've always been. Oh, not because she's pretty. She's not nearly so pretty as me. I always detested the way Papa bragged about her mind. I hated the way the servants respected her. I resented the way she would bravely face any crisis and see it through without shedding so much as a single tear. There were times when I would gladly have given up my beauty to be as smart as Olivia. As wise. As brave. She even went into this farce of a marriage with dignity, knowing you wanted her for only one reason and that was her dowry. Yet . . .

"Yet she even made this ridiculous relationship between you work. Rumor is, you and Olivia have become . . . very close. For the first time in Olivia's miserable life, she's happy. Isn't it ironic that she stumbled into this arrangement because of me . . . now it will end because of me as well."

Olivia slowly shoved open the door. Standing in the threshold, her eyes meeting Emily's, she said, "Emily, I've never asked you for anything. But I ask you now. I beg you now." Briefly, Olivia closed her eyes and willed back the desperate tears and the fear that made her thick voice vibrate with emotion. Never had she witnessed such hate in her sister's features, such malicious intent. "For Bryan's sake. For my sake. Have mercy on me. I can't lose them now."

Leaving her chair, Emily glided across the room, a vision in pink taffeta and white eyelet lace. Her pale hair was fixed at the nape with a black net, and black satin ribbon. She threw herself against Miles, who turned rigid as a rock in her arms.

Her knees shaking, Olivia moved into the room, her concentration fixed on the scene before her: her sister with her arms around Miles—her husband—his hazel eyes boring into hers and his features dark as a thundercloud in its anger and confusion. At last, he closed his hands around Emily's arms, and forcibly shoved her away.

"Stay the hell away from me," he said through his teeth.

"Come now, Miles. You know you've loved me all along. That first day in November when you responded to my father's letter—you said yourself that you thought I had written it. You only married her because she's my sister. Surely you can understand why I chose to marry Clanricarde. Only for his money, I assure you."

Miles turned to Olivia. Looking up into his beloved face, she ached to touch it one last time, to beg his forgiveness—

"She claims she gave birth to Bryan," he said.

Olivia attempted to smile, to nod. She could do nothing but stare into her husband's confused eyes while her heart felt as if it were renting in two. "I . . . did what I thought was best for everyone. Father had such plans for Emily—such grand dreams for her marriage. I was convinced that I would never marry. I was too plain. A bluestocking. My tastes for life and comfort were far too common.

"And besides," she continued, looking him straight in the eyes. "There was only one man whom I loved. If I couldn't have him I simply refused to settle for less. Surely you can understand, then, how Emily's pregnancy seemed to be a miracle for me. If I could not marry the man I loved, at least I could be the mother of his son . . . and love him with all my heart."

For a moment, Miles stared at her without blinking, then, little by little his face drained of color and his body became rigid. A thousand emotions appeared to cross his handsome features in those few seconds. Confusion. Anger. Disbelief. Each with an intensity that cut Olivia's soul like a knife.

He closed his hands around her arms, and the grip felt excruciating—made more hurtful by the raw pain reflected in his gray-green eyes as he attempted to speak, and was unable to.

Without taking her eyes from his, she said softly, "You're Bryan's father."

"Emily—"

"Is his mother. He was never really mine."

Emily moved up beside them, and took Miles's arm. Like an automaton, he faced her, his face blank with shock—or fury. Olivia couldn't tell.

Merciful God, how he must hate her, Olivia thought, as she backed toward the door.

Her smile becoming brittle beneath the intensity of his attention, Emily said, "You can understand why I didn't tell you, Miles darling. All I could think of was getting away before my father found out about you and me . . . and our baby. So Olivia suggested our visiting France until after the child was born—that way no one would know—I could farm him out to some family who wanted to adopt a child. It wasn't until we settled outside of Les Sables d'Olonne that Olivia came up with the idea of passing the child off as her own. It was the perfect solution, of course. My reputation would be saved. It was simply fate that my father chose you, of all people, to marry Olivia. But I'm certain you can agree that our family should be together. Mother. Son. And his father . . ."

Olivia turned up the gallery and found Armand, Sally, Jacques, Gustavea, and a scattering of the new servants standing rooted in the shadows, their features slack with discomfiture, concern, and compassion for her.

"Olivia!" Miles roared behind her.

She froze.

He shouted, "Look at me!"

Woodenly, she turned. Miles stood at the end of the gallery, half in, half out of the shadows, his hands fisted at his sides. His soiled and tattered shirt hung loosely from his shoulders. His glorious dark hair spilled in wild disarray over his brow and shirt collar. She thought, in that moment, that he was the most exquisite creature she had ever known—even more handsome than he had been those many years ago, when she had first seen him at Margrave Bluff—when she had only fantasized loving him, holding him, marrying him.

"Is it true?" he demanded, his voice hoarse and breaking. Even from her distance she could see that he trembled; his dark eyes glistened with tears of hope. "Is Bryan my son?"

Nodding, she replied, "Yes."

Emily hurried from the room and sidled up against him. "We'll be married, of course—" she began, but he flung her away and stalked up the corridor, toward Olivia, who, suddenly, could not find the strength to retreat. If he chose to murder her for her deceit, then so be it. She would rather die than live with the idea that he hated her for loving him so.

Stopping before her, he struggled with his thoughts before speaking. "Why didn't you tell me?"

"I . . . was afraid. You'd made it quite clear that you didn't love me when we married."

Her shoulders began to shake; she couldn't help it. All the strength seemed to melt from her legs and she sat down hard on the floor, her elbows on her knees, her face buried in her hands. She wept openly, ashamed by the sound of the horrible retching, of the miserably disgusting way her nose ran rivulets of water.

"Later, I feared that if you learned the truth, you would condemn me for lying to you. And while I took comfort that you would remain with me as long as you needed my money, I knew if you located that new vein, which you did, you would become incredibly wealthy—you wouldn't need me at all any longer. And you don't."

Slowly, Miles went to one knee before her. He took her face in his hands.

Tears streaming from her eyes, she cried, "The two of you are mine, dammit! I may not have given birth to Bryan, but I've raised him. I've loved him. I couldn't love him more if I'd grown him in my own womb. He's part of the man I love . . . he's part of you."

Struggling to regain her senses, infuriated, suddenly, by the terrible weakness she was displaying, Olivia shoved her husband's hands away and tried to stand. He caught her, held her tight against his chest, one hand buried in her tumbled hair, gripping it fiercely. Closing her eyes, Olivia allowed herself to absorb the feel of him, the smell of him, the taste of him, and she thought she might die from the painful pleasure of it.

Finally, she whispered, "Let me go. Emily was your first choice—you cared for her once. You only married me for my money. Business only. Perhaps you grew fond of me because you had little choice. But now you do have a choice. There's not a woman in England who wouldn't find you acceptable now. Don't you see, Miles? You can start all over and do it right this time. You can marry the woman you honestly love, and this time marry for all the right reasons."

For a long minute, he said nothing. Then, very quietly, he replied, "You're right. I should marry again. Only I'll be marrying the woman that I love, and by God, I'll go about it right this time."

Emily, who'd remained motionless at the doorway, broke into a smile and started up the corridor, only to be brought up short as Armand and Gustavea suddenly flanked her on each side, and grabbed her by her arms.

She almost hissed. "How dare you! Take your hands from me this moment. Who do you think you are?" Fixing her burning eyes on Miles, she screamed, "Do something, you idiot!"

"Oh, I intend to, Emily." He smiled and glanced toward the servants lining the corridor, their faces concerned and watchful. Sally glared at him with her hands on her hips, cap cocked askew and red ringlets springing around it like frizzy corkscrews. Jacques stood in the dining hall doorway, face, hands, and apron coated in flour.

Then Miles looked up the stairway where Bertrice held Bryan in her arms. He took a breath. "Bear witness that I, Miles Kemball Warwick, being of sound mind—" He slowly turned back to Olivia where she continued to wait, immobilized by a weakening of her backbone and a pounding of her heart as she watched him go to one knee before her, and reach for her hand. "Being of sound mind, and heart, do hereby ask Olivia Devonshire Warwick, and mother of my son, for her hand in marriage—to be my wife—to be my love—my *only* love—for the remainder of our natural lives."

Olivia closed her eyes, too moved by relief and joy to speak. Then a child's voice called from the top of the stairs, "Say yes, Mummy, or I won't have nobody to play the Black Knight with me no more."

"Oh." She sighed. "Oh yes."

The wedding was held in Braithwaite's rose garden, amid the scores of brilliant blooms that filled the June air with heady perfume. The sky was cloudless and vibrant blue.

Three hundred guests attended the ceremony. (Olivia ran out of favors!) Folks came from Gunnerside. From Middleham. From London. They spread out over Braithwaite's immense gardens surrounding the house and watched somewhat misty-eyed as Olivia and Miles stood upon the raised platform of a rose-covered gazebo and renewed their vows before a minister. As Miles slid the heavy gold wedding ring onto Olivia's finger, a roar of approval rose up from the miners.

Jacques was in heaven as the guests oohed and ahhed over his seven-layer wedding cake and champagne punch. Armand complained that they would be forced to build a new wing on the house to store all their wedding gifts, and Sally got tipsy by drinking the dregs of punch remaining in the bottom of glasses.

As the day's festivities drew to a close, Olivia and Miles Warwick stood in the receiving line and shook the hand of each guest who passed by. As Miles's best man, Earl Warwick stood at Miles's side. Janet attended Olivia, but wandered off occasionally, only to be found in deep conversation with Charles Fowles, who appeared to take great pleasure in explaining to her the peculiarities of running a top-notch stable.

Once, much to Olivia's dismay, she discovered Bryan embroiled in a shockingly fierce wrestle on the ground with Earl Warwick's oldest son, Patrick. Miles and Damien dragged them apart while Bonnie, the Countess Warwick, and Olivia stood to one side, eyebrows lowered disapprovingly as their husbands set the boys on their feet.

"Hey ho!" came a voice from the crowd. "My money's on Bryan!"

"And mine on Patrick!"

"There's simply no question," announced the third voice. "My shilling's on a draw!"

Frederick Millhouse, Philippe Fitzpatrick, and Claurence Newman, friends of Earl Warwick and Miles's, surrounded the boys and argued heatedly over which cousin would oust the other, while Miles and Damien stared at one another a long tense moment, then burst out in laughter. Then Damien offered his hand to Miles and said, "Welcome to the family, Mr. Warwick."

As was customary, after all the guests had departed, the Braithwaite servants lined up and accepted tokens of appreciation from Olivia. There were new caps and aprons for the maids, and new gloves for the men servants. Each beamed their appreciation and voiced their best wishes for Olivia and Miles's happiness. When all the help had departed, Bertrice lingered in the shadows, humming to herself, and casting furtive glances at her employers.

Miles gave Olivia a wink and said, "Come here, Bertrice."

With her gray hair in tufts, the old woman waddled up the foyer and stopped before Miles. She regarded him somewhat skeptically.

"I have something for you as well," he explained.

Her penny-shaped eyes widened with surprise and pleasure.

"Bryan!" he called.

Bryan walked from a drawing room, hefting a fat yellow tabby in his little arms. Bertrice's eyes welled with tears, and she clapped her plump hands. "Oh Lud," she declared, "y've found me—"

"Kitty!" Olivia, Miles, and Bryan cried in unison.

Putting the purring cat into Bertrice's waiting arms, Miles said, "I'm certain you and Bryan will find a way to entertain Dickens throughout the remainder of the evening. Won't you, dear?"

Her mouth curved in a smile. " 'Course." Taking Bryan's hand, Bertrice turned and started for the door, pausing only long enough to look back and say saucily, "Dickens was black."

Miles slid his hands in his trouser pockets. "Ungrateful old woman," he muttered. "I should fire her."

"But you won't." Olivia drew her arm around her husband's and smiled up into his face. "Now for your wedding gift."

"A wedding gift for me?" He grinned like their son; his eyes danced with excitement.

Olivia pulled him toward the open front door, where Armand waited, looking very distinguished in his black suit and white gloves, one eyebrow raised in amusement.

Olivia and Miles stepped from the house. Twilight cast a rosy glow upon the countryside, and at the foot of the stairs stood Charles Fowles, doing his best to calm the pawing, prancing black Arabian that whinnied the moment its liquid brown eyes saw Miles.

Miles stopped short. "Gdansk."

"It took months to track him down," Olivia explained, immeasurably moved by the emotion that tightened the muscles of her husband's face. "Since he was auctioned off last December, he was sold three times. Seems he'll allow no one to ride him but you. He'll make a grand sire for Perlagal's foals, I think."

Miles closed his eyes, then, with no warning, he swept her up in his arms and returned to the house, mounted the Jacobean staircase while Olivia threw back her head in laughter and declared that he would surely break his back before reaching the spiraling summit.

But he wasn't so much as breathing hard by the time he slid her to the floor in his bedroom. For a long time, they stood before the cheval mirror and watched their images, together, reflected in the glass: she wearing an exquisite wedding gown that countless Warwick wives had worn before her—including Damien's wife, Bonnie—and he, Miles Kemball Warwick, her husband, wearing a stunning short frock coat of blue cloth, with a velvet collar edged in silk cord. His waistcoat was of white drill, and his trousers were dove-gray. A snow-white rosebud peeked from the buttonhole on his coat.

"I love you," he said at last.

Olivia closed her eyes and thrilled in the fresh rush of pleasure that robbed her of breath.

His fingers moved slowly down her back, releasing each tiny button until the gown slid, with a gentle rustle of silk, over her shoulders, to the tops of her breasts, exposing the pale pink rose on her white skin.

Miles touched it lightly, traced the delicate image with his fingertips, all the while his eyes holding hers in the mirror. "Did I ever mention to you that I adore roses?" he asked.

She nodded as, with an easy flip of his hand, he nudged the gown further, so it slid to her waist, barely noticing as it shimmied by her hips and pooled around her ankles. Her vision, her senses, were focused on the magic his hands were working on her body, her breasts, her thighs, and in between, where the hot sexual heart of her warmed and ached with the anticipation of loving him again.

Miles nuzzled behind her ear. "The first time I took you, I hurt you," he murmured. "You were a virgin and I was too damned hurt and drunk to realize. Yet you forgave me. You saved my life in every way imaginable, and I rewarded you with pain. I'll spend the rest of my life making it up to you."

She did not speak. She felt too marvelously weak. Too incredibly alive.

Somehow, he removed her corset, chemise, and drawers. He slid her shoes from her feet and peeled the filmy embroidered stockings from her legs. Then he laid her on his bed of white silk sheets and scattered red rose petals.

And soon he joined her, naked as she, aroused, touching, tasting, tongue against tongue, upon nipples, sliding into the wet heat of her until she cried aloud and quivered with the delicious ecstasy of love found and fulfilled, until they lay spent and shivering from the night wind blowing through the open window.

"Thank you," he finally said.

Olivia smiled. "For what?"

"For believing in me. But mostly for loving me." He took Olivia in his arms and held her tightly, until the warmth of her body suffused his, until the passion became hot once more and he rolled her to her back, spilling her hair like a dark rich fire amid the pillows and petals. And he entered her again, slowly, exalting in the rhapsody of her welcoming body.

"Thank you for my son," he said.

She gasped, and sighed, the rapture too intense, the transport almost more than she could bear.

"There's only one thing that could make me happier than I am now," came his gentle words through her heaven.

"Tell me," she breathed. "Quickly, husband, and I will do all that I can to make it happen."

Miles kissed her, lightly, and drove himself home as he whispered, "A daughter who looks just like you."